SOLDIER COWBOY

HEATHERLY BELL

PROLOGUE

*W*e're happy to report that after our *Mr. Cowboy* reality show ended, we've enjoyed several young women moving permanently to Stone Ridge. These ladies are nobody's fools. They got a good look at the handsome cowboys we have us around here and what do you know, many decided to stay. Can't say I blame them.

But so far, the only official engagement has been that of my niece, Bonnie Lee Wheeler, to the love of her life, Sean Henderson. Yes, thank you very much, I *did* engineer this reunion. Sure, I partially blamed myself for the demise of their relationship in the first place. But what can I say? All's well that ends well.

No engagements to speak of but give them time. They're brand-new relationships, and quite a few of them. We do, however, quite unexpectedly have an unfamiliar woman in town. Colton, the last Henderson brother, has returned with a fiancée. Hearts broke all over Stone Ridge at the news that he didn't come home alone. I hear rumors that several of our single women were holding out for his return. Well, ladies, that's what happens when you wait. We have plenty of cowboys, so you have no excuse.

Actually, Colton has been gone so long that some of us forgot what he looked like. We have heard stories of all his bravery overseas, yes we have. But it seems he is done with all that, and back in Stone Ridge ready to be a cowboy again. Good for him.

We have no idea what to make of Jennifer so far, except that she's as nice as could be. However, I can't help feeling there's something special going on out at the Henderson ranch and I'm not just talking about Bonnie Lee's nuptials. Colton and his fiancée are rarely seen apart. Whenever she comes into town, wouldn't you know Colton is right behind her. He even tried to attend the ceremony for the gifting of the marriage quilt, an annual Ladies of SORROW Stone Ridge tradition! Why, men are absolutely *forbidden*. We made him stand outside and he did, like a sentry. We can't discuss the men of Stone Ridge with one of them in our midst!

Honestly, love is one thing, but he acts like more of a... well, for lack of a better word I'd say *bodyguard*.

Why on earth he feels he must protect his fiancée in Stone Ridge is beyond me. This is the place where all our men look out for the few women we have. Nothing will ever happen to her on our watch.

Either way, we're sure glad Colton is back, and he was kind enough to bring his woman with him.

~ Beulah Hayes, President of SORROW (Society of Reasonable, Respectable, Orderly Women) and keeper of the *Men of Stone Ridge* bible, tenth edition. ~

CHAPTER 1

*C*olton Henderson closed his laptop and surveyed his dreary motel room. Double twin beds, coffeemaker with horrible coffee, desk. Nothing special, but this was a quick stop. One night and he'd finally be on his way to Texas.

Just when he thought he'd completed his last mission for the US Army Special Forces, tonight he had a meeting with an old friend and former mentor, and had already been informed a "big ask" would be forthcoming. The whole cloak-and-dagger feel had him wondering what would come next. No phone calls discussing the subject were allowed, as if interceptions were suspected. They were to meet in person and there would be an "exchange" should Colton agree. Many soldiers eased into civilian life by taking dangerous high-paying work all over the world, but Colton hadn't done anything like this. He understood he could make a lot of money, but he wasn't interested. Trouble, of any kind, was behind him.

Unfortunately, no matter what would be asked of Colton, it would have to fit around Sean and Bonnie Lee's wedding. He'd just emailed his brother tonight to let him know he would be there, and there was no way he would miss it. Colton had been gone too long from his small town, and even if he wondered whether he'd still recognize Henderson Grange, he remembered his ranch. Hill Country was a post-card that lived in his mind. Large stretches of flat land with the occasional hills dotting the landscape filled with wild-flowers and tall grass. Lupine Lake, where he and his brothers had learned to swim. The Longhorns, cattle, and fields were waiting for him. His brothers were waiting for him. It was past time to go home. Even so, he'd agreed to this meeting out of respect for the man who'd asked.

The smoky casino in Winnemucca, Nevada, was pretty much what he'd expected of the small mining town between Utah and California.

He found Horace Walker waiting for him at a red vinyl booth with a Formica- covered table in the restaurant tucked near the back, past the gambling tables and slot machines.

Even out of uniform, even in his own country, now offi-cially a civilian, Colton hesitated a second before he sat. This was still a whole new world he'd entered, one in which he didn't always need to have his guard up. There were fewer rules. Less violence. Less breaches of decorum.

It would take some time getting used to all this.

"At ease," said his former superior, as though he under-stood Colton's dilemma far too well.

Colton took a seat across from him and when the wait-ress came by, he ordered a coffee.

"Are you getting settled?" Horace asked.

Polite conversation, and Colton recognized it. He just wasn't accustomed to this new world. He wanted orders, um, the *request,* so he could get this over with. He wanted to see whether or not he could work this "big" ask around his brother's wedding. But more than likely he wanted to tact-fully let his friend down easy and explain that his fighting days were behind him. He'd been lucky, too lucky, and like a gambler who won big at the blackjack table, he planned to cut out and take his winnings home.

Colton nodded. "I got in late last night."

"I know this is probably not what you expected, and I appreciate you meeting with me. I want to assure you this is not a job that will pull you back into any more overseas battles. That's over."

"Yes, it is, sir. No offense but I don't need your approval for that. The United States Government agrees I've completed my service and we have separated."

Horace chuckled. "I always liked you but more importantly, I *trust* you. And I would not trust anyone else with this. It's too important to me."

Colton took a sip of his coffee and waited. Out of respect he tried not to look at his wristwatch, but he really wanted to get a move on and finish driving to Texas. He planned to surprise his family.

"I remember you being a man of action and few words. So, here's the issue. Someone very dear to me is in trouble." Horace slammed the rest of his drink down and scowled. "You remember I have a daughter?"

There hadn't been a whole lot of downtime between missions overseas, but Horace and Colton had gotten particularly close. That sort of thing happened when you were part of an extraction team and wound up one of two survivors. For a long night, Colton and Horace had huddled together and waited for reinforcements. They would be friends for life. Colton fully expected to ask Horace to his wedding someday, and expected to be asked to Walker family weddings and baptisms. Horace was like a second father to Colton.

"You've heard of podcasts?"

One of Colton's buddies regularly listened to a UFO

podcast and others were fans of true crime. Colton, for his part, preferred to relax and decompress with cooking shows, both video and audio. Late at night, when he couldn't sleep, Colton usually pulled up a show and listened as the cook chopped garlic and onions and stirred them in sizzling butter. He'd never been so relaxed in his life. It was his secret, and he'd go to his death never revealing he loved to listen to or watch people create interesting meals.

"Do you remember that old movie, *Play Misty for Me?*"

"Clint Eastwood?"

"My daughter has a podcast, pretty popular, from what I understand. So much so she seems to have acquired a stalker." He made a face as if the words he'd said smelled foul when they came out of his mouth.

Colton shook his head. At this point he was truly confused. What did any of this have to do with him? This was so far out of his field of expertise that he had no idea what he was even doing here.

"Basically, she needs a bodyguard. My daughter isn't who she used to be. She was confident, happy, and outgoing, and now Jennifer is glancing around corners, afraid of her own shadow. She's stopped working. Stopped living."

Colton shook his head. He had compassion for the situation, but he wasn't a babysitter *or* a bodyguard.

He'd just been through three months of therapy himself, wanting to be more of a whole person before he returned to his family. It had been hell, rehashing through everything, living through every battle again and again. Putting in the hard work to be mentally healthy. But he'd gotten through. Barely. He had his coping skills and understood on one level that he'd never be the same. And that would have to be okay. A wedding was happening, and he had to get home, ready or not.

"I trust you more than I trust anyone else." Horace

glanced behind Colton with a scowl. "Here she is. The restroom is one of the few places she goes by herself these days. I'll let her tell you the rest."

Colton would have to finesse his way out of this scenario. He hadn't ever met Horace's daughter, but knew she was one of two children of Horace and his first wife. She'd died when the kids were young, and Horace's sister had helped raise them while he was on long deployments. Colton sympathized with their situation, but he still hadn't decided whether or not he'd agree to this favor. There were too many unknown factors. Besides, he was going to a wedding and bringing a woman home with him to Stone Ridge would be...complicated. In a small town like his, questions would be asked. And asked. Then if they weren't answered satisfactorily, the rumors would fly.

Did this somewhat famous podcaster want everyone to know she had a stalker? Did Horace?

Colton followed Horace's gaze and they both stood from the booth as she approached, crossing slot machines and blackjack tables. And...

Holy God.

Colton was thunderstruck. Maybe he'd been away too long, which might be influencing his perception, but he found this woman...gorgeous. She wore jeans and a plain dark T-shirt and carried a colorful patchwork bag that said, "New York City." She looked nothing like her hooked-nose father who was a great leader and a good man but wouldn't grace the cover of any magazine. She had long, straight, nearly black hair and huge blue eyes.

Lust slammed into him, and a coil of longing hit him hard in the gut.

This would be a *bad* idea. Or a very, very good one but for...other reasons.

At the same time, he felt a decidedly unfamiliar sensation.

This was ridiculous and embarrassing. He was already almost in love and this kind of thing didn't happen to him.

Then she gave him a shy look from under lowered lashes and there was no "almost" about it.

She slid into the booth on Horace's side and wouldn't meet Colton's eyes.

"Honey, this is the man I told you about."

"He's a soldier." She glanced up at him briefly and in two seconds had him dialed. "I thought you wanted me to hire a bodyguard."

"This is someone I trust with my life. He will keep you safe for the next few weeks."

Reluctantly, Colton interrupted, "Wait. Weeks?"

"I would expect the stalker danger to be less of an issue then. Moving in with me isn't really an option and I'll be traveling back and forth to Maryland next month. I also think it might be too easy for him to make the connection and find me, too, so I'm at a loss."

"I don't want to move from my condo and let him win," Jennifer said.

"He's already winning."

Colton watched the exchange before he butted in. "I'm sorry I can't be of assistance, but I'm on my way to Texas."

Horace cocked his head and eyed him. "That small Podunk town you always talked about? The one where every man looks out for the few women in town? The one *without* WiFi?"

Jennifer's gaze snapped to her father as if he'd suggested she go visit the blazing hot planet Mars. But Colton saw where Horace was going with this. It was somewhat of a running joke because with their superior satellites he'd gotten better reception in the desert than he ever did in Stone Ridge. But he hadn't been home for years. Things may have changed in more than one way.

"Yeah, that was true then but I'm sure it's improved since."

"How many acres on your ranch?"

Colton ignored the question, shook his head, and traced the rim of his glass.

The truth was that the Grange, the family ranch, and Stone Ridge, happened to be the perfect place to hide out. But from now on, he would not have any other job besides cattle ranching.

"So…you want your daughter hiding out in Stone Ridge. With me."

"I trust you. And she needs protection from a certain man." Horace frowned.

So, the stalker was a man. They were, in fact, rarely women.

Colton quirked a brow and tried to meet Jennifer's averted eyes. "Ex-boyfriend? Ex-husband? What about the court system? Restraining order, all that?"

"Yes, but he…he keeps on trying. He hasn't done anything to hurt me, but he seems obsessed. I went on *one date* with him."

"We're talking about a possibly mentally unbalanced individual. He seems to think they're getting married," Horace spit out. "Tell him how you changed your number when he sent you three hundred text messages daily. Now he shows up unannounced, making a scene when she won't open the door. The police have been called but he hasn't technically broken any laws. Yet."

Jesus.

"I must have done something to encourage him, but I don't know what I did." Jennifer folded into herself, biting her lower lip. "I suppose I responded to the text messages for a while. He needs help and I wanted him to get it."

Colton's body tightened. This beautiful girl somehow blamed herself.

"I don't want to hear that. You did nothing wrong," Horace said, taking the words from Colton's mouth. "But until he finally moves on and finds a new obsession, you need to be safe."

"Maybe if someone besides me and the police talks to him," Jennifer tried. "Gets him to understand."

Colton snorted and downed the last of his horrible coffee. People like the man she described wouldn't listen to reason.

"They've already talked to him," Horace said. "If he won't listen to them, he won't listen to anyone else. The only thing that will stop him is to be caught in the act and we can't let it get that far. Jennifer, meet Colton Henderson. Your bodyguard."

CHAPTER 2

*J*ennifer Walker surveyed the man seated across from her in the booth. He was tall and imposing. Words like scary and *intimidating* came to mind. When he'd stood as she approached, he'd towered over her *and* her father. He had short chestnut-brown hair and piercing dark eyes. Complete with a square jaw and light dusting of beard stubble, he might have just walked out of central casting.

I'm here to audition for the part of G.I. Joe.

Ugh. Maybe she'd lived in Los Angeles too long.

Growing up in Maryland, Jennifer had wanted to get as far away from home and the family military dynasty as possible. She loved her father, truly she did, but he was an alarmist. Always looking for trouble over his shoulder, assuming the worst of people. She understood why on one level. He had a skewed view of the world through no fault of his own. The soldier sitting across from her was probably similar. Like her father, a man she both adored and feared a little.

All to say that she could hold her own with these alpha men. But she didn't like to fight as much as they did.

"I don't need a bodyguard but thank you. Fine, I'll just go away for a while."

A minute ago, the man snorted when she'd suggested maybe Dan Gates would listen to someone. It was a Hail Mary pass but even she realized it was too late. People given to the kind of behavior he'd demonstrated had mental health issues. They needed help. Possibly medication.

Dan had been so nice on their one and only date, opening doors, complimenting her. She was used to lousy boyfriends, and he'd been the exception. It had all gone so wrong and there had never been another date. Still, he was a fan of her podcast and somehow became obsessed with her. Maybe because she was the only woman to ever say no to him.

"Yes, you *do* need a bodyguard," her father said now.

But it was strange to introduce a relative stranger to her hot mess. Colton didn't know her. He didn't know that from the time she'd been a little girl, all she'd ever wanted was the truth. Her parents gave up on the Santa Claus myth early on because by the time she was five she'd wanted to interview him. She had to know how in the world he'd trained reindeer to fly. She was often told that she asked too many questions. That was nothing new.

It was what made her good at what she did. She'd studied photojournalism, but it was her podcast, *Truth Salad*, that gave her a job and reliable income from sponsors. More important than the truth she'd found a way to help others. A way for them to feel connected and not so alone.

And then came her stalker.

Before long *she'd* become the story. Rumors flew that she had a stalker of her own and sponsors began to drop. The career that meant so much to her might be over. Jennifer understood that she had to stop broadcasting, but she didn't know why she had to be relocated.

"I love you, Daddy, but this is your worst idea to date."

Colton straightened. "I'm afraid I have to agree with her. This isn't a great plan. As I said I have to go to Texas."

"And there's no way I'm going to Texas."

Colton smiled then, just a little quirk of his mouth, but it transformed his face. He was definitely less frightening for a nanosecond.

"You heard her, sir."

But her father's scowl had gone to full-scale mode. "Don't listen to her. If you're going to Texas, she's going with you. This would just be temporary, Bug."

At the sound of her pet name, she softened. But go somewhere with *this* scary guy? Already her throat constricted at the thought of being stuck in an airplane with him. Sharing all that recycled air. Her knee bumping into his. Him, eerily quiet the entire time. He didn't want to do this, that much was clear. No doubt he was another soldier indebted to her father.

"Why can't I stay home and have him look out for me there?"

"Your stalker knows where you live. I won't take chances with this man's life any more than your own."

"How long would I have to be in Texas?"

"Until you're safe."

"I still don't think—" Colton said.

"Please," her father interrupted.

To her knowledge, her father had never begged *anyone*. As she worked to recover from the shock, Colton, too, blinked in surprise. No one spoke for a moment in which Jennifer heard the sounds of cards shuffling and slot machines rolling in the near distance.

Colton held out his hand and shook. "Done."

Outside, within minutes, her suitcases were loaded into the bed of Colton's truck. That's when she understood they were *driving* to Texas from Nevada. Not flying. A twenty-four-hour road trip with a stranger.

She couldn't believe this was happening. All because of one truly bad date and a man who didn't understand that they weren't right for each other.

"Give your father your phone," Colton ordered.

"Wh-what? No!"

She glanced at her father for help. Rescue me, she sent via mental telepathy. How would *she* get help if this man hurt her? But she knew better. Her father would never hand her over to someone he didn't fully trust. Someone who would lay down his life to protect her.

And someone, she figured, he could easily find should the need arise.

Her father held out his open palm. "Phone. It's the best way to track you."

Her *phone*. "But, how will I communicate with you?"

"You can use mine." Colton slammed the tailgate shut. "And landlines."

"Both of you check in with me often," her father said. "Your safety is the single most important thing to me."

An hour later, Jennifer was on the road to Texas with a man she'd just met. It was apparently enough that he was former military, her *father* knew him, and that he obviously trusted Colton with his own life. Still, how odd to be traveling with a virtual stranger. Colton informed her they would be arriving in the wee hours of tomorrow morning and that she could relax and take a nap if she'd like.

At least he was a courteous stranger, one who had loaded her bags into the back of his truck. He held the door open for her and waited until she had buckled in before starting to drive. But as she'd suspected, he was the silent, brooding, quiet type.

God, she *hated* the quiet type.

"Look, I have an idea. Drop me off in Utah. That's another two hours from here and then we'll part ways."

He quirked a brow. "What are you going to do in *Utah?*"

"Not be in California, which is the point."

"I'm not going to drop you off at some motel room and leave you there."

"Why not? You're not a babysitter or a bodyguard and you don't really want to do this."

"Who said I don't want to do this?"

"Um, your eyes, your body posture. Oh, and also your *words*. And I quote 'this isn't a good idea.' Sound familiar?"

"It wasn't a good plan because I'm starting a helluva long drive, and I figured you wouldn't appreciate that. I can't fit into your schedule, so you have to fit into mine. But your father thinks this is important and now so do I."

"Because he said 'please'? I admit, I've heard him say please exactly once before today. I understand how it must have affected you. But that doesn't mean you have to go through with this. Drop me off. Really, I won't tell him."

"I'm not *dropping* you off."

"Wouldn't that be called kidnapping?"

"You got in this truck willingly."

"And I'd like to get out willingly, too."

"I'd pull over if we had another day. We just don't have the time for Utah. Another time, okay?"

He made it sound like she wanted to do some sightseeing instead of unburdening him of this obligation.

"And anyway, if I drop you off at a motel in Utah, I'll have to call your father and advise him of the development."

"You wouldn't!"

"Yes, I would. You would leave me no choice."

"Arrgh!" Jennifer growled and turned her body to face the passenger side door.

He growled back.

Was he actually being funny? She honestly couldn't tell.

For the next few hours, he didn't initiate any conversation on his own. You would think he'd want to find out more about her life, or maybe how she'd wound up with a stalker. If it were her, she'd certainly be curious enough to ask.

"Can we stop in an hour so I can stretch my legs?"

"Two hours."

"Okay. Unless I have to use the ladies' room."

"Let me know. I'll pull over on the highway if you do."

"Pull *over*?"

"Yes."

Now, he seemed to be speaking through a tight jaw. He expected her to hike out on the side of the freeway, pull down her panties, and find a tree. No different than trips with her father, who'd practically held her and her brother hostage on "road trips." Joe had peed into a bottle, just because he could.

"How far is it to Stone Ridge?"

"Here." He handed her his phone. "Look it up on GPS."

"But I wanted to hear it from your perspective."

"My perspective is the miles. Look it up."

"Are we going the fastest way?"

"Yes."

She peppered him with more questions such as how long he'd lived in Stone Ridge.

He'd been three when he and his brothers became foster kids and were later adopted. His parents were dead.

Did he have any other family there?

His mother's best friend, two brothers, a sister-in-law, two nephews and a niece.

God forbid he volunteer any information not requested first.

Never even the slightest elaboration. He obviously resented being begged to take this job, feeling he couldn't say no simply because he felt a deep loyalty to her father. Not love. *Loyalty*. There was a difference. Loyalty was the military way. Decisions were made and actions taken from a place of blind allegiance. From the beginning, Jennifer hadn't fit into her family. She couldn't believe in anything or anyone without first knowing all the facts and making an informed decision. *Her* decision. She was the antithesis of the military complex and definitely her mother's daughter.

Sometimes the ache for her hit at odd and quiet times of reflection. Such as now when Jennifer wondered what her mother would have to say about all this.

Jennifer fell asleep somewhere between Utah and New Mexico, waking several times to find Colton still wide awake.

"Don't you want to let me take a turn driving so you can nap?" She yawned and stretched.

"No."

"I *can* drive. You can trust me with your precious truck."

He snorted. "It's not precious."

"Even better." She sat up straighter and rubbed her eyes. "Can I at least get some coffee?"

"I didn't bring any," he said, heavy on the sarcasm.

"Or, you could pull over to any one of these many truck stops along the way." She watched with longing as one after another they passed by them, leaving rest stops in their rearview. "Plus, I have to…you know. Use the *facilities*."

He sighed deeply, and made her wait twenty more minutes, while she squirmed in her seat and complained. Finally, he pulled over at a twenty-four-hour station and snack shop off the interstate. One look at the gauge and she realized he'd only done so because he needed *gasoline*. So, she refused to appreciate the fact she had an actual toilet instead of squatting by a thicket on the side of the highway.

But when she walked outside, she found him leaning against the truck, holding two coffees.

He held one out for her.

"Thanks." She took a sip, not caring it was too sugary and creamy for her taste.

It was the nicest thing he'd done for her.

Other than agree to sacrifice his time alone to possibly save my life.

She should be grateful. And she was. She'd simply find a way to make friends with him for the next couple of weeks until it was time to go home to California. During that time, she'd plan how to get her life back. She missed the way things used to be, when she'd easily walk to the farmer's market on Saturday mornings or meet for drinks with friends. Gradually, her friends had slipped away when she stopped attending parties and events. She'd tried to explain her situation, but no one seemed to understand.

Just tell him you're not interested. What's the problem?

But she had, many times, and Dan didn't *hear* her. She had been prepared to take time away from the podcast, but wasn't warned that she'd be going all the way to Texas.

At least this surly cowboy was someone who she was certain would grow on her. Eventually. It helped that he was the opposite of Dan. She now understood that scary people came in all shapes and sizes. Dan was a handsome and tall broker who wore suits and wingtips.

And he'd once tried to break down her door.

The coffee, as always, managed to keep her awake and she had her eyes wide open when they rolled into town well after midnight.

"We would have been here sooner except for all the stops."

Welcome to Stone Ridge, established 1806 by Titus Ridge
Population 5,010
Women are especially welcome
Women eat free every night Tuesday at the Shady Grind

"What's with the sign?" Jennifer turned to get a better look at it as they passed by. "What's this about? Why are women eating free every Tuesday at the Shady Grind?"

Colton grunted. "We don't have many women."

"Why?"

"I don't know."

"C'mon, surely you do. Is this a misogynist town? Did you *drive* them all out?"

He gave her a patient look before responding. "No."

"There must be a reason."

He didn't answer. If he had any information, he did not plan to share it with Jennifer.

They passed through downtown and the closed shops, The Shady Grind (where women ate free every Tuesday), a church, a small school, the general store, a medical clinic, and a veterinary clinic. She didn't see much else other than a town green in the center and only saw *that* because the headlights displayed it as he turned on to a single-lane country road.

Then a few yards down, came a huge billboard, looking terribly out of place. An extremely handsome cowboy smiled wickedly into the camera, his arms crossed.

Mr. Cowboy, the sign read. She was about to ask Colton what this was all about, when he almost ran off the road.

"What the hell?" He pulled over and now looked up through the windshield at the huge billboard.

"I take it you have no idea what this is?" Jennifer didn't want to point out that a simple online search would give them the answer. She no longer had a phone, but he did.

"That's *Sean.*"

"And Sean is…" She'd try this new approach to asking questions. Fill in the blanks.

"My brother."

Bingo! Another question answered.

"And this surprises you because…"

"I have no idea *what* Mr. Cowboy is." He shook his head. "Been gone too long, I guess."

"Lots of changes. You could look it up on your phone."

"Or I could talk to the man himself." He pulled back on to the road.

"Right. We'll be there soon?"

"Yeah."

Of course, most everyone would be sleeping at this hour. They'd been on the road for nearly twenty-four hours. Colton didn't even appear to be sleepy. He was like a machine.

"Listen. I think we need a plan. But I'm not sure you're going to like this."

Progress. He had *initiated* conversation, talking in full sentences even if what he'd just said didn't sound too promising. Maybe she should be worried. He might make her sleep in a tent.

"What is it? What won't I like?"

She prepared herself to hear she'd be sleeping outside, or of a jealous girlfriend who might not appreciate his spending so much time around Jennifer. If the girlfriend was the worst she had to deal with, she'd be lucky. She'd been through far worse and would simply make friends with the woman. Assure her she had no intentions of taking someone else's man. That's not how Jennifer rolled.

"People in Stone Ridge tend to ask a lot of questions. How comfortable are you with everyone knowing the details of your situation?"

"Not comfortable at all."

"That's what I thought. And I'm not particularly at ease with my family thinking I brought home my work."

"I'm not *work*. I'm a favor for my father."

"Either way. I need everyone to know the military part of my life is over."

"Got it. You don't want them to worry about you and think you've still got a foot in the military complex because of me."

He quirked a brow. "Not how I would have put it but yeah. If we're going to hide out, I'd like to protect your privacy as much as possible."

"I appreciate that."

"There's a way we can spend a lot of time together and no one will wonder a thing."

"Sounds like a plan."

"We can minimize the questions and protect the real reason you're here and the fact that I'm technically your bodyguard."

"Awesome. What do we do?"

"Pretend we're engaged."

CHAPTER 3

*I*f Colton had known it would be this simple to get Jennifer to stop talking, he'd have suggested a fake engagement five hundred miles ago. Except for the several blissful hours when she slept, she hadn't stopped talking since she got in his truck. Once she'd figured out he didn't appreciate being grilled, she entertained him with her life story. Her *entire* life story.

She had an older brother who'd also been in the service. Born and raised in Bethesda, Maryland, which he did already know. Mother died when Jennifer was twelve and an aunt helped raise her. Horace had told him all this, of course. But he now knew more about her than he did some of his best friends. No one talked as much as she did. No one in the world. Surely, she'd broken some kind of a record. The Guinness books should know about her.

"*Excuse* me?" She blinked now and, in the darkness, the moonlight gleamed in her blue eyes and on a shaft of her nearly black hair.

"You heard me. I don't like it either but it's the easiest way. We can live together without any annoying questions or judgements. You'll be welcomed into town as my fiancée. No questions asked as to why we're always together. We're in love and it's that simple."

"And what will we tell your family when I go back to California?"

"It didn't work out and you don't like small-town life. No different than most servicemen reacclimating into civilian life."

Her eyes narrowed. "But that's a *lie.*"

"Yeah, no kidding. So is our engagement."

"That's two lies." She held up her fingers.

"Good, you can count."

"This isn't a good idea. I don't like lying to people." She crossed her arms. "I thought you trusted everyone here."

He had thought he would, but no longer. Everything was...different. The ridiculous sign was the first clue. Sean hadn't mentioned he'd become a model. In the brief emails, he'd mentioned Bonnie Lee came back home, they reconciled, and were getting married. Seemed he was missing some important details.

"What I now know is that this place has changed while I've been gone. You saw the billboard. I've never seen anything like that in Stone Ridge. It's like seeing a tank parked next to a church. There's also a medical clinic and a school that were never there before. I may have missed some emails here and there. I know my brother Riggs married a Nashville celebrity so who knows how many people have moved here since? Maybe some of her fans followed her. No, I *don't* trust every single person in this town. Not anymore. Until I know what we're dealing with, I won't trust anyone but family."

A fine time to come to this realization when they were already here. They could have gone anywhere else. But he'd wanted to come in time for Sean's wedding, so Stone Ridge it was. For better or worse, this was still his hometown. He'd find a way to make this work.

"Why can't we just say I'm a friend?"

"A friend who's going to live with me? A friend I'm going to have to follow around everywhere?"

"I see what you mean. Unless you tell them you're literally my bodyguard, it's going to look…odd."

"And they will ask questions such as why someone like you needs a bodyguard. I'd rather my family not think I came here because I thought it would be a great place for us to hide out." He wanted Sean to realize he'd come here for him and Bonnie. "I didn't plan on…you."

"I'm sorry to be a tag-a-long but I'm not sure this is the best idea, either."

"You know what won't look odd? An engaged couple, living together, rarely seen apart for however long this takes. Think about it. You don't need to decide right away."

A few minutes later, he headed up the familiar small hill on a dirt road. The moon was full and bright, and other than his truck's headlights and a smattering of brilliant stars, the sky was as black as he remembered. No house-lights were on anywhere at this time of the night, and there were no streetlights. Nothing but darkness surrounded them in the quiet and still night. This, however, was a familiar comforting darkness and not one that set him on high alert.

"Since we're getting here this early, we'll stay at Delores's cottage on the back property. Sean recently told me that she's moved in with Riggs and Winona when they renovated and added on rooms to the main house. This way we won't bother anyone. I know where she used to hide the key and I bet she still has it hidden in the same place."

"And Delores is…?"

Jennifer had taken to asking him questions in a strange

way, but it had started to grow on him. It felt less like an interrogation.

"I know I mentioned her. She was my mother's best friend growing up. And after my mother died, she kind of adopted all of us boys as her own. Except that we were grown men by that time. She stayed on with the ranch as a caretaker, making meals for the ranch hands, and helping Riggs out with the housework."

His words felt like they were suddenly coming out rapid-fire and he hoped this didn't show that he was nervous. He'd planned this as a surprise and had planned to be alone. He hoped that he'd be welcome. Riggs would no doubt be pissed he'd been gone this long. He'd never wanted Colton in the military. Even Sean might be upset he'd stayed away for such a long time. Colton had emailed as frequently as possible even if on some missions the access had been limited for weeks at a time. The last few emails from Sean, the only one who emailed him, were often pithy:

Are you alive? Please reply.

"They're not expecting me today. I wanted to surprise them."

"So, they're not even expecting *you*. They're certainly not expecting *me*. And I'm supposed to be your fiancée?"

"We'll say it's sudden. My family understands. I've been out of touch for a while."

Colton didn't want to elaborate, but the facts were that his family worried about him. If he came home with a woman, they'd worry far less. They'd see it as a sign that he'd moved on, that he was ready to settle down. He pulled up to the back of the house, the headlights gleaming on a cute little one-story with yellow trim and a porch filled with flowers.

"I knew she'd still take care of this place even if she doesn't live here anymore."

"Maybe she's kept it up for you."

"Maybe. Delores is one-of-a-kind. You're going to like her."

Colton hopped out of the truck, and shone his phone light, bending to look in a ceramic pot of pink flowers. He came up with the key, *exactly* where he expected it to be. Such a comfort to find that some things never changed. Good old Delores.

He was finally, at long last, home to stay.

* * *

JENNIFER STARED at the *almost*-smile from Colton as he held up the key he'd found in a potted flower. The corner of his mouth curled up.

He'd probably be a smoke show of a cowboy if he smiled *all* the way.

When he moved, his leather jacket unfurled briefly from his side, and she noticed the holster. He was *carrying*. She shouldn't be surprised but she still hated guns. And yes, she knew how strange this was for a girl who'd grown up around them. A girl who'd been taught a healthy respect for their power and function. She'd been okay with guns when she was younger, and she knew they had their place. Her father had insisted everyone learn how to operate a gun from the time they were thirteen. She'd felt safe then, next to her father, who tended to command a room. Nothing bad would happen to her while next to him.

Then Dan began to send photos of himself, one of them holding a 45, declaring he'd protect her from all the criminals in LA. All the homeless people. All she had to do was marry him. But she didn't need protection from the guy pushing a shopping cart filled with clothes down the street. She required protection from a man she'd dated exactly *once*.

The man who in his life presented himself to be a respectable broker and businessman. *He* was the big, bad wolf.

And now she was in cowboy country. With a soldier. This imposing man seemed concerned with her reputation and privacy as much as he did her safety.

Colton switched on a light, giving her a full view inside. Considering she was used to a one-bedroom in LA. this was plenty of room. Cozy. A leather couch with colorful Aztec throws and pillows faced the red brick fireplace. Framed photos of horses and cattle graced the walls giving it a decidedly western flair. The walls were paneled with wood, flannel-style curtains gracing the windows. A bookcase was filled with several shelves of paperbacks. Beyond the front room, there was a kitchen with a gas-powered stove and a rack filled with hanging pots and pans.

Two bedrooms, thank you, God. One of them seemed more like a guest room containing a dresser and a small twin bed with a faded green-and-white patchwork quilt. She'd take that room because she couldn't see a man the size of Colton fitting on the bed.

"This is nice," she commented as Colton brought in her suitcases and his own.

One. He had one bag. He set them down in the foyer and shut the front door.

"That's it? *One* bag?"

"I travel light. Figure some of my clothes will be at the main house in my old room. And I'll buy new stuff if I need it."

He ran a hand through his closely cropped hair and scanned the room as if looking for something he recognized. Sometime during their long drive, short dark beard stubble had made an appearance. But rather than make him look tougher, now he just seemed…human.

And a little bit out of sorts, which made him somewhat endearing.

She studied the man who'd suggested they pretend to be engaged. The idea had shocked her to the point of being speechless, a rare thing.

The real surprise was she was actually *considering* it. She hated lying, but some lies were necessary to get to the truth. Ironically. As a budding independent investigative journalist, Jennifer didn't lie when she reported. She always tried to be unbiased even if she sometimes failed due to the reason of *also* being human. Occasionally, in order to get close to a subject, she had stretched the truth.

I'm friends with your sister (acquaintances). She mentioned the problem (briefly, and on another news report). I'd like to know more (exclusively).

And there were always the occasional lies of omission. Not her preference, but nothing law enforcement didn't also do to get to the real truth. If the end justified the means, it had to be done. This was at least one way in which she and Colton understood each other. A lie that wouldn't hurt anyone was harmless.

And maybe if she'd lied to Dan, told him there *was* someone else, he might have stopped.

Colton's expression after he'd suggested they pretend to be engaged, eyes fixated on the road, had ranged from impassive to unreadable. But she'd heard something in the tone of his voice she recognized. He reminded her of her brother, Joe, the year he'd come home from his service overseas. An obvious separation from those he remembered because the setting had changed, if not always the people. While any soldier was gone from his normal life, life moved on. Some businesses closed. People moved away. In theory, every soldier understood this, but the reality of experiencing coming home could be entirely different for each one of them.

Her heart ached for Colton, who might feel like Joe had a few years ago, struggling to reintegrate into civilian life again. Family was important to him. She owed him the same compassion and acceptance she'd give to her brother. The compassion she should give any soldier simply following orders given by command. In this case, her own father.

Maybe he wanted to lie because he wanted his family to think he was fine, had managed to find a solid relationship. He was rooted. Healthy. Nothing to see here, folks.

"Is there another reason you want me to pretend to be your fiancée?" She'd decided if he gave her honesty, and was open about this, she would consider the ask far more seriously.

"The first reason is a little embarrassing. If anyone thinks you're single in this town, there will be a line out the door with suitors by tomorrow."

Not at all what she'd expected him to say. He looked awfully serious to be making a joke. Plus, she got the distinct impression he didn't know *how* to be funny.

"How does that work, exactly?" She decided to play along.

He sighed. "There have never been many women in our town, as I explained. So that means the ones that are here, and single, are frequently chased. Looking the way you do you'll have to beat them off with a stick. It will make my job a thousand times more difficult, especially if you actually want to date any of these cowboys."

Looking the way I do? She was wearing jeans, a T-shirt, and her trusty red-and-white high-top Chuck Taylors. If this was a backhanded compliment, he'd failed.

"Oh, I'm not dating *anyone*. Not for a long while."

"Kind of figured you were soured on the experience. There won't be an issue. If you're my fake fiancée, you won't have to date anyone. It will be hands-off because you're taken."

While this sounded crazy pants, she would be the first to admit to being out of her element. Having never lived in a small town, she had no idea if he was making this up as he went.

"Colton? I *really* don't want a line of men out the door. Even if they mean well."

Coming from her recent experience with Dan, the idea of being a hot commodity chased by a man sounded as unnerving as jumping off a bridge. While on fire. She wanted to disappear at this point.

"These are good men, don't get me wrong, but it's not what you need right now. And I get it. I wish I could think of another option, but we didn't have much time to plan."

All her father's fault, of course. He'd put them in this predicament simply because he relished controlling situations. And people.

"Can't I just be your girlfriend?" If they were okay with two engaged people shacking up, surely they'd be okay with him bringing home and living with his girlfriend.

"Yeah." He sighed and ran a hand down his stubbled jawline. "This is where you might help me, just a little. You don't have to, of course, but I'd appreciate it. I've been trying to think of a way I can assure my oldest brother that I'm serious about staying home. He's a little jaded because I never managed to before. But this is different. I'm done with the military, and I'll be staying. Riggs is pretty traditional, more so than Sean or me, and having a fiancée will go a long way to convince him I'm putting down roots."

It was just as she'd thought.

He needed her.

The compassionate side of Jennifer, the one that had done a podcast special on returning soldiers, the one who'd witnessed Joe's struggles, didn't have any reasons left to say no.

"I've thought about it enough, and I'll pretend to be your fiancée if you think that's the best idea. I trust you because my father trusts you." She pointed to the smaller room and grabbed a suitcase. "And I'll take this bed."

He nodded. "I'm going to take a shower. You can go after me if you want. If I'm not up by seven, it's okay to knock on the door. Around here, everyone is up early. We'll have company as soon as day breaks and they see the truck."

"There's something we forgot." She hesitated. "If we're going to lie about being engaged, shouldn't we get our stories straight?"

"Right." He shut his eyes and pinched the bridge of his nose. "Any ideas?"

"Well, we can say we met through my father. The best lies always have a little grain of truth to them."

"Right. We met years ago through Horace, and when I got back stateside, we reunited and had a whirlwind courtship. I asked you to marry me and you said yes."

"You're getting the hang of this." She tried a smile. "Is your family going to believe you'd get engaged to someone you barely know?"

"I'm just as crazy about a gorgeous woman as the next guy. Why not?" He shrugged.

Dan had called her *gorgeous*. Then he'd tried to own her, possess her like a piece of furniture that would look good in his home.

"That's not why people get *engaged*," she said.

"I know. Sorry. You're right."

The apology just slid out of his mouth like it didn't cost him anything.

Colton headed into the bathroom, where she heard the shower going. Sitting on the edge of the bed, Jennifer tried to imagine her next two weeks on a ranch in the middle of nowhere. It might be good. Or terrible. At least she wouldn't have any of the distractions of social media.

And the hope was that eventually Dan would lose interest or feel threatened enough by legal action that she could go back to her regular life.

After a few minutes, Colton knocked on the door to her bedroom.

"Come in."

He had towels with him, which he dropped into her lap unceremoniously. "In case you want to shower. Have a good night. Tomorrow we'll talk some more."

"Colton? What about a ring?"

"Right." He ran a hand through his damp hair. "I haven't thought this through all the angles."

She would imagine he was exhausted, too, and running on fumes. "We can say that you wanted me to choose one because I'm picky."

"Good idea."

Jennifer had brought her hair products and soap with her, and good thing because there was only a white bar of soap in the stall. Wet from Colton's touch. As she lathered up, she couldn't help thinking that Colton had been in this same spot only a few minutes ago. Naked. And wet and…Okay, she would *not* go there. Once you got past the scary factor, yes, he was attractive. Rugged and handsome. Anyone with good eyesight could see that. But for all intents and purposes he was a hired bodyguard, and they were here together only out of obligation. Not a good way to start any relationship. Not that she would start any relationship with a *soldier*.

Colton still had that rigid posture, the hallmark of a returning soldier. If she did nothing else while here, she was going to get him to slouch at least once. Consider it her civic duty.

The warm water sluiced down her hair and body and she relaxed for the first time in weeks. She'd been terrified, wondering if Dan would show up with his gun, and try to get her to leave her apartment.

After which she might never be seen again.

Now Dan was thousands of miles away and had no idea she'd left town. By the time he figured it out, maybe he would have found something else to obsess over.

Either way, she was safe.

After drying off, she crossed the hallway to her room, dressed in her pajamas, and crawled under the sheets for a nice long nap.

CHAPTER 4

*J*ennifer slept, waking with a parched and dry throat. She still felt out of sorts after sleeping in a moving vehicle for several hours, never quite managing a deep REM sleep. She was now sleeping in a strange home in a new town. After rolling out of the bed, she padded into the kitchen. Finding the kitchen light, she switched it on. The refrigerator was bare, so she found a glass from the cupboard and filled it with tap water. She took a heavy gulp of fresh cold water and sighed.

All things considered she could definitely do far worse than staying in this little cabin. She'd think of it as a retreat. At least she'd brought along her camera so she wouldn't go completely stir-crazy. Photography was her first dream, a dream she'd put aside so she could actually pay her bills.

Shaded only in the ambient light of the kitchen, the great room looked warm. Cozy. This place reminded her of the cabins from the trips her family used to take every year to the mountains, when her mother was still alive and commanded vacations. She could do this. When Dan gave up on her in a couple of weeks, she'd go home. It was Texas, so

34

she expected some uncomfortable temperatures and heat but at least it wasn't summertime. As soon as dawn broke, maybe she'd wander outside. Or at least look out the window to see something besides complete and utter blackness.

The front door handle jiggled as if someone on the other side was about to open the door.

Hadn't Colton locked the door?

Why hadn't he?

Was this one of those country things were no one bothered to lock their doors?

It wasn't yet sunrise but approximately three a.m. according to the digital clock on the kitchen wall. *Oh my God, what if Dan followed us here?* She'd had her phone with her up until Nevada, after all. If he'd followed her there, and already had them in sight, he could have followed them all the way into Texas. *Stupid, stupid, stupid.* She should have left her tracker behind before she got to Nevada. He would have been lying in wait outside to break in at a time when Colton would be his most vulnerable. Now it wasn't only her that would suffer. It was another good man who was only trying to help.

No, she was not imagining this. Someone opened the door.

This was real.

This was happening.

Her vocal cords constricted, and she could barely take in a breath, let alone yell.

"Colton," she whispered. "Help."

The door opened, and there was a man. Carrying a rifle. Pointing.

"What are you doing here?' he shouted.

"Please don't kill me!" she screamed, and hit the floor, curling into a fetal position.

Colton would hear her, hopefully, and come to her aid.

Dan had found them. But wait. If it was Dan, why had he asked what she was doing here? He would know she was running from him, and he'd be pissed. He certainly wouldn't sound as if he didn't *recognize* her.

Colton came barreling down the hallway at the sounds of her scream, gun in hand.

The rifle lowered and the other man stepped more clearly into the kitchen light.

And it wasn't Dan.

"What the hell?" the man said.

Colton immediately lowered his gun and grabbed the man in a bear hug. She saw him really *smile* for the first time.

And it was a hell of a show.

"Surprise." Colton chuckled. "I didn't mean to scare you. Thought you'd be asleep."

"I could have shot you," the man said. "Bonnie Lee is freaking out."

"Thanks for not killing me."

A moment later, Jennifer was still on the floor, hands over her ears, when both men hovered above her, twin brows furrowed. Definite lookalikes these two. Yes, the *brother.* The man on the billboard. Of course.

When Jennifer kept staring at the weapons with what had to be wild-eyed terror, both men seemed to realize. They slowly laid their weapons down. Colton offered his hand and heaved her up. As if he quickly realized the state of her panic, he drew her into his arms. She clung to him, shaking. He felt like the only steady place for her right now, the only solid ground.

"Sorry, I guess you scared her."

"Well, no wonder. I don't usually greet people with my rifle. I'm really sorry, ma'am."

"That's okay, we shouldn't have surprised you like this."

Colton led her to the couch, hand on her back. "Sean, meet Jennifer. My fiancée."

Sean let out a hoot. "You got a fiancée? Damn it, I'm even sorrier about this now. Not a great way to meet my future sister-in-law."

"I'm…hi, nice to meet you." She stood and held out her hand.

Sean pulled her into a bear hug. "Oh, c'mon, we're family. But tell me how you got this knucklehead to finally settle down.

"Oh, well. You know, he's a knucklehead."

"She threatened to cut me off." Colton grinned again.

Oh. Wow. That smile changed the entire landscape of his face. She found that she was staring.

Sean broke out in hearty laughter. "That'll do it."

"We met through her father. He was my superior," Colton said.

"My father," Jennifer repeated inanely.

"When I came back stateside a couple of months ago, we happened to run into each other again. Kind of a whirlwind."

"Whirlwind." Jennifer nodded. It would be good if she could come up with words of her own at some point.

"Boy, I'll say." Sean grinned. "Not like Bonnie and me, finally getting married after nearly twenty years."

"I had to say yes," Jennifer said, feeling she wasn't carrying her weight of their deception. "I love him, you know."

"What's not to love, right?" Sean clapped his brother on the back. "Man, I am so glad to see you."

"Told you there's no way I'd miss your wedding."

Wedding? There's a wedding?

"Oh, shitfire! Let me use the landline and call Bonnie. When she saw me get the rifle, she freaked out."

Sounded like a kindred spirit.

With Sean in the kitchen on the phone, Colton sat next to Jennifer and draped a big and warm hand on her knee.

"Are you okay?"

"I-I thought I was going to die," she said, trying to ignore the callused hand. "I thought it was Dan. That maybe he'd followed us from Nevada. I was stupid to think I could keep my phone."

"He's not going to hurt you while we're here."

"Colton, I have a confession to make. I hate guns."

"*Hate* them?" He narrowed his eyes.

"Well, I'm afraid of them."

"That's better."

"You mean it makes more sense than just hating them on principle?" She quirked a brow.

"Well, you *are* practically part of a military dynasty."

"And I never joined up." She threw a glance in Sean's direction. "Do you think he bought it? Us?"

"Sean is way too happy to pay much attention to anything else but Bonnie right now."

"Other than someone breaking into his property."

"Yeah, that was my fault. I should have figured he'd notice."

"I shouldn't have turned on the light when I came into the kitchen. But…it's so dark out here."

"Speaking of that, what were you doing up and wandering the house?" He glanced down at her, taking in what she wore.

It was only then she realized she was wearing her most comfortable nightgown, the thin white cotton one she'd used so long it was practically…see-through.

"Oh my God!" She leapt up, covering her bosom with her hands. Her *heaving* bosom? Lord, she hoped not! "I'm so embarrassed."

"Don't be." Colton gave her an amused look. "It's perfectly normal that you'd be wearing that since we're engaged."

With that she ran down the hallway, stopping between bedroom doors. His room? Hers? Did it matter? Would Sean notice? Would he think it weird she was covering her boobs with her hands?

Is this my life?

From the kitchen, Sean leaned into the hall, holding the long old-fashioned cord and handset. "Sure, I'll ask her. Hey, Jennifer, would you like to come over for breakfast? Bonnie wants to meet the woman who locked Colton down."

"Sure!" Jennifer shouted, then ran into the bathroom, the least complicated choice among doors, and shut it behind her.

"BONNIE SAYS you shaved two years off her life and gave her another gray hair. She might need to punch you once, but she forgives you."

"Sorry I wasn't great about keeping in touch. I did the best I could considering. But I feel like I've missed…a lot."

Colton hoped Sean took the hint and would now explain how in the hell he wound up on an eyesore of a billboard.

"The sign…it should be coming down soon." Sean ran a hand down his face. "And before you say anything, I'm not proud of it."

"Mr. *Cowboy?*"

"It was a reality dating show Beulah talked me into. She's been pulling out all the stops to bring more women to town. This was her bright idea. But as it turns out, it worked out fine for me because Bonnie Lee happened to be one of the contestants."

"Bonnie was a contestant?" Colton choked back a laugh. "Talk about stacking the deck."

He shrugged. "It's not like I knew she'd come back."

"You *should* have." Colton shook his head.

"Yeah, yeah. Everybody says that. The truth is, I had my own selfish reasons for doing the show before I even knew Bonnie Lee had signed on. They couldn't pay me a salary, but they offered to make a large donation to my wild horse foundation."

"No kidding."

"When I went with Bonnie Lee to Canada for the *Kavanaugh's Way* reboot, I wound up with even more donors. You ought to come out later this afternoon to see the mustangs I'm keeping here."

"Well, congratulations on both. You and Bonnie. Finally, you locked that down."

"And speaking of locking it down..." Sean glanced down the hallway. "Um, how did you lock *that* down? She's way out of your league, bro."

"Hey!" But Colton knew it was true.

After seeing her lying on the floor, her sheer nightgown hiked up over luscious legs, he'd had a good long look at his fake fiancée. Spending time guarding her wasn't exactly going to be a hardship.

"She looks like that woman...who was that singer you crushed on so hard? She wasn't even a country singer if I recall."

"Katy Perry." Colton hung his head.

Damn brother knew where all the skeletons were buried.

"And I still think she's hot."

"No argument from me even if I prefer redheads." He grinned.

"So, what else has changed around here? Because it feels like...pretty much everything."

"You'll get used to it. The important things remain the same. Delores still makes the best fried chicken in the state.

Riggs is still cranky and ornery but now he has three children so he's less of a curmudgeon. You should see him when Mary makes him wear a princess crown. I laughed so hard I almost split a rib."

"I'll have to get over to see him today."

"I'm sure he'll be at breakfast."

"I hope he remembers me."

"Are you kidding? No one has forgotten you, bud. We were just waiting for you to come back. And every time we thought you were finally done, you re-upped."

"They make it tempting. I'm only thirty-five and I can officially retire with a pension that starts in two years."

That didn't explain why Colton had rarely taken any of his leaves at home. Sean was kind enough never to ask or pry too deeply. The short story was that he had a fear if he came back, he'd never want to leave. This town…well, it made him feel vulnerable. Weak. Wonderful things had happened to him and his brothers here. Wonderful and horrible. He'd come back for his mother's funeral, then his father's not long after. Those were the only times he'd been back, which might have something to do with the vulnerability associated with the trips. And then there was the betrayal involving Taylor, his oldest friend. Though that hadn't kept him away, it hadn't encouraged him to run back home, either.

But there were good memories, too.

The first time all three brothers had arrived at the foster home of Calvin and Marge Henderson they were dirty, hungry and abandoned by their drug-addicted parents. It could have been temporary, but once his mother laid eyes on them, she swore she'd never let them go. All three were adopted. There was biological family, and there was found family. He'd *found* his parents and then lost them again. But he'd lost a lot of friends, too, along the way and learned to live with grief.

"Hey, where'd you go?" Sean elbowed Colton, who snapped out of his daze.

He knew. Of course, he did. They were practically twins. Both raised by an older brother who practically took on the role of father. Riggs. Colton had disappointed him so many times it became another reason coming back was going to be tough. But it was time.

"I'm okay. It's just…a lot to take in."

"Then do it slowly. One step at a time."

Colton wouldn't mention he had a job to do while he readjusted to life. A job to protect Jennifer, his so-called fiancée. Let Sean believe he was happy and settled. The expression on his face said it all. And maybe it would be a nice distraction. Later, he'd explain, and Sean would understand why Colton chose to keep him out of the loop.

He always did.

CHAPTER 5

*I*n the bright light of day, Jennifer breathed in the clear and fresh morning air. As she'd known, the house they were staying in was set on a hill, but outside the land stretched as far as the eye could see. Mostly beautiful flatland, accompanied by the occasional hill dotting the landscape in the distance. There were the boonies, and then there was the *countryside*. This beautiful patch of land fell on the peaceful side of country. A person couldn't feel alone and stranded out here. The beauty of the white cotton clouds so fluffy in the achingly blue sky seemed to show off. Not a hint of smog in sight. Heaven.

It took only three minutes to walk the several yards down the hill to Sean's home, passing live oaks, pecan trees, and abundant colorful spring wildflowers. Sean's home had a wraparound porch, complete with a porch swing and decorative pillows. Beautiful potted flowers were hanging from the porch ceiling, sitting along the rail, and on each step leading to the front door. Blue hydrangeas, birds-of-paradise, and columbine made up the landscape of their lush front yard. Jennifer had been walking side by side with

Colton, talking very little and trying to mentally prepare for this meeting. He still hadn't told her much about his past. There'd been no time because she'd dominated the conversation. But their cover story at least fit the fact that they might not actually know each other well. Whirlwind romance, he'd said, and she'd repeated like a parrot.

Maybe not a *romance*, but this arrangement was definitely hasty and impetuous. Wonder what her father would think if or when he heard they were pretend engaged. Would he wonder in awe at Colton's brilliance under pressure, or have him court-martialed?

Sean stood on the porch watching as they approached, his arm around a beautiful redhead who must be his fiancée, Bonnie Lee. She looked oddly...familiar. Jennifer had the annoying skill of never forgetting a face. So, whether it be her grocery store clerk, her dental hygienist, or the stewardess on a flight, she had perfect facial recall. Names she forgot, but someone's face was forever imprinted on her mind. Both a good *and* a bad thing. She kept thinking she might know a person, when really, she'd run into them once in her life.

Colton grabbed Jennifer's hand and pulled her a bit closer. They'd been walking about a foot apart, which didn't exactly give them the appearance of being in love.

"To make this look real," he said, answering her unasked question. "Sean knows I'm affectionate with my girlfriend."

His hand was warm and strong, and she struggled not to feel like she was on a first date with a man. Because essentially, she was.

"Did you...leave your gun behind?"

He wore a light denim jacket, and she couldn't tell if he wore a holster underneath. "No. It's going with me everywhere we go. Remember, I'm also on the job."

"Right."

She would argue nothing could possibly happen to her on their property, that the point of coming here to the country-side was they'd be safe here. But this morning she'd thought Dan might have opened the door to the cabin. The memory was still fresh in her mind, right along with the thought that she wanted to live. Badly.

"Don't worry," he said as if he was also remembering. "You're safe with me. *Always.*"

A sheepdog rushed past them, a streak of black-and-white fur going up the porch steps to join Bonnie and Sean.

Bonnie walked down the steps to meet them halfway.

"Colton, you rascal!" She went into his arms, causing him to let go of Jennifer's hand. "You gave me another gray hair and gray doesn't look good on a redhead."

"Bonnie Lee. It's been a long time."

There was that smile again, so honest, so...open. Another Colton was in there, a younger version, and a more carefree one. This Colton didn't have his soldier guard up. This Colton wasn't at all frightening.

Bonnie broke the hug to smile at Jennifer. "I'm sorry. I haven't seen this guy for years. We all grew up together. I knew Colton *before* he was a soldier. I knew him when he was a skinny kid, throwing pebbles at Sean and me."

"You shouldn't have been making out in the *barn.* Easy target."

"I'm Jennifer Walker." Jennifer stuck out her hand.

Bonnie ignored the outstretched hand and pulled Jennifer into her arms. The woman gave great hugs, she had to give her that. First bear-hugged by Sean, then Bonnie. Jennifer wasn't used to this type of affection. She didn't come from a hugging family. In her family they were far more likely to salute each other than hug. Good to know Colton had enjoyed a healthy balance between the harshness of the mili-tary and a warm and loving family.

She, on the other hand, had not. Neither had Joe.

"Have we met before? You look *so* familiar."

"I've got that kind of a face?" Bonnie smiled.

"Meghan Kavanaugh," Sean called out. "In the flesh."

It all came together in a matter of minutes. She was older now but still so beautiful.

"You're Meg! *Kavanaugh's Way*? I watched that show when I was a teenager."

Bonnie grinned and covered her mouth. "You're making me feel old."

"When the streaming service brought it back, I binged all the old seasons so I could watch right where the show left off. You were such a badass on that show."

"As the oldest daughter of an Irish mafia family, I had to be." Bonnie blew on her fingernails like a lady boss. "How old are you, honey?"

"Twenty-five."

"You're not just a rascal, you're a cradle-robber!" Bonnie called out. "He's thirty-five, you know?"

"Um, sure. I do."

She did not know this. He certainly didn't look much older than Jennifer. But she and her new fake fiancée had a bit of an age gap going on. Well, that was okay. Probably.

"I've dated younger men and there's no comparison with the experience of an older man who knows what he's doing." She elbowed Jennifer. "But love is love, right? Sue me, but I'm a romantic. Sean and I fell in love at sixteen. We're only now getting married. Second chances are the best. And all the rage."

Colton had moved up the steps, where he squatted to pet the dog. "This must be Beer."

"Forgive my fiancée and his poor taste in names," Bonnie said. "He thought it funny and original to name his dog Beer. He *won't* be naming our children."

Sean chuckled and waved them inside. "C'mon in before the rest of them get here."

"The rest? You're expecting more company?" Jennifer asked as she followed Bonnie inside.

"Just family."

Just family turned out to be the oldest brother, Riggs, and his wife Winona. They had three small children, two of them twins. The famous Delores was here, too, herding the twin boys who seemed to love to chase poor Beer's tail. The little girl was adorable and riding high on her dad's broad shoulders. The moment their family unit arrived the decibel level went up by at least fifty percent. Less than twenty minutes later, everyone had arrived, and hugs were exchanged.

"This is my mother, Maybelle Wheeler, and my aunt, Beulah Hayes." Bonnie placed a hand on Jennifer's shoulder. "Ladies, prepare to be shocked. This is Colton's fiancée, Jennifer."

"His *fiancée*?"

Beulah Hayes wore an outfit that could best be described as country chic. The dark blue jeans looked like they'd been pressed, and she wore a pink-and-yellow scarf matching her pink-and-white gingham blouse. Her sister Maybelle dressed in a similar fashion but without the scarf and pressed jeans.

"Well, now isn't that something. Congratulations," said Maybelle.

"Um, thank you." Jennifer didn't know what to do with her hands, so they fluttered in front of her like birds. "I love him, of course."

Both Maybelle and Beulah cocked their heads, observing her like she was a strange oddity. Not entirely unpleasant, but out of place. A Los Angeles pigeon among all these bluebirds.

"Of course, you love him," said Maybelle as though speaking to a five-year-old.

"People don't usually get engaged unless they're in love." Beulah's twang was thicker than Maybelle's.

Something about this woman said "lady in charge" and "queen bee." Jennifer should stay on her good side or this ruse of theirs wouldn't last the day.

She caught Beulah staring at Jennifer's empty ring finger and quirking a brow. "Did the ring need to be sized?"

Yes, that would have been a better idea.

She held up her naked finger. "Colton wanted me to pick out something I'd like."

"Nothing worse than a piece of jewelry you hate," Bonnie said. "And have to wear for the rest of your life."

"Then how did he propose?" Maybelle asked.

Fortunately, as a journalist, Jennifer thought fast on her feet. "It was…romantic. Um, he had a box, wrapped very prettily and he dropped to one knee and everything."

"That does sound like a man of Stone Ridge. But what was in the *box?*" Beulah cocked her head.

"It was empty."

"Empty," Maybelle repeated, as if dumbfounded.

"And in it, there was a little note that said I should pick whatever I wanted since I would be wearing it for the rest of my life."

"Aw," Bonnie said, hand on her heart. "Sweet, *sweet* Colton."

"Ours was a quick courtship," Jennifer said, trying to remember all the particulars. "We met through my father, who knew Colton. He introduced us."

Best of all none of this was a lie. The two ladies clucked their approval and nodded.

"*Where* did you meet?" Bonnie said.

This they had *not* discussed, or if they had, she could not recall.

Jennifer swallowed and pulled on her pinky finger, a nervous habit. "Well, it was…we met in—"

"Los Angeles." Colton appeared at her side, draping his arm around her waist. "That was the *first* time we met."

"Well, now, Colton, sweetheart." Beulah shook her head. "I sure do thank you for bringing along your fiancée but hopefully you're not getting married too soon. Because we're not quite ready for her."

"You should have called ahead," Maybelle said, nodding.

Called *ahead*?

Not quite *ready*?

Jennifer glanced at Colton, but he just shrugged. "Not anytime soon, so don't worry, but we can pass on the quilt. Right, honey?"

"Um…uh sure."

Quilt?

"You will most certainly not pass on the marriage quilt, young man!" Beulah shook a finger. "That's bad luck."

Wait. What? *Marriage* quilt? This felt like the *Twilight Zone*. As if she'd stepped into an alternate reality and time traveled back to the Old West.

"Miss Beulah, please don't scare Jennifer off with your old-school traditions. She's a modern woman," Colton said.

"And my *niece* isn't a modern woman? We're still putting the finishing touches on Bonnie's quilt. Then we can move forward with Jennifer's so it's ready for your wedding, whenever that may be. We will call in reinforcements if needed."

"You make it sound like you'll rally the troops." Colton skimmed his hand low on her back and it felt…kind of nice.

"That's exactly what we'll do. I just make one phone call to the top of the phone tree, Anne Abernathy? And then it just goes on down the line until we get to Helen Zelinski." She turned to Jennifer. "We make marriage quilts for all the brides in town. You'll have your own marriage quilt some-day, sugar, handmade by the Ladies of S.O.R.R.O.W."

"It isn't as weird as it sounds." Bonnie laughed. "These women head up the Society of Reasonable, Respectable, Orderly Women. Also, that *sounds* a lot worse than it is. Think of it as a club that does good works and most of them are for women's causes. They're kind of like the junior league, but Stone Ridge style."

Jennifer's mother had been a junior league member, so she understood a little something about this and wasn't sure she'd like it much. Part of the appeal of staying single had been avoiding all the wedding hoopla her aunt Betty and her friends would put her through. Tea parties and cocktails parties. After all, Jennifer was to have married a career military man and proceeded to pop out children one right after the other, supporting her husband as he possibly ran for office. No, *thanks*.

If anything like that was expected of her here, she'd have to pretend to be ill for weeks.

THERE WAS nothing quite like a big breakfast on the Henderson ranch. Even if Colton was so tired he might soon need toothpicks to hold up his eyelids, he ate a little bit of everything. With everyone bringing a dish or two, Bonnie served a breakfast worthy of Delores's best spreads. Hash brown casserole, bacon, green beans, fried okra, apple bread and southern cheese grits.

He hadn't eaten this well in years. No wonder Riggs had called him skinny. He hadn't hugged him like Sean had, but he also hadn't yelled at him. So, he'd count that as a win. Riggs had always expected a lot out of both him and Sean. When their parents died, they'd been left acres upon acres of land in Hill Country. Maybe, biologically, they weren't

Hendersons, but that hadn't mattered to Cal and Marge, who'd left them everything they owned. A few cousins on Cal's side hadn't liked the idea much, but there'd been nothing they could do about it.

Riggs's position was that the brothers could never lose this land, not a square inch of it. He'd gone to law school to protect his adopted family's heritage, specializing in contract law. And he wasn't wholly convinced that Colton had the same kind of passion for the land Riggs did. Colton would just have to prove himself to Riggs. Prove to him he was settled and staying. Just because he'd let another cause come before his family for a time, this didn't mean that he wasn't ready now, to do what he had to do. To *keep* this Henderson land for generations to come. For little Cal, Joey, and Mary. For the kids he assumed Sean and Bonnie would have soon.

And for his own children, someday, even if that seemed light-years away.

Conversations around the table ranged from the hideous billboard the production company still hadn't taken down to all the new cabins the Stephens family was building around Lake Lupine.

"It's an economic boom," Beulah insisted, since apparently, she held most of the blame for all this progress.

"Seems like Beau Stephens and his family's construction company is getting the most out of all this." Riggs scowled.

"Unless you want to count all our single cowboys." Beulah sniffed.

Yet another reason Colton was glad for this charade with Jennifer. If not, Beulah would be trying to marry him off.

"They can't build those cabins fast enough," Winona said, balancing Mary on her lap while she tried to eat.

"Jackson isn't doing too badly, either, with the Shady Grind," Sean said.

"And we have a school for the first time in decades," Bonnie said.

"And don't forget the new medical clinic!" Beulah stated triumphantly.

"Did all these people move here for you, Winona?" Colton said, knowing that his beautiful sister-in-law had quite a fan base.

Winona shook her head and laughed. "Women? Moving here for *me*?"

"They moved here for *Sean*." Bonnie ruffled Sean's hair.

"Or to be on TV." Sean shoved in a helping of cheese grits.

"It was the best idea I've ever had," Beulah said. "And it worked. Just because the town's going to change a little, well, that's the price you pay for a few good women. We need to make room for them."

"Here, here," said Delores.

"And if we could get a spa or hair salon in here soon, that would be good," Bonnie said.

"Hush up! Your cousin's going to do your hair just fine for the wedding," Beulah said.

"Oh, I know, but not everyone has unlimited access to my cousin like I do."

"So, it's just the Stephens family building these units? Beau and them?" As Colton asked, he suspected he knew the answer. "Or are we going to have more stragglers hanging around?"

Beau and his father operated a large family-owned construction company, but they hired on workers all the time. Mostly these were cowboys who were looking for a little extra cash, but with the added need, he worried they would be hiring from all over. More strangers who would blend in easily. And one of them could be Jennifer's stalker.

"Oh, don't worry none." Maybelle waved her hand dismissively. "They're just workers coming through for the job and moving on when it's done. Besides, at least you don't have to worry about more competition for our few women."

Colton couldn't care less about the men-to-women ratio. But a job that transient and temporary was perfect for men with a record. And men trying to blend in, too. He had to force himself to think about these things now. Here, on their ranch, they were safe.

When Riggs and Winona gave each other a goofy smile and Sean and Bonnie kissed, Colton knew he had to do *something*. But a kiss? Now? He was supposed to be a man in love. If he was actually engaged to this woman, he wouldn't keep his hands off her. They'd be sleeping together, oh hell yeah, and that kind of intimacy would *show*.

Jennifer bumped his knee, but he didn't know if that was a prompt or an accident. She wasn't making any moves, simply holding her fork poised over the grits and staring at Sean and Bonnie.

Well, when in Rome...

Taking her free hand in his, he brought it to his lips and brushed a kiss across her knuckles. In what he assumed was her knee-jerk automatic reaction, she pulled her hand back.

He met her eyes and something in them switched and clicked into place.

"Oh," she whispered and didn't give him any more resistance. "Right."

He kissed her wrist, then lowered his lips to her neck, spending a little time there, breathing in her sweet flowery scent. He brushed a kiss to her neck, just under the fleshy soft skin behind her ear. There. Good enough.

When he finally came up for air, he figured he'd done his job. If the rest of them didn't fall for his display, he didn't know what else he could do.

Jennifer stared at him, her eyes soft and...surprised.

Hopefully because he knew how to appreciate a woman.

How to make her want more. She probably thought he'd been in the desert too long. Much like his family. Well, he was here to prove to everyone he'd come back whole. He could do relationships. He could handle commitment and a family.

When he turned to face the table, all eyes were on him. Sean and Bonnie were grinning. Riggs and Winona had moved on from kissing and were trying to stop their children from starting a food fight. Delores beamed. Beulah and Maybelle silently nodded and clucked their approval.

Yeah, this was going to be a good thing for Jennifer and him both. It suited two purposes.

Now, no one would worry about him adjusting back into small-town life after fighting a war for several years.

"And on that note, we have an announcement to make!" Sean stood and offered Bonnie Lee his hand.

"We know, we know. You're finally getting married," Winona quipped.

"Not that." Sean shook his head. "Bonnie and I decided a month ago after a lot of thought and prayer. We're officially applying to be foster parents right after the honeymoon. After what Cal and Marge Henderson did for me and my brothers, it's the least we can do."

"Oh, Sean," Delores said, hand to her heart. "That's beautiful. Your parents would be so proud."

Riggs stood up to shake Sean's hand, and then so did Colton. The thought that they would continue the family tradition of giving stray kids a home—the same that had been done for them —was a nice welcome.

CHAPTER 6

All the food nearly put Colton into a coma. He should run two miles after that kind of feast but instead he walked Jennifer back to their cabin. It had been decided at breakfast that he and his "new fiancée" would stay here until he started construction on his own home. He assured Riggs, in an effort to confirm he was putting down his stakes, that he would soon. Truthfully, he was in no hurry. This small cottage was good enough for him.

Sean had built his house not long after Riggs married Winona. The plan all along had been that the three brothers would build houses on their cattle ranch. It was Cal and Marge's dream for their adopted sons to always be together and, side by side, raise their families. It hadn't been enough to foster three brothers, then adopt all three so they could stay together. Even after death his adopted parents continued to give.

But for years, Colton hadn't gone along with the established program. He'd wanted to see the world first and Cal understood. Much as he'd loved his parents, family and obligations were dead weight when he was eighteen. Now, he *had* seen the world, and far more he wished he could unsee. Turned out Riggs was right. There was no place like Texas. So, sure, he'd build his home once Riggs released those funds from the trust. It would be solid proof he wasn't going anywhere and by then it wouldn't matter that Jennifer was gone.

In the meantime, he'd live here comfortably. A week or two with Jennifer if all went according to plan, then later, after assuring his family he was okay after their "breakup," he'd find someone else. Maybe one of those new women who'd moved here after *Mr. Cowboy*. He only hoped this time with her wouldn't ruin him for anyone else. Her scent alone was intoxicating and all he'd done was kiss her hand and neck.

She'd hardly looked at him after that kissing overture and he worried he'd gone too far. He wanted to inspire her trust, not grow fear for yet another man. Sure, her father trusted him, and she'd lent him that trust.

Now he'd have to prove himself.

"You should sleep," Jennifer said when they got back.

"Just a couple of hours is all I need. I am pretty whipped. You woke me up mid-dream with that shriek of yours. It rivaled some of the best slasher movies I've seen."

"I thought Dan had found us." She studied the ground. "And your brother has a big rifle."

He shrugged. "He's smart. You know what they say, don't bring a knife to a gun fight."

"How about we don't have any *fights* at all?"

In a perfect world, sweetheart. In a perfect world.

"Fine with me, but if we come across your stalker, don't expect me to engage in a conversation with him. I'll neutralize him and ask questions later."

"Sure, tough guy." She gave him an eye roll. "I can see why my father asked for your help. He's the same way."

Colton nodded, knowing how much of this was the truth. "Hey, I'm sorry about the kiss."

"That's okay, I know why you did it."

Well, she knew one of his reasons. The secret reason, the fact he'd wanted to kiss her, that would remain need to know. She was skittish and had good reason to be. He would not be one more male in her life who didn't listen.

"From now on, I want you to be the one to initiate anything physical between us. I'm going to back off. If that makes it look odd, then so be it. It's our fake relationship. It can be whatever we want it to be. I don't want to scare you."

"Thank you." She hesitated. "But I'm telling people I love you, and I'd appreciate it if you did the same."

"Why else do people get married?"

"Um, you told your brother it's because I threatened to cut you off."

"It was a *joke*."

"One I didn't appreciate."

"Consider it done. I'll tell everyone I adore you." Halfway down the hall, he turned one last time to Jennifer. "You'll be okay while I sleep?"

She saw the question in his eyes. He wanted reassurance she wouldn't be a difficult person to guard.

"Don't worry, I won't go anywhere without you. And if we're going to stay here, we need supplies. You do have a store around here?"

"Downtown. I'll take you there."

"Maybe you can go, and I'll stay here."

"You're coming with me. The answer isn't going to be for you to hide out in this cabin like you did in your apartment." He opened the door to the bedroom.

"Do you…think we were followed here?" She pulled on that pinky finger again.

"Probably not. But we can't be too careful."

Colton sat on the edge of the bed and picked up his phone. *No service.* Not a surprise there. Still, he was due to check in with her father. He picked up the handset on the nightstand. There were several of these around the house and they also served as intercoms. Not that he would need one in this small house.

"Walker," said the gruff voice on the other end of the line.

"It's Henderson."

"I didn't recognize the number. How is she?"

"We arrived before dawn and had no issues."

Horace whistled. "You made good time. Is she giving you any trouble yet?"

"What *kind* of trouble?"

"She might want to go off plan. Take off without telling you, that kind of thing. Always been a bit of a free spirit, pain in the ass."

Free spirit. And probably a free thinker. Horace wasn't a fan, and in this situation neither was Colton, so he'd be sure to be aware. There were times to go off script and there were times to follow the plan.

"No trouble at all. And I think she's subdued now. My brother accidentally surprised us this morning when he thought someone had broken into the house. He carried a rifle with him."

Horace chuckled. "I imagine she's going to be fairly quiet for a while."

Colton hesitated letting Horace in on their fake relationship situation. This was on a need-to-know basis, too, and he didn't mind falling on the right side of that command for once.

"We still have no Wi-Fi on the ranch, so this is the number to reach us. I'll have my phone on me because it works in the downtown area. Have there been any additional threats?"

"Not that I know of, but I will alert you if there are. For now, I've been driving by and the apartment is clearly unoccupied, which is what we want her stalker to realize."

"You have her phone. Have you turned it off?" He hardly needed to remind Horace, but one never knew. Colton liked to cover all angles.

"Yes."

After a few more particulars and promising to get in touch with any changes in location, Colton hung up.

Then he slept. Like the dead.

WHILE COLTON NAPPED, Jennifer unpacked. She'd taken everything she could fit in three suitcases when her father informed her she'd be going out of town for a while. For her protection.

If only she'd never agreed to go out with Dan. Maybe none of this would have happened. He seemed so nice, so normal, and then like a flipped switch, he became someone else. She should have known someone who had asked her out ten times and wouldn't take no for an answer was not normal.

But then one of her friends would remark, "Derek asked me to marry him seven times before I finally said yes."

Or "At first, I thought Tom was a jerk and that he had to be conceited with those good looks, so I turned him down. Four times. Thank God he never gave up on me!"

So, it wasn't unusual for a man to press if truly interested. Jennifer hadn't dated much since her college boyfriend, and she kept thinking maybe it was time to get started again. Mistake number one: she agreed to one date.

Dan was handsome in a Ken doll sort of way and put together in his suits and wingtips. Perfect hair, perfect straight white teeth. Completely unthreatening and about as far from a military man as possible. He worked at a local real estate brokerage firm and drove a BMW. Not that she cared about money, but he obviously had the ability to function in the world.

Only later would she wonder how.

On their first date she learned he was a fan of her podcast and confessed that's the first time he'd heard of her. It should have been a wake-up call. He'd looked her up on social media, and the fact they'd run into each other at her regular coffeeshop was no coincidence. But she did not realize any of this at the time.

"What you do is a service to the community," Dan had said.

She was flattered he appreciated her up-and-coming podcast.

"That's my intention. Do you know of anyone who suffers from PTSD?"

Her recent podcast series had focused on the need for treatment for returning soldiers. A subject near to her heart.

"No, but I give regularly to the Wounded Warrior Project."

"Oh, that's nice."

After several more comments on how much money he had, and how much of it he donated, Jennifer realized *this* wasn't going to work. The man was obsessed with money and his sense of pride over his achievements (fancy home, a flashy car) seemed over the top. Weirdly, he spoke of himself in the third person, lauding his numerous accomplishments. Plus, he was mean to the waitress.

He got no kiss at the door and only a quick hug with thanks for the meal, even if she'd insisted on paying for her half.

Dan called her the next day. She made excuses as to why she couldn't go out again, busy with research and interviews for the podcast. All of this had the benefit of being 100 percent true. But it turned out she wasn't ready for a relationship.

Dan:

> Are you sure there's no one else? You can tell me if there is. I'll understand.

She typed back:

> No, there's no one. I'm just a busy professional, which I'm sure you can understand.

Dan:

> I think I get it. That's okay.

She'd breathed a sigh of relief when the text messages stopped. Dan got her unspoken message. There would be no more dates. But a week later, he sent flowers. Flattered, she'd texted him but set the tone from personal to professional:

> Thank you for the flowers. Listen to the episode tonight, it's a good one.

Dan:

> You know I will. I like to fall asleep listening to the sound of your sultry voice.

Okay, kind of creepy, but she'd been told before that she had a smooth radio-style-personality voice so maybe this made sense. Still, she didn't like the idea. It was the first highly personal thing he'd said to her, and she didn't see it as a warning except in hindsight.

The messages started up again, at first just compliments about the podcast and her guests. Suggesting people to interview and resources. Just when she thought he'd accepted their "friends only" rule, the new flurry of text messages began.

> I sensed a connection between you and the soldier you interviewed. What is his name?

> Tell the truth. Is he your new lover?

> Have I been forgotten so quickly?

> I won't be ignored.

Yes, he'd sensed a connection between her and the soldier she'd interviewed. Her brother, Joe. He'd wanted to remain anonymous for many reasons, every one of which Jennifer agreed to. But despite the innocence of it all, it wasn't any of Dan's business if she was dating someone else. She ignored him.

Things got progressively worse after that day. Jennifer would often wake to three hundred text messages on her phone.

> Why won't you accept there's something between us? I want us to get married. Stop denying your feelings. It isn't healthy.

Healthy! Ha. He was going to talk to her about healthy. She made the mistake of texting back:

> Please seek professional help. There's someone special out there for you but it isn't me.

It only made him worse. That time he hurled insults at her intelligence and that she shouldn't try to be a faux therapist. She should just stick to what she knew. Interviewing far more interesting people than she'd ever be.

Yes, it hurt, but she didn't respond.

"Why did you ever let him pick you up at the apartment?" her friend Mallory had asked.

"That's not fair. It wasn't like I knew this would happen."

It wasn't the first time Jennifer's friends made her feel as if all of *this* was her fault. She'd encouraged it somehow. She hadn't been firm enough in her rejection. From time to time she thought she felt Dan watching her from outside and she wouldn't allow any of her male friends into the apartment, lest he get the wrong idea and start harassing them next. Eventually, it wasn't much of a problem as one by one she lost friends. Once, Dan had shown up in the middle of the night banging on her door, threatening suicide if she didn't let him in. It was a particularly sensitive subject for Jennifer, one he should understand, and it had sent her in a downward spiral. She'd called 911 but he was gone before they arrived.

A new phone accomplished the fact he could no longer text her, but it didn't stop him from watching from across the street. Mallory had gone with her to the police to file a restraining order, but since then Dan hadn't technically done anything wrong. If he showed up at the apartment and knocked on her door, he would have violated the order, and she could technically call the police and have him arrested. Jennifer didn't want to do that. If he lost his job, he'd be even more despondent with far more time to obsess over her. And he'd be angrier because now she'd done something to truly hurt him.

When he could no longer text her, he sent flowers and cards. He watched her from across the street. She'd caught him once, as she tried to swim laps in her condo's pool. Her favorite way to unwind and she hadn't been able to indulge in weeks.

"Have you told your family?" Mallory asked. "You need to tell them what's happening. Maybe they can *do* something."

Once she'd confided in her father, who'd never been thrilled with her choice of occupation, he was the one to suggest/order time away from home to let matters calm down. But how much time would be enough? Should she wait for Dan to give up and move on to some other poor and unsuspecting woman? She felt trapped and resented allowing Dan to win by forcing her to retreat. To rearrange her life. But as her father pointed out, he was winning anyway when he forced her to live in fear.

For now, she'd issued a statement that the podcast was on hiatus. *She'd* never mentioned her issues with an obsessed fan, not wanting to make herself the story. Even now, she didn't see how she could ever talk about this. It was humiliating. She should have known better, but she'd never dreamed of the kind of popularity the podcast had brought her. Now it would be best called notoriety and if she didn't get back to podcasting soon, she was fairly sure she would be done.

Colton was still resting after she'd unpacked, so she wandered through the house inspecting every nook and cranny. It was her nature to snoop, hence her choice of profession, and surely Delores wouldn't mind. This was her house, after all, and the lovely woman reminded Jennifer of her own grandmother. She found the kitchen stocked with pots and pans, cookie sheets and pie pans. Silverware in one drawer, a rolling pin and cookie cutters in another.

In one drawer, a matchbook labeled "The Shady Grind" alongside a pad and several pens and pencils. A list labeled "phone tree" was of interest. Beulah had talked about this as a system of disseminating information like people must have done in the olden days. Jennifer would love to know more of this antiquated system.

She made her way over to the paperbacks, sliding her

finger across the spines. There were several western novels, some self-help, and plenty of historical romance. All good choices which further validated her high opinion of Delores. Then, Jennifer hit the jackpot. Photo albums and scrapbooks.

Her own mother had scrapbooked for years when Jennifer and her brother were young, so she recognized the stencils, cut-outs, and stickers. Delores had beautifully decorated pages and the center of her subject was clear: the brothers. They were seen in photos from the time they were children.

"First week at home with Marge and Calvin" the page read. There were photos of a younger Riggs, recognizable though thin and scrappy. Still clearly in charge of his younger brothers, one hand draped around each one protectively. Sean and Colton were look-alikes even then, their wild brown hair lightened by the sun, similar expressions of mischief in their eyes.

They were close, clearly, and once more the pebble of regret formed in her throat. She missed the easy relationship she'd had with Joe before he'd entered the service. Even now, even though he had improved, they weren't as close.

The photos and pages progressed and ended with Colton dressed out in his Army fatigues. Obviously at the start of his career and not the Green Beret he'd become. He looked so much younger, thinner, eager. It was a story she understood far too well. She put the scrapbook down and went for another album, flipping through pages of picnics and proms and days by the lake.

There were photos of Sean and Bonnie Lee, and also Colton with a blonde girl who appeared often in the photos. It was only when she heard the knock at the door that Jennifer realized she'd spent hours immersed in her study of the Hendersons.

She peeked through the curtains and found Delores's happy smile on the other side.

Jennifer unlocked and opened the door. "Colton is taking a nap. He drove us straight through for about twenty-four hours."

Delores handed Jennifer a paper bag. "That's okay. I brought some supplies for y'all."

"We were going to the store later."

"Now you won't have to." Delores went back to the ATV she had ridden over to fetch more boxes.

Jennifer set the bag on the kitchen counter and began to unpack. Flour, sugar, butter, eggs, milk. Canned soups and chili. Rice.

"This is one of Colt's favorite." Delores placed her hand on the can of Tex-Mex chili con carne.

Jennifer helped Delores put the groceries away. "Thank you for this. I'm sure Colton really appreciates it as well."

"I for one am glad he's sleeping, and we gals have a chance to chat."

Gosh, she hoped Delores wouldn't grill her on details she'd have to remember for Colton later.

"I see you found my albums." Delores gestured to the couch where Jennifer had been sitting just before she arrived.

"It's nice looking at him and his brothers grow up through photos. I...really don't know that much about Colton. We're still getting to know each other."

Jennifer loved the way this sentence was also 100 percent true.

"Well, sometimes love happens that way. Riggs and Winona were also an unexpected surprise. Both were married before and found each other later in life. Happened very quickly. The physical attraction was pretty immediate, but love wasn't far behind. Now those two have one of the strongest marriages I've ever seen."

"How about Colton? Was he…ever married before?"

Too late, Jennifer realized it might be a question she should have already asked. But Colton was thirty-five, and an early marriage would have been possible.

"He didn't tell you?" Delores blinked. "Not our Colton. Oh, he had a teenage sweetheart, but they didn't last. He was pretty singularly focused on the military early on. We tried but couldn't quite wash it out of him. I figure it's because Calvin had been in the service and Colton admired the heck out of him. He figured he could always be a cowboy later."

"I've never been married, either, but I'm only twenty-five."

"Oh, an age gap. You seem quite mature for your age." Delores walked to the couch and Jennifer followed. "Are you from a big family, too?"

"No, just me and my brother, Joe." Jennifer didn't volunteer any more information.

She didn't like talking about her brother and guarded his privacy. Joe had been through enough and finally seemed to have reached a good place.

"Do you think you and Colton will have many children?"

Jennifer blinked and Delores laughed and waved her hand dismissively. "You probably haven't even talked about this yet. I'm sorry to spook you. I always thought Colton would have a bunch of children but he's getting a late start."

He'd been busy with other matters, Jennifer guessed. She tried not to think of those other matters.

"I want children." This was true. "Someday."

"Do you have a career?"

Of all the questions, this one was the toughest. "I…used to be a journalist. I had a popular podcast."

"Wonderful. You're taking a break?"

This was the easier answer. "Yes."

"One good thing about writing is you can do it

anywhere." Delores went on, not waiting for a response. "My husband and I couldn't have children of our own and neither could Marge, my best friend. When she and Cal adopted the boys, they became like my own. And, with Marge gone I'm all they have."

"Colton speaks so highly of you."

"Well, although a mother doesn't have favorites, just between you, me, and the wall, he may have been Marge's favorite. Such a sweetheart. Those beautiful eyes and sweet smile. He's always been a looker."

Jennifer was about to comment on the resemblance between Sean and Colton, but Delores kept talking.

"He won't say anything, of course, but I'm sure his ex-girlfriend is going to be brokenhearted when she hears he's engaged. But the breakup was her fault anyway, so she should talk. I'm so glad he came home with someone kind like you."

So, there was yet another reason Colton might want a fake fiancée. A bit of bitterness between him and his ex? She didn't appreciate being put in the middle of this drama.

"I hope she doesn't hate me."

"Don't be silly, honey. Us women stick together in Stone Ridge. There are so few, and so many eligible men that there's no room for petty jealousy or bitterness. Well, mostly. And if Colton loves you, we will all love you." She stood and went hands on hips. "Now, should I teach you how to cook Colt's very favorite meal?"

CHAPTER 7

olton woke and for a brief moment he did not recognize his surroundings. He sat up ramrod straight while his heart pounded against his rib cage. But then he noticed the pale blue ruffled curtains with bright sunshine spilling through them. A framed photo on the wall of his mother, Marge, and Delores when they were much younger. The throbbing in his chest slowed and eased. Gradually he relaxed in the knowledge that he was no longer in Germany, going through debriefings. Putting himself through therapy. He was home.

The commonplace was important, the familiar and routine key to readjustment. Today, he'd go riding and get reacquainted with his horse, Freya. He'd have to figure something to do with Jennifer. He hated leaving her alone for a few hours, even in a place where she should feel safe. It would take her time, too, since she'd been through her own form of terrorizing. He had to be patient and simply do his job. Um, favor.

Look out for Horace's daughter until the threat was gone.

The scent of garlic and onion wafted through the house

and smelled delicious. His therapist told him that familiar scents would be therapeutic and help with any flashbacks. He rose from bed and pulled on a shirt. He wouldn't bother shaving, and dragging a hand through his hair was the most he'd do today about his appearance. There was a woman, sure, but she wasn't his, and he would do well to remember that from now on. No need to impress.

"And that's Colton's first sleepover with his best friend, Taylor."

"Delores, what are you doing?" He found both women on the couch, a photo album settled on both of their laps.

"Taking a walk down memory lane, Mr. Popular," Jennifer said.

"Hello, sleepyhead." Delores stood and reached up to tousle his hair like he was still nine. "You'll be happy to know I brought y'all some groceries."

"You didn't have to do that."

"I wanted to. And guess what? I showed your fiancée how to make your favorite meal. You're welcome."

"What's my favorite meal?"

Delores knew this even if he didn't. Colton used to eat whatever was put in front of him.

"Pot roast, of course!"

He scratched his beard stubble, so thick it made a sound. "Oh yeah, I forgot."

"You'd forget your head if it wasn't screwed on!" Delores waved a hand dismissively. "Anyway, it ought to be tender and succulent for supper. Just keep checking the water, Jennifer. I'll leave you two lovebirds alone."

Jennifer stood. "You don't have to—"

"I'm afraid I do. I promised little Cal I'd play hide and seek with him after his nap. His favorite game. You should see how he plays! When it's his turn to hide he just covers his little face with his hands. He's adorable. We don't have a lot of baby photos of Riggs, but I still see his face in that little boy."

"Don't let us keep you." Colton bent to kiss her cheek. "Don't tell anyone, by the way, but you're my favorite."

"Aw." She beamed. "I'll see y'all tomorrow. I'm so glad you're home."

"Bye, Delores." He shut the door behind her.

"Colton?"

He turned to Jennifer. "What's up?"

"I feel terrible lying to your family. Delores is so sweet and caring. And she's *so* happy that you're engaged."

"I know." He pinched the bridge of his nose. "And I thank you for that."

"But she's going to be angry later. I don't want her to hate me."

"No one's going to hate you." He made his way to the kitchen stove and lifted the lid to peek inside. "You should at some point stop caring what other people think of you."

She behaved as though he'd slapped her, her neck swiveling back. "I...I don't."

Realizing he'd hit on a nerve, he back pedaled. "Okay. I believe you. Look, let *me* be the bad guy when the time comes for truth telling. This isn't your fault."

"Fine." She crossed her arms and jutted her chin. "And I hope this hasn't given you the idea that I'm going to *cook* for you every night. I wouldn't do that even if I was your fiancée for real. I was happy to peel potatoes, but Delores seems to think I want to be some kind of domestic goddess for you."

"Are you kidding me? I wouldn't let you in my kitchen if you tried."

That seemed to stop her short. "*Excuse* me?"

"No offense, but I'm going to do all the cooking around here." He held up both palms. "It isn't that I don't trust you, far from it. But cooking relaxes me. So please, let me handle this."

"*Cooking* relaxes you?"

"Don't believe me?" He chuckled. "I listen to all the cooking podcasts. I'm finally going to have time to make all the food I've been dreaming about."

She narrowed her eyes. "I can't decide if you're teasing or telling me the truth."

"The truth. I'm always going to tell you the truth. No lies between us. Let's lie to everyone else but never to each other."

"Okay."

"Don't you have something that relaxes you?"

"I used to swim every day. There's something about the water and the sound it makes that comforts me. We have a pool at the condo complex, but I haven't been swimming for weeks."

"Why did you stop?"

"I was…afraid he'd see me." She bit on her lower lip and wouldn't meet his eyes.

Jesus. He felt like he'd been punched in the gut.

"Right. The reason you're here."

She pulled on her pinky finger. "You know that thing you said a minute ago? That I want people to like me? That I care too much what they think?"

"Don't listen to me—"

"No, it's true. I should have been meaner to the man. But he was a fan of the podcast and believe it or not I didn't want to alienate him." She shook her head. "Crazy."

"Not crazy. That makes sense."

"You wouldn't do it. No man ever would. It's only us women, for some odd reason, who believe *everyone has* to like us."

"Um, I've known a few women in my life who don't care who likes them."

"Yeah? I want to be more like that." She paused for a beat. "Well at least I didn't move from my complex. It was the only stand I took. I won't move from a place I like just because of him."

"And now here you are."

"Yes, here I am. I know what my father would say, but what do you think? Is he winning?"

"I think he was winning when he terrorized you to the point you couldn't enjoy the pool. When you were afraid to leave your apartment. But I *don't* think he's winning now. He's losing. You're no longer an object within his reach. Sooner or later, he'll realize it and move on when he can't get a reaction."

"But what if he doesn't? What if he hurts himself?"

The hint of fear in her eyes made him wonder what she'd seen or experienced, but he wouldn't go there. What he would do, sometime when he had access to Wi-Fi, is listen to a few of her podcasts. He'd learn something about who she was and what mattered to her. And maybe he'd learn what attracted this stalker enough to obsess over her.

He tipped her chin to meet his eyes. "If he's going to hurt himself, he will do it with or without you. You're not responsible for him. Understand?"

"Yes, I know you're right." She nodded.

But he saw it in her blue eyes. She was worried about the man.

"I'm going to go shower and shave." He raked a finger through the beard stubble, deciding that he should probably make an effort to clean up. "Then I want to show you my horse."

. . .

A FEW MINUTES LATER, Jennifer shut off the stove before they left and peeked under the lid. Delores was right. The roast was the most tender she'd ever seen, meat flaking off like butter. Hopefully Colton would cook it for her another time. Being banished from the kitchen was not the worst thing to ever happen to her. She was a regular take-out person and even had an account with a delivery service once she'd stopped leaving the apartment.

Before Colton took her on this so-called tour or walkabout, she grabbed her camera just in case. This kind of scenery begged for its photo to be taken. And, when she was long gone, she'd have memories of this magical place.

"I have to admit, I'm not too fond of horses," Jennifer confessed as they walked to the stables.

"Not fond of horses, not fond of guns. I see a pattern. You're probably not fond of cowboys, either."

She sped up her walk because he had longer legs than she did and an equally long stride. "Shockingly there aren't many of them in LA"

"Yeah, I know. Sean tried for a while, but he couldn't hang."

"Sean lived in LA? Why?"

"Back when he and Bonnie were trying to reunite the first time. She had to live there for her profession, and he *couldn't* live there. It was a problem."

"I see why it would be."

"Yeah, glad they worked it out. After almost twenty years."

"That's too long if you love each other." She paused because what did she know about love? Not much. "I think."

"Definitely not ideal."

"Speaking of love, Delores seems to think your ex-girlfriend's heart is going to break when she hears you're *engaged*."

"I don't know about that."

"It would be sad to keep you away from someone who has always loved you."

"You let me worry about that."

He hadn't denied there might be someone else, but he also wasn't sharing more. Big surprise there. He was going to be the one to worry about it, which, fine, made sense. But if he was going to be sneaking out to meet a former girlfriend while pretending to be engaged, she should know about it. Probably. If one lovesick old girlfriend found out they were not actually engaged, word would spread quickly. Maybe that was for the best, even if she'd like to pretend for a while longer that soon she'd be a part of Colton's family.

He wasn't touching her anymore, not holding her hand or walking too closely. Instead, he walked a respectable distance from her, giving her space. He'd obviously been serious about letting her set the pace of their PDA. She was okay with the distance for now, but not because she didn't enjoy being close to Colton. It was mostly because she'd become aware that she might be enjoying it a little too much. One thing she'd never do again is lead a man on. And yeah, she understood on one level that Dan's obsession wasn't *her* fault, especially since they'd only had one date, but she still blamed herself in some ways. Good to know Colton didn't judge her. Maybe now she'd try not to judge herself.

Meanwhile, she was living inside a countryside postcard. A long white fence stretched across a grassy plain. Another much longer one divided sections of the property. In the distance, she noticed horses running wild, chasing each other, then stopping to graze. She snapped photos, one after the other, capturing one horse midgallop as graceful as if the wind were pushing him.

"Don't you keep them in the stables?"

"Those must be Sean's wild horses. He has a foundation.

We don't have enough land to keep all the ones he'd like to help, so the foundation leases land where the horses can graze and live freely. Most of them are unbroken."

Unbroken. Jennifer rather loved the word. She would use it somewhere soon, maybe as a title for her next podcast. Whenever she was able to go back to regular life.

"So…no one is ever going to put a saddle on them and ride them? Work them?"

"Probably not. No." Colton stopped and leaned over the fence, ignoring her camera. "But we do have horses to ride. Or we did. I guess I should check on all that."

He went quiet for several minutes. Jennifer thought he seemed pretty lost at times, at once seemingly comfortable and at home, at other times an awkward stranger. It was like this for all the returning soldiers, including Joe. She understood more about the subject than she'd ever wanted to know.

"Hey, where did you go?" She pressed a hand to his arm. "Are you okay?"

He met her eyes, shaking off whatever memory had taken him somewhere else. "Yeah. I'm fine."

"Is it weird being home again, with everything so different?"

"It's not all that different. That's the best thing about our land. It doesn't change the way people do."

"That's true. My brother, Joe, he—"

"Hey, you two!" Sean called out from several yards away. "Want to go for a ride?"

"I know it's probably a dumb thing to ask, but how's my horse doing?" Colton said. "I'm hoping she's still around."

It was only then that Jennifer realized he might have been stalling. Afraid to look and see for himself whether or not he still had a horse.

The smile dropped from Sean's face. "I would have told you if she wasn't."

"Sometimes a soldier thinks nobody wants to send him the bad news." There was something in his tone, laced with pain, that told her he'd received bad news before.

She thought of his father, dying while he was away.

"She's older now, but still hanging in there. No major issues. She's twenty-five and ready for pasture. Living the easy life. She's been waiting for you to come home."

All three of them ambled to the stables, a large gray-and-white building with the classic X on the door. Four separate corrals opened to the adjacent stables.

"There she is." Colton pointed. "Freya."

Colton's horse was a beautiful mare, black with only a streak of white on her forelock. She was on the farthest end of the corral from them when they walked up to the fence.

"Hey, Freya. I'm back."

The mare turned, clearly responding to the sound of Colton's voice. She trotted to the fence and bent her head low toward Colton. He was tall enough to reach for her, and she lowered her head to his shoulder. And smiled contentedly.

"She's smiling," Jennifer said, dumbfounded. "I didn't know a horse could smile."

She snapped away, shot after shot of Colton's back and the horse's muzzle on his shoulder.

"I haven't seen her this happy in *years*." Sean petted her alongside Colton. "Good girl."

Jennifer stopped taking photos to pet her forelock. "Freya? That's an unusual name for a horse. Is it—"

"The Nordic goddess," Colton said. "Freya was the goddess of war."

"Perfect name for the horse of a soldier," Sean said.

"But she's also the goddess of love, fertility, and death," Jennifer said and both men turned to her.

"That's right," Colton said, sounding surprised. "You know your Nordic mythology."

"It's been a long time but there's some stuff I remember. Her death was never mentioned and even after the religion died, she was still worshipped."

"Her chariot is pulled by two cats." Colton chuckled. "Ironic because this Freya hated our barn cats."

Sean, who had walked inside the barn, came back out and held out his hand. "Here, give her a treat and make friends with your fiancé's first love."

Jennifer held out her hand and Freya noticed her for the first time. Turning her large head as if to say, "Who in the world are *you?*" she sniffed her hand for the treat before licking it off Jennifer's hands.

After that, she went right back to Colton, who didn't need a treat for her undying devotion.

"I guess there's nothing quite like your first true love." She grinned at Colton. "Don't worry, I'm not the jealous type."

Not only was she not the jealous type, but Jennifer was gratified that this soldier already had some equine therapy right here at home.

CHAPTER 8

*J*ennifer spent the next hour watching Colton lead Freya to the open pasture, not bothering to saddle her. He uncinched her and let her go free in the larger fenced-in area by the tree line, watching as she trotted along, stopping to chew on some grass. It made a pretty picture through Jennifer's lens. Colton stayed with her, hanging back, but never far behind. Freya never lost sight of him.

Jennifer had heard a lot about equine therapy and that it wasn't always accessible to everyone, especially not in LA. Joe would have enjoyed something like this, as he'd always loved animals. She would check in with him tonight. He was doing so much better now but still didn't enjoy phone calls, and she remained the only one in the family he'd talk to at the moment. The estrangement between him and their father was still going strong and nothing Jennifer said would get him to talk to their father.

Then again, their dad had taken too long to recognize or acknowledge Joe's issues and his need to step away from the military service. Even when Jennifer had tried to intervene, expressing her concern over Joe's obvious depression, her father didn't take it seriously enough. Until the day he'd been forced to acknowledge it. But the fact it got that far was something Joe was still struggling to forgive of their father.

"Have you heard of equine therapy?" Jennifer asked Sean while they watched Colton and Freya getting reacquainted.

Since Sean was a horse rescuer, maybe he'd be interested in rescuing soldiers, too.

"I'm interested in the theory behind it." Sean turned to her, his booted foot on the fence rail. "You and I haven't had a chance to talk. What were you doing when you met my brother and he swept you off your feet?"

"How do you know I didn't sweep *him* off his feet?"

"I have no doubt you did."

There was something about this family, this setting, that made Jennifer feel freer than she had in a while. She could feel herself coming back slowly, her old spirit returning, the fear slowly seeping out of her. Colton and his family felt so safe. She'd forgotten what it was like to be this secure. But it wasn't just the distance from LA. and the remoteness of this area putting her at ease. It was this family.

"I guess it was mutual sweeping." Jennifer tucked a stray hair behind her ear. "I was…when I met him…I used to have a fairly popular podcast."

It hurt to think of it all in the past. The podcast had meant so much to her because of all the good she'd done, all the people she'd helped.

"Yeah? What's the name? Bonnie and I love the true crime ones when we can get them out here."

"I called it *Truth Salad*. I interviewed all kinds of people on a range of subjects but had started a special on PTSD when I…when I had to take a break."

"Did Colton want you to stop? That doesn't sound like him."

"No, um, I just wanted to."

Lie number two. She should keep track of them and later send this nice man a letter asking for his forgiveness.

"I hope you get back to it. I understand that you can do a podcast from anywhere. Even if we don't have WiFi here, we have dial-up. I always like to say it's slow but worth waiting for. Hey, thank you for coming here in time for the wedding, by the way. It means a lot. I wasn't sure Colton would get here in time. I'm glad you all made it out."

"This is all pretty amazing to a big-city girl. I feel like I'm on the set of a Hallmark movie."

"Once you live here, it's hard to feel comfortable anywhere else. The land just settles into your bones."

"I can see that."

She'd expected for the quiet and lack of Wi-Fi to grate on her nerves. But instead of frustration, this place had begun to sink into her with the warmth of an old and well-loved blanket. A blanket so worn-out, it ought to be replaced but never would be because it was soft and perfect.

Colton rejoined them and Sean suggested they grab a couple of ATVs and ride out to the pasture where he let the wild horses graze. She hopped on the back of Colton's ATV, strapping her camera to her, grabbing on to his waist and initiating the first physical contact they'd had today. And my goodness, his was a strong back. Her legs pressed and gripped against the taut muscles of his thighs. She pictured all that sinewy skin and fought against the mental image of Colton not wearing any pants. Disgusted with her basic thoughts, she immediately put his pants back on in her mind and focused on the view ahead.

They followed Sean's ATV down a small hill, then along a well-worn path of flat land. He came to a stop and pointed in the distance to a field filled with horses grazing.

"Are all of them mustangs?" Colton said.

"So far. Levi, our local horse whisperer, wants a crack at one or two of 'em. It's a smart idea because if they're trained, they're far more practical to have on a ranch. They can at least earn their keep. Right now, no one wants them."

"Except you," Jennifer said, snapping a shot of Sean pointing to the horses.

"I wish I could keep more of them, but it isn't just the vet bills. The grazing land is the problem. And I can only afford to feed a limited number of horses. At least that's what Riggs tells me. Before many of these were captured they were out running free on the range on land owned by the Bureau of Land Management, but often starving to death. They were destroying the range and yet there still wasn't enough to keep up with them. There are so many unwanted mustangs. That's what my foundation does. Raise money to lease land for other mustangs, feed them, and pay for veterinary bills."

"That's amazing, bro. Very proud of you."

"Well, you've been off fighting a war. I had to do something." Sean chuckled.

"Believe me, I didn't do half as much good as you have right here."

Jennifer heard the regret in his voice, far too familiar. "I want to interview you for the podcast. What you're doing here is amazing."

"I'm in, but let's wait until after the wedding."

But Jennifer might not be here for the wedding. "Oh, right. You and Bonnie must be so busy."

"Had I known it would be quite like this I'd have suggested we elope. But the show offered to pay for part of the wedding so long as we allow a photo shoot for *People* magazine."

"*People* magazine is going to be here?" Colton spoke up.

"Yeah, don't worry. It will just be me and Bonnie and we'll let the rest of the wedding party off the hook. We didn't have to do it, but it was a compromise. They wanted to roll into town and do a whole spectacle. TV, everything. We shot that down."

"Good for you. You don't need that many people involved," Colton said.

"When's the wedding?" Jennifer probably wouldn't be here, but she'd send a gift.

"This Sunday."

"*Excuse me?* Did you say this…this Sunday?" She whipped her head around to glare at Colton.

She'd assumed Sean and Bonnie would marry later, a few days or weeks after she went home. He could have warned her.

"Sorry. I thought I told you," Colton said, and his eyes communicated: *why did you think I was in a hurry to come home?*

Sean shook his head. "Colton probably thought you'd be happy to wear jeans to the wedding. Which is fine with us, of course, but I know how Bonnie would feel about that. Besides, I'm breaking it to you now, bud. You're going to be wearing a tux and your fitting is scheduled for tomorrow."

"Thanks for the heads up." Colton scowled.

It would seem everyone in this family was late on relaying important details.

Sean shrugged. "Hey it was in an email."

"Must have been in the fine print," Colton muttered.

Jennifer needed a dress. And shoes. And her hair done.

A wedding. Dammit!

Guess I'm going to a wedding.

"ALL I'M SAYING IS you could have told me *sooner*," Jennifer said.

She was still a little flushed, a little pink in the cheek with semi-righteous anger. So, let's see if he had this straight. Colton was in a fake relationship, and he'd already disappointed his fake fiancée. He had a gift.

They were sitting at the dining table enjoying Delores's roast. True to his word, Colton hadn't allowed Jennifer in the kitchen when he prepared mashed potatoes worthy of his own cooking show. And he wasn't bragging. They were buttery and fluffy just like the recipe said they would be. The secret was a ton of butter. During the time he'd peeled, cut, boiled, and mashed he'd kept his mind occupied with nothing but pleasant thoughts about how good this was all going to taste. Not one thought about the anxiety he'd felt at first hearing there would be an entire crew from Hollywood descending on their small town.

It was bad enough there were workers building cabins and now there would be God only knew how many strangers. Taking photos. For a major magazine.

He took a bite of the roast and set the fork down. "I already said I'm sorry."

"It wouldn't have mattered until I became your fake fiancée."

"Hey, no one forced you to agree to that." He was still wondering why she had. Unless she thought word might get back to her stalker somehow and he'd finally give up.

Colton thought that would likely only further enrage him.

"Fine, but I agreed to be your fiancée without realizing I would still be here for the wedding. Now I *have* to go."

"I can always say you're sick."

"Oh no, buddy. No." She held up a finger, shaking it. "That would be lie number…you know what? I'm starting to lose count. No more lies unless they're necessary ones."

"You should really be worried about the fact there's an entire crew coming to take photos of my brother and his famous wife. We'll be sure you don't even wind up in the blurry background of one of the photos. That's the last thing we need."

"It's amazing how little you know of what's been going on while you were gone."

She'd hit on a sore spot without realizing it.

Yes, he could see the world had moved on without him. "Well, that's why I'm here. To catch up."

"You didn't tell me about the mustangs. That's really…interesting."

"Sean got into that the last few years and I didn't have all the information." He met her eyes. "Besides, we've had a lot to digest in the past two days. We don't really *know* each other at all."

"That's because someone kept his mouth shut for almost the entire drive here. I had to pull information out of you. Is there anything else that's important and I have to know? Are there any more events happening while I'm here?"

"Hard to say because we don't know exactly how *long* you'll be here."

She slumped a little in her chair. "I know. But I want to get back to my life. I have friends, too, and a career. Or, I had one."

"You still do. He won't take that away from you and you can't let him."

"What do you mean? I already *let* him. Take a look at where I am." She gestured around the room.

"Not for long. Think outside the box. You could always take photos like you have been doing."

"Oh, you noticed that?"

"Hard not to. You almost disappear behind that camera."

"In a good way. I feel like I see everything better through the lens. No one can hide their true feelings from me there." She paused and slid him a significant look. "Hey, maybe when this is all said and done, I could have you on the podcast."

"Uh, that's a hard pass."

"Why? I interviewed *Joe.*"

Colton didn't think this was a conversation she'd want to have with him. "I heard."

"The podcast, or did my father mention it?"

He didn't see a way out of this one even if he'd love to avoid the subject. "Your father talked about it."

"Then you know he doesn't believe in post-traumatic stress. He thinks every soldier should suck it up. My brother was struggling!"

Colton thought he ought to change the subject but didn't know how. He didn't want to talk about this. A therapist had diagnosed *him* with PTSD. It was still tough to accept because he'd always believed those with PTSD far worse off than him. But different soldiers handled trauma in different ways, the therapist had explained. There were so many factors involved in the outcome, such as a family history of depression, family support, or suicidal ideation. And yes, there were soldiers who'd decided it would not happen to them or those they'd raised. It was a sign of weakness. Horace was definitely one of those old-school types. A great man with a fatal flaw. What else was new.

"Your father is a good man."

"I'm sure you believe that. Maybe you're just like him."

"I'd like to think so."

Colton took a breath and went for the words he wanted to say. The connection he wanted to make. It wasn't easy. Being vulnerable never was. "I honestly believe he's always done the best he could, and he wanted the best for his son. Just like he wants the best for you."

"He has a funny way of showing it." She took a bite of the

potatoes almost menacingly. Then she moved from narrowed eyes to wide ones. "Hey, these are *really good.*"

He pushed the serving platter toward her. "Have some more."

She put another spoonful on her plate. "This doesn't get you off the hook. I'm still mad I don't have a dress to wear and proper shoes. With heels."

"We can take care of that tomorrow."

And so it was that Colton found himself the next morning, after a quick breakfast, on the road to Kerrville for his tux fitting with Jennifer in tow. Bonnie and Winona had wanted Jennifer to wait to go dress shopping with them later and make a day of it. But Colton made excuses that he didn't like being away from his fiancée for too long.

There was no way he could leave her in Stone Ridge while he went to Kerrville. And she could not go shopping anywhere without him. So, the solution was clearly to pretend they were madly in love and couldn't be separated. He was lovesick, that was all. It had never happened before but there was a first time for everything.

"Aw that's so *sweet.*" Winona had held a hand to her heart and Colton figured he'd scored a direct hit.

Driving out of town now, he noticed the changes far better in the clear light of a bright and sunny April day. They passed a group of Longhorn steer. Long fields of pastures.

The billboard was still huge and alarming.

Jennifer cocked her head as they passed it. "Kind of scary. It's a little like seeing you up there larger than life. A matinee idol. If you smiled, you'd look a lot more like Sean."

"I leave the smiling to him."

They arrived at the tux rental place early for his appointment, so Colton drove Jennifer to a shopping strip mall nearby. There was a large department store not far, but he'd determined in order to keep a closer watch he'd prefer a small place without as many exits.

"There should be something you can find here."

He parked, then held the door open and followed Jennifer through the small shop as she picked up and put down about twenty dresses. Any of them would have looked good on her and he grew more irritated with every passing second.

"Aren't you a patient one?" The clerk winked. "Good for you. Most men wouldn't follow their woman around without complaint."

He wanted to shout: *I'm her bodyguard! I'm not following, dammit, I'm leading. I'm working here.*

But yes, he was following her.

"I'm going to wait by the entrance," he told Jennifer when he'd had enough of following her around in circles.

He should have thought of parking himself here earlier but didn't want to announce to the entire world he was security detail even if that's exactly what he was. There wasn't any reason to keep up the pretense of lovers in public with people they didn't know and might never see again.

Colton stood near the door, arms crossed, shades on, doing his best not to look like a guard. Every now and again he glanced at his watch to be sure he wasn't going to be late for his fitting. All this wedding stuff was bad enough to deal with, on his own, but now he had Jennifer along. He'd known this would be the case, but the practicalities of their arrangement were beginning to drain him.

She was…a lot. And not just because she was beautiful, and he had a difficult time keeping his hands off her. She wanted to discuss things he'd rather not. PTSD. The whole situation with Horace and her brother. The fact Colton had been disconnected from his family for so long. He knew better than to think she'd let it go. She'd only put the subject on hold for now because she wanted a dress. Well, he'd take his distractions and interceptions when and where he could.

The door to the shop opened and closed several times while Jennifer took eons to choose a dress. Then shoes.

"Oh my God, what are you doing *here*, Sean?"

When Colton and Sean were younger, people often mistook the two brothers. But Colton, who'd had a late growth spurt, was now a good inch or two taller than Sean, at six-two. His hair was shorter than Sean's, he had a scar over his left eyebrow, and quite a few others on his back. A coiled-snake tattoo half sleeve covered most of his right arm. Yet they were still being mistaken for each other.

He peered at the woman over the rim of his shades. "I'm not Sean."

"I can see that now, but gosh! You look a lot like him. You must be Colton." She stuck her hand out. "I'm Tabitha, runner-up. Yes, that's right, had destiny gone the other way I might be getting ready to be your sister-in-law. Hoo boy, but if I'd seen you first…"

He nodded. "Nice to meet you."

Colton really should watch this *Mr. Cowboy* show which had apparently had its streaming run over six months ago. His brother had dated *this* woman right alongside Bonnie Lee. What a wonder everyone still had all their major limbs intact. If he recalled, his sister-in-law-to-be had matched Sean dollar for dollar in the jealousy department.

Two more women waltzed in right after the pretty blonde.

"Guys, check it out! It's Sean 2.0." She waved over to them. "Colton, this is Jessica. And this is Angela. We were all in the final four with Bonnie Lee."

"You all decided to stay in town?"

"Not me," the one named Jessica said. "I got married not long after the show ended."

"And I'm working in New York City," Angela said. "But the show invited all of us to attend the wedding of the year."

The wedding of the year.

Colton felt his jaw turn to granite. "Yeah, I had no idea this wedding was going to be so well *attended.*"

If so, he would have actually told Horace that Jennifer might be safer staying in LA. But no, surely that wasn't true. She was safe here, far from the stalker, as long as he kept his edge.

"Wouldn't you like your boyfriend to see how you look in the dress?" The attendant said to Jennifer.

"Oh, no, it's fine, he's not my boyfriend."

Colton watched as Jennifer turned to see him standing with the women and she almost visibly jerked and straightened her posture.

Colton stilled. Jennifer didn't yet know these women were coming to the wedding. He could always hope they hadn't heard Jennifer. If he were better at mind reading or she could read hand signals, he would relay the information to her. Even so, he tried to deliver an SOS with his eyes.

"And who is *this*?" Tabitha turned to watch Jennifer as she paid at the register. "A friend of yours? A cousin?"

"That's Jennifer Walker. She's also coming to the wedding of the year." He rubbed the back of his neck. "Isn't everyone?"

Tabitha laughed and tossed back her hair, reaching to squeeze his bicep. "You're so right! Just about everyone. But I *moved* here. I'm a nurse and I actually live in Stone Ridge. Just in case you need a plus one to the—"

"I'm ready, honey." Jennifer came up to them, resting her hand possessively over his other bicep. "Sorry I took so long."

"Yeah," he said, raising the arm Tabitha had been holding so that he could glance at his watch. The move also managed to skillfully shake her off. "I'm going to be late for my tux fitting if we don't get out of here in exactly three point five seconds."

"How weirdly precise," Tabitha said. "Hello, I'm Tabitha. And how do you know Bonnie Lee?"

"She's going to be my sister-in-law someday. I'm Colton's fiancée. Nice to meet you." At this she stuck out her hand and smiled.

"Oh, hell's bells, I'm sorry I was flirtin' with your fiancé." Tabitha eyed him. "He didn't *mention* you."

"Aw, we're new. It happened so fast sometimes I even forget we're engaged." She laughed.

Yeah, he had to get them out of here.

"I'm sorry, but we have to go now," Colton said, holding the door open for Jennifer. "See ya'll at the wedding."

With that, and a quick wave, he took Jennifer's hand and hustled her out the door.

She rushed to keep up with his longer strides. "Who were those women?"

"They're all former contestants on the stupid show and were invited to be at the wedding."

"You're *kidding*. I thought maybe one of them was an ex-girlfriend or something and I didn't know what to do. I didn't want to cramp your style with the beautiful blonde."

He held the passenger side door open. "But…?"

She threw in her packages, then turned to him. "But you gave me a *signal*. Didn't you?"

"What signal?" He was at once both shocked and pleased she could read him so well.

"With your eyebrows." She made a motion with her hands, hovering them above her eyes.

"My *eyebrows*."

"Well, you were wearing those aviator shades, which by the way isn't a good idea if you want to send me an eye signal. But your eyebrows. They were going up and down and quirking. Like they were having a seizure. I figured something was wrong and you needed rescuing." She paused and took a breath. "Was I wrong?"

"You weren't wrong. And that blonde isn't even my type." He shut the door when she climbed inside, then went around to the driver's side to buckle up.

"Thanks for reading my eyebrows. If I tell anyone about our lie, it's going to be Sean first."

She held a hand to her chest as if the news delighted her. "And you're going to tell him?"

"I might have to after today. I'm not sure they bought what we were selling."

"I'd feel much better if at least Sean knew. I don't like lying to him."

If anyone would understand the need for a little misdirection, it would be Sean. He wouldn't judge. And once Colton told him about Jennifer and the need for privacy, seclusion, and protection, he'd be on board.

Colton was almost sure of it.

CHAPTER 9

After returning her to the cottage and showing Jennifer how to plug in to the dial-up connection, Colton left Jennifer alone.

As he'd told her right before he left to talk to Sean, it was time to check her emails.

It had only been a few days since she left her apartment complex, but knowing Dan's history, he'd have already tried to contact her.

She found nearly two hundred unread messages. He had her exclusive email address for the podcast, another mistake. A few fans were wondering how long of a hiatus the show would be taking. More sponsors had pulled out, unwilling to wait it out. She composed a few quick replies, careful to be as vague as possible.

Fear swirled through her to find that nearly all of the emails were from Dan. She opened the oldest one, taken the day she'd left town.

I'd love to take you to dinner tonight, to apologize for the misunderstanding. I can see now how I must have scared you. My intensity can be difficult to take at times.

The next one, same day, asked for a reply soon so he'd have time to make reservations.

Time to make reservations. It was as if he hadn't heard her at all. He lived in his own delusional world. What had she done to encourage him? Had she simply been too kind? She hit reply on one email to ask him to please stop this madness. Then she changed her mind. Do not engage. She continued to read so she could report back to Colton as he'd asked.

It appears you're gone. There's no one living in your apartment. Now I'm worried. Your neighbors haven't seen you in days. You've left me no choice but to come after you. Wherever you are, you're not safe. The podcast has stopped, and I can't even listen to your voice each night. How can you be so cruel? I'm the only one who cares about you, can't you see this? No matter where you go, I'll find you. I have resources.

As each day passed, the emails grew more hostile and threatening until Jennifer couldn't read another word.

She'd show these to Colton and ask him what to do next. Admittedly, though she resented being taken from her home and all that she knew and loved, she felt safer here, more than she'd imagined. She felt grounded in a good way. And, on the chance that Dan found her somehow, Colton would be here. Fake fiancé or not, he inspired security. Safety. She'd never had to rely on anyone else for that sense of security, not since she was a small child. But there was good reason now to allow someone to protect her. She'd resisted that for so long, from both her father and an older brother who'd been over-the-top protective from the beginning.

But there had never been a reason to be overprotective until now.

Now, she could finally admit the situation was out of her hands and control. She could admit that she'd stopped living before she'd been pulled from her environment.

A knock on the door made Jennifer jump and she had to

shake her head and remind herself of where she was. She was no longer in LA where the knock on the door could be from Dan. She was safe for now.

It was Bonnie Lee on the other side of the door.

"Hey," Jennifer said, holding the door wide open for her to walk inside.

"I *have* to see the dress."

"My dress?"

She wasn't aware the dress had to meet inspection. A little trust, perhaps?

"Well, the men were talkin' and I got bored even before they left for a ride. Colton told me you found a dress and sent me to come look. Can I see?"

For a moment, Jennifer panicked, wondering if the screen saver would turn on before Bonnie could accidentally see one of the angry emails. The last one was in big, bold letters in caps and in an extra-large font size. This whole situation had spiraled so far out of control. If Colton's family heard of her stalker, she'd put a pall on the entire happy-wedding proceedings. And besides, she didn't want any more judgement from people who didn't understand. Who couldn't possibly understand. Who thought maybe Jennifer should have managed to stop him earlier. Sooner. Should have been firmer in her refusals.

Maybe she should have realized Dan had become dangerous, but if she were to give herself the benefit of the doubt like she would for any other victim, she refused to blame herself. Not anymore.

"I'll get it and be right back."

She considered leading Bonnie to the dress, but then she might see Jennifer and Colton were sleeping in separate rooms.

On the way to the closet where she'd hung the dress, she realized Colton must have made an excuse to send Bonnie over. So, Jennifer wouldn't be alone for long. He was definitely taking this favor he was doing for her father very seriously. Then again, Colton didn't look like the kind of man who took anything lightly.

Jennifer came out and held up the royal-blue gown up to her neck.

"You look good in blue." Bonnie Lee folded her hands in front of her. "I'm going to be honest. I didn't come over just to see your dress. Unlike Colton, I trusted whatever you chose would be fine. With the men, we had to put them in a tux lest they come in slacks and a nice flannel shirt, wearing their yellow work gloves. Cowboys are cute but kind of hopeless when it comes to fashion."

"Why are you here then?"

"First, let me just say that I think you're lovely."

Uh-oh. This sounded like the start of a dressing down, pun intended.

Jennifer would bet Bonnie Lee had already realized something was not quite right in paradise.

"Thanks...but..."

Bonnie laughed. "But nothing. It's just...from where I stand the relationship looks lopsided between you two. Now, I have plenty of experience with this. Twenty years ago, when we first met, Sean loved me more than I loved him. I was sixteen, stupid, and flighty. He knew from the moment he met me that he loved me and wanted marriage and children for us. It took me a bit longer to get there. Now, some days I know I love him more than he loves me."

"I doubt that."

"It's because I came so close to losing him for good and it's okay. I know from experience it will even out again. Some days, we're both in the same place and honestly, it's overwhelming. Like I might die from all the happiness. Other days, somebody just has to love a little bit more."

"Like a balance?"

The idea sounded wonderful and were she in a real relationship, she could definitely appreciate it. Especially compared to obsession.

"Yes, exactly. And that's why I can see that at the moment, Colton loves you far more than you love him. And because he's like my own brother, I worry."

"I…I think you're wrong. We just got engaged and I—"

"Exactly. *That's* why I'm worried."

"Don't worry, I love him."

Honestly, it was beginning to feel a little bit true.

Who *wouldn't* love Colton? He was loyal, strong, and kind. He loved his family and would clearly lay his life down for a friend. Then there was that whole other thing he had going on with the extremely good looks, which she was not *weighing* heavily in his favor. Because that would be shallow. But those smoldering looks sure didn't hurt anything, either.

"Okay." Bonnie sighed with relief. "Whew, I feel so much better now. We were all so worried about Colton."

It was exactly as Jennifer had feared. Colton didn't want them to worry, and he was right to assume they would.

"You were? But why? He's so *capable*."

"I remember the young kid who'd finally found a home with Marge and Cal. He was the youngest, so he barely remembered his parents. All he'd experienced was a succession of relatives who bounced them from one home to another until they wound up in foster care. All the brothers have a bit of abandonment issues but none more so than Colton."

Jennifer swallowed hard and her stomach pitched and roiled. She did not like picturing that sweet little boy she'd seen in photos worried he'd be left yet again.

She wasn't helping Colton at all but possibly harming when she abandoned him. Her only hope was that he wouldn't make an investment in her. Bonnie Lee was wrong about her assumptions that Colton loved her. She was only seeing what she expected to see. He cared about her, sure, and wanted to keep her safe from an unstable man.

Maybe this was a gift. Later, Jennifer could say she'd listened to Bonnie Lee and decided to slow things down. That would be her "out" and the reason she'd leave.

"You're still getting to know each other. Sounds like this all happened…fast."

"Do you think that wasn't such a great idea? Rushing into it?"

"Not at all. You both seem to be in a good place and if it works, it works. You look like the kind of woman who honors her commitments."

"Yes, I am." Jennifer swallowed hard.

She was, in fact, exactly that kind of a woman, which is why leaving her life had been so difficult. She'd abandoned her listeners, and her sponsors. The few friends she had left.

Next, she would have an entirely new group of people who would be terribly unhappy with her when she left Colton.

Stop caring what other people think about you.

The words had been Colton's, and really, wasn't this how she got into this predicament? Mistakenly caring what *Dan* thought of her. She reminded herself that Bonnie, Sean, and Delores were strangers to her, and she didn't owe them anything. Even if it didn't feel that way. She felt accepted and welcome and as if she'd found a second family.

"The truth is," Bonnie said. "we've all been worried about Colton for quite a while. The army was the right place for him no doubt, but it also changed him."

Jennifer hated to hear that. But she understood how active duty could alter someone's perspective. The same thing had happened with Joe.

"It happens to a lot of soldiers."

"And I don't think Sean would mind me sharing this with you, after all you're Colton's fiancée now. It isn't fair if you're kept in the dark until he decides he's ready to share. I know how that can be. This is too important."

Bonnie took a seat on the couch.

"The truth is, Colton joining the service caused a rift between him and Riggs. Unfortunately, I had a firsthand seat for the drama. Sean was always the proverbial middle child brokering the peace between the two brothers. And Colton and Sean are the closest, too, for obvious reasons. Ever since Colton came back, we all know Riggs is not convinced he'll stay. I have to admit, your engagement went a long way toward convincing him that Colton may actually stick around this time. For so many years, even though he had leave from the army, Colton never came home. The last time I saw him was at his father's funeral. There was somewhat of a blowup at that time when Riggs realized that Colton would re-up for even more time. For Riggs, it's always been about family. Family first and foremost, and for a long time the brothers were the only family any of them had."

"But now?"

"Well, Winona came along, and Riggs is now the father of three. He has Sean, but he also wants and needs Colton's help and loyalty. It would be nice to know he's going to stick around."

"He's given me every indication that he will. That's why we're here."

"Sean and I worried he'd only come here for the wedding. We know he wouldn't miss that. Sean has wanted him home many times before but only our wedding got him here."

"It's not just the wedding. You should have seen him with his horse. I think he missed his home."

"Then why didn't he come back sooner?"

"Maybe…maybe he first wanted you all to know that he's fine. In my experience, sometimes soldiers know their families will be the first ones to notice if there's something missing. And a brother would know before anyone else would. Or a sister."

It was why Joe had stayed away from their family, and especially from her. She would be able to see right through him and know he wasn't okay. Not fully functioning. And at one time, he hadn't even believed he deserved help.

"Those were my thoughts as well. Sean would know and even Riggs would see if Colton was struggling."

And then Jennifer knew what Bonnie Lee really wanted to hear. It was the entire reason she'd agreed to this farce, and it felt good to know she could help in some small way.

"Colton and I have a very, um, solid relationship, and I think I've been good for him. Coming from a military family and that dynamic, I understand more than most women would. He feels comfortable with me, and I think that's how…uh, how we fell in love so quickly."

"That makes sense." Bonnie stood and moved to the door. "I feel so much better about all this, which is a good thing. Tomorrow is my meeting with the Ladies of SORROW and the old-fashioned gifting of the marriage quilt. It's kind of like a wedding shower."

"Are you really *doing* that?"

"Oh, we all do. And it's my family. My Aunt Beulah is their official 'president.'" Bonnie held up air quotes. "And it's all meant in the spirit of community. You should come, so you'll see what you have in store when it's your turn. Winona is coming and it would be nice to have you there, too. We're all three going to be sisters, after all."

"Right."

Jennifer followed Bonnie to the door.

Once she was gone, Jennifer locked the door and double-checked it twice. She couldn't afford to get complacent, not after the emails she'd read. She had to talk to Colton the moment he returned. Not only had Dan made more threats, but Colton should also know that his family was seriously worried about him. And if he told Sean, he'd tell Bonnie Lee. She'd tell Winona, who would undoubtedly tell Riggs.

Maybe it *wasn't* time to tell anyone the truth.

CHAPTER 10

Colton had every intention of telling Sean about his fake engagement and the reasoning behind it. He'd been trying to find the perfect time to bring up the subject between moments of riding in the back of the ranch's weathered pickup truck and unloading bales of hay.

"Brings back memories, doesn't it?" Sean laughed, stopping the truck to help pitch a bale of hay for the horses. "Thought it would be more fun this way."

Colton shoved another one out. "I was driving the truck at fourteen, so yeah, good memories."

"Sure have missed you around here."

He didn't know how to tell Sean, arguably also his closest friend, that he'd stayed away because every time he came home, he lost his edge. Coming home made it all the tougher to get back to a mission he questioned more with each passing day. Delores remained the only tie left to strong memories of his parents, to their kindness, big heart, and sense of family. Unconditional love. All of these had no place in this soldier's head except to keep them in mind as an end goal. In the meantime, he'd made a commitment to the US Army and stayed alive to honor it.

Riggs might never know it but his tough talk about loyalty to family still rang in Colton's head like a nonstop lecture. He'd failed to honor one commitment while making room for another. There hadn't been space for both and some days the guilt pressed and weighed on him, not allowing him to breathe. He'd made a mistake staying away from home for so long. This was what he wanted, to be here in the quiet of Hill Country and the beauty of the land. With Freya. Why had he ever chosen a different life? Well, there was no going back now. Only forward.

In therapy, he'd learned to stop the punishing scenes rolling in his head twenty-four- seven reminding him of everything he'd done wrong. He replaced them with uplifting images. Soothing voices. Peaceful and calming aesthetics. That's how he'd gotten into cooking shows in the first place. It involved all the senses. Chopping and stirring offered both a tactile experience and a soothing sound. Scent was a given when cooking, and a good visual presentation essential to most above-average cooks. Tonight, he would bake a chocolate cake similar to the one his mother made for him on his birthday. He had a recipe that involved chocolate chips and espresso powder.

And routine, such as this one with his brother, was also comforting. When all the bales were unloaded, Colton and Sean sat on the tailgate like old times and drank cold beer. Only this time they hadn't had to sneak it out of the fridge when their parents weren't looking.

"Welcome home." Sean tapped the neck of his bottle with Colton's.

"Good to be here."

"Just so you know, Riggs is the happiest I've seen him since little Mary was born."

"Yeah?"

"You coming home engaged, well, let's just say that put to rest some of his biggest fears."

"*What* fears?"

"In Riggs's mind, anyway, you're more likely to stick around with a wife and later, children. You know, a family."

"Pretty 1950s of him."

Sean snorted. "Well, you know Riggs. He's old-fashioned and it works for him in this town."

"Yeah, shocking he's with Winona of all women."

"You'd be surprised by how much they have in common."

"Well, I'm glad he finally believes I'll stay. But I don't think I needed a wife to do it." Colton grunted.

"A partner just centers a man. Grounds him. And I know you've had a tough time sitting still."

"That was then."

"Regardless, I was worried about you, and I wasn't the only one. You didn't come home, and I occasionally wondered if you ever would again. At first, Riggs thought it was because of *her*…and well, you know."

Her.

Everybody in town thought he'd taken that abandonment a lot harder than he had. When Cherisse left him, he'd been pissed, but not for long. He was far angrier with someone else.

"And when I take a good look at our lopsided town… actually, I figured you were coming home for the wedding, only to leave again. But hell, when you came home with Jennifer, I knew you'd be just fine."

"I've put in my time and the rest of my life is going to be this ranch. This family."

"That's good to know." Sean cocked his head, a smile quirking his mouth. "And you don't think you'll ever feel stir-crazy again? Like you need to see the world? Or at least another part of Texas?"

"Not going to rule out another part of Texas. You know I love Galveston, but I've seen the world. Or enough of it."

Sean clapped Colton's back. "It will be good to have you around because that means I get to leave now and then without worrying. You're looking at an international traveler. We're home most of the year, but Bonnie Lee and I go to Canada when her series films. It's only a few weeks. At the moment, they're talking about bringing another season of the show with filming sometime next year."

"What do you do there while she works?"

"A lot of smooth talking. Last time I was there I made all those rich actors put their money where their mouth is. Plenty of donations to my wild horse foundation."

"Canada." Colton chuckled. "Only Bonnie Lee could get you off the ranch."

"Yep, I've loved that girl since I was a teenager."

"Not all of us can wind up with our first love. Speaking of love, when I took Jennifer dress shopping in Kerrville, we ran into some of your exes."

"Exes?" Sean quirked a brow. "Who?"

"Tabitha, Angela, and Jessica. The triple threat."

"Ah, yes. I guess they are technically my exes because we 'dated' on the show." He held up air quotes. "Didn't so much as kiss one of them."

"Bonnie is okay with them coming to the wedding?"

"We've both grown up a lot and aren't insanely jealous like we used to be. But in answer to your question, she doesn't love it. The show begged, and she finally relented. They're not going to be part of the wedding and we won't see much of them. Think of them as the audience. It's likely the crew will take photos of them at the reception so they can do their thing."

"So, you don't see yourself talking to any of them?"

"No time. I think I'll be pretty busy with my wife that day."

Colton swallowed the last of his beer. "Can you imagine what it would have been like if I'd brought Jennifer here, as my *girlfriend*?"

"Ha! You were wise. It would have been open season until you put a ring on it. That's what I had to deal with when the show took a break, and I wasn't supposed to see any of the women until we resumed filming. Bonnie Lee had a line out the door of men coming to court, just in case I didn't pick her."

"That must have been fun for you."

He scowled. "Before that, I'd had a taste of what it was like to have women chase after me for a change. Got to say, I didn't hate it."

Even though he'd had every intention, this didn't seem like a good time for Colton to bring up that he'd lied about his engagement. He had more than one reason now. He had wanted everyone to believe he was fine. But he'd never realized what an impact it would have in demonstrating he was perfectly capable of having a solid relationship. Perfectly willing to make a lifetime commitment. And even if it annoyed him to no end that a wife was what it took everyone to convince them he was sticking around, he was not going to back down now that he'd won Riggs's approval for a change.

"What's it going to be like around here on your wedding day? I expect a crew, but how many? Will they all be vetted?"

Sean looked at him quizzically but if he thought it a weird question to ask, he didn't say so. "No one gets on this property that doesn't have a press pass. Don't worry, both Riggs and I have been adamant about that. And it should be a small crew. None of the former contestants were even allowed to bring a plus one."

"What about at the chapel?"

Everyone in Stone Ridge was married at Trinity right in town.

"The ceremony is assured to be only family and close friends. We insisted on it."

Hours later, when Colton got back from chores around the ranch and visiting with Freya once more, he was hot and sweaty.

On the way back to the cabin, Delores waved until she got his attention.

She jogged to close the distance between them. "I have something for you."

"What now? You did enough by stocking the kitchen."

"That's not enough! After Bonnie and Sean's wedding, we'll have to celebrate yours and Jennifer's engagement."

"We don't need that. Or expect it." He dragged a hand through his hair, wishing he could somehow get her to drop it.

"Well, darling boy, you may not need any fanfare, but I assure you your fiancée does. You can't just get married at one of those drive-through chapels in Reno and be done with it. We're your family and we'd like to celebrate with you. You'll be married at Trinity like everyone else. And what about a ring?"

"Yeah, we'll go shopping for one soon."

"Or…you don't have to." She took his hand, opened it up, and deposited a ring box. "It was my wedding ring and I always hoped I could give it to someone. Winona and Bonnie Lee already had their rings, so this one has just been waiting for you. I like Jennifer, or I wouldn't let you have this ring. But it would mean a lot if you would take it."

"Delores, I can't—"

"I realize it's not a big fancy diamond but it's a classic. You might say it's practically an antique. My husband bought it for me, and Marge helped him pick it out. She knew what I liked, and what he could afford."

Colton opened the box and stared at the ring inside. It was a plain gold band with etching on the sides and looked both old, understated, and classic. Like Delores. The connection to his mother and Delores was like a band stretching across the years, binding them together.

"It's really beautiful."

Refusing the ring would hurt her feelings, but accepting it was…he didn't know what, other than deception pure and simple. For a brief second, he considered taking her into his confidence. Then he saw the shimmering happiness in her eyes.

"I'm so happy for you. After what happened with that… that *woman*, well, let's just say that loyalty is a scarce commodity for some of the women of Stone Ridge."

"Delores, that was a long time ago."

Sooner or later, he should have known that Delores would bring this up. He didn't know how else to spell it out for everyone: he was over it. Over Cherisse, and had been for some time. Sure, it was a little embarrassing, and now that he considered it carefully, word getting back to Cherisse about his upcoming marriage was going to be nice. Very nice. She'd married Taylor, after all, and that kind of thing was tough to forget. But Colton was angrier with Taylor than he was with Cherisse. In one short email, he lost both his first girlfriend and his oldest friend. It wasn't exactly the best news a soldier could get from home. Followed shortly after the death of his father, it had been particularly heinous timing.

It happened to a lot of servicemen, in fact, and none of them came from a town like his where a girl had plenty of choices. A woman here didn't have to wait for her first love to come back or worry whether he ever would. And Cherisse had moved on, which was her right. Even if it had turned both of them into a cliché. She'd sent him a Dear John letter only it was the twenty-first century version. An email. He'd been torn up about it for a while, but it felt like forever ago.

"Now you have Jennifer…she's so perfect and down to earth. She fits right in with your family. I knew the second we sat looking through old family photos that she was a keeper. And she loves you so much, I can tell."

"Um, yeah." Colton removed his hat and scratched the side of his head.

Poor delusional Delores. Jennifer might not love him, but he couldn't disagree she was a nice girl, uh…woman.

"Anyway, see what she thinks of the ring. If she really hates it, then I'll take it back."

"She's not going to hate it."

"I'm just glad I never gave it to you before. *This* is the right moment. *This* is the right woman." She smiled and waved her hand in the air. "I'm happy my ring is going to have a good home."

Colton pulled her into his arms and gave her a hug, the kind that he reserved only for Delores. Then he bussed her on the cheek and listened as her laughter trilled all around them. He tucked the ring in his jeans pocket, wondering how best to handle all this. Guilt pressed through him, but he reminded himself he was making everyone around him ecstatic. With a lie.

Jennifer greeted him at the front door like she'd been lying in wait.

"Oh my God, you're here!"

"What's happened?" He startled and immediately flew into full scale alert. "Are you okay?"

He'd been stupid to leave her here for a few hours, but

damn it, if she wasn't safe inside this house, on a private and secluded ranch, she wasn't safe anywhere at all.

"Oh, nothing. At ease, soldier." She threw up her palms. "You didn't tell Sean, did you? I would have intercepted you, but I wouldn't even know where to find you."

"No, I didn't get the chance."

Jennifer launched into a long discussion involving Bonnie Lee's visit earlier, ending with her opinion that they should continue to be faked engaged. She had a good argument for staying the course and he let her keep going as if she had to convince *him*.

He was probably going to hell for this. "Hmm, you sure you're okay with this?"

She nodded several times. "It's for the best. And after you see my emails, you're going to want me to stay here for a while longer."

"That bad?"

"I don't want to take him seriously, but I know better. It's smarter to be cautious and assume the worst no matter how far away I am. I get it now."

"I'm glad, because your safety is important to me."

"Thank you. That means a lot." She stared at him for a long minute before lowering her gaze.

Concern spliced through him even if they were almost certainly safe here. The point was, he didn't know what she'd do when she had to go back, which he knew was inevitable at some point. And he certainly couldn't go with her to continue to be her bodyguard, protector, and fake fiancé. That was a short-term plan at best. He was staying in Texas and making a life right here on this ranch. Everything else would fall into place and he no longer had any doubts it would.

But her safety had become far more important than he'd been prepared for it to be, because this was no longer simply a favor he would do for a mentor. She was helping him, too, and she was not only beautiful but smart, loyal, and kind.

"I'll make dinner after I take a shower. Then I'll read those emails." He headed toward the shower, throwing off his hat, and ripping off his stinky shirt on the way. "Until then, you don't want to get within three feet of me."

JENNIFER'S GAZE followed Colton as he walked down the hallway toward the bathroom, shirtless. Oh, mama. Thank you, Jesus. Shirt-less. He'd walked in the door and honestly, she hadn't even noticed the smell. She was too busy paying attention to the sweat trickling down both sides of his neck under that sexy cowboy hat. For some odd reason, Jennifer had never been attracted to a sweaty male before that moment. Even when ex-boyfriends would work out, just to have the enviable six-pack abs, she found them disgusting until they took a shower. But Colton even made sweat look sexy. The first thing she'd noticed when he one-handedly pulled his shirt off was the tattoo. She wasn't surprised to see it, because so many in her generation had one or two, especially military men.

But Colton's tattoo was somewhat a work of art. A half sleeve over his left arm, of a coiling and colorful snake. There were scars on his muscular back. A scar also partially bisected his eyebrow and gave him the scary look that had been so off-putting the night they'd met. Colton was not a pretty boy, but she couldn't discount his appeal and deep attraction. He was a rugged man who suggested danger and edginess. She'd never dated anyone like him and no longer felt immune.

How ironic that the man who had inspired fear at first glance was her safest bet. Her bodyguard and protector, while the man in a *suit* wanted to hurt her unless she could be his. Nothing made sense anymore. Not this crazy arrangement between them or why she felt bound and determined to protect him when *she* was the one in need of protection.

When Colton emerged from the bedroom, he'd shaved (dammit!) and changed into jeans and a long-sleeved, pearl-button shirt. As he walked into the kitchen, he plunked something small on the table.

"Almost forgot. This is for you."

"What is it?"

She came away from the couch where she'd been watching one of the few shows they could get with their rabbit-ears antenna. It was one of those gossipy celebrity-obsessed "news" shows. Lately, since her life had started to resemble a true crime show, she'd switched from her steady diet of *Dateline* re-runs and moved to Hallmark movies when she could get them. Those inspiring movies were the equivalent of painting a room with bright colors, which were scientifically proven to make people happier. Somewhere there was probably a study that monitored the lowered blood pressure of viewers after a rom-com.

When Colton didn't answer, but simply started banging pots and pans around, she joined him in the kitchen. In the center of the small round farm-style table sat a little pink box, looking suspiciously like it might hold a ring inside. Surely, he hadn't…oh boy. She picked it up and twirled the box in her hands.

"Did you…"

Please don't say you spent your money on a ring.

"We needed something while we keep up this charade." He set a skillet on the stove. "It belongs to Delores, and she wanted you to have it. It's probably not something you'd prefer, and I'll expect to get it back from you at some point. But for now, it will do."

Jennifer opened the box to find a shiny plain gold band with etching on the sides, giving it a unique appearance, like someone had carved beautiful swirling lines through the chunk of gold.

"*Delores* wanted me to have it?"

"She likes you. I'm sure you can tell. Guess you won her over when you looked through those old photo albums."

"This is a gorgeous piece of jewelry. It's like an antique."

"I told her you'd like it. She wasn't sure since it isn't a diamond. Go ahead, put it on."

Yes, of course, because it would make absolutely no sense for *him* to put it on her. She slipped it on the ring finger of her left hand and turned it toward the light, admiring it. Funny, she'd never even tried costume jewelry on this finger, thinking there would be only once in her lifetime when she'd wear a ring there. How wonderfully and spectacularly naïve of her.

Life had taken some strange turns along the way. Here she was pretending to be engaged to this hot and surly cowboy who loved to cook.

Is this my life?

"Does it fit okay?" He glanced up from the cutting board where he was at work chopping green onions.

"Yes." It was actually a little snug but not significantly so. It should work fine for their purposes.

"Good thing I don't need a ring. Cowboys are forever taking off their rings, so they won't get them caught in machinery, or God forbid, inside of a heifer giving birth. Sometimes we have to help pull out a calf." He smiled as if the thought pleased him.

She thought she might lose her breakfast. "Eww."

"Right. And the other half of the time we're wearing gloves. No one notices a ring or lack of one."

"Hmm, it seems a little unfair. Like I'm branded but you're not."

"Let's not forget neither one of us is, as you put it, branded."

"Right. It's just for show." She wiggled her finger, wondering what her old friends would say if they could see Jennifer now.

Colton's meal began to overpower the smell of anything else in the room. She could no longer smell his clean fresh scents of soap and leather. He wasn't following a recipe but had apparently memorized many of them from the cooking shows he'd listened to and watched. The scents of onion, garlic, and butter wafted through the small kitchen as he seemed utterly involved. He chopped, he stirred, and he boiled.

Eventually they sat down to a dinner of stir-fried rice with chunks of chicken, peas, and eggs. They sat and ate like an old married couple that neither bothered to talk nor have sex anymore. Except they weren't old. Or married.

Or had ever had sex. She would definitely remember that.

She wished he would talk a little more. Silence was uncomfortable, this empty space that felt stifling and oppressive.

"Delicious," she said, to fill the quiet.

"It is."

"So, um, tomorrow? The quilt thing."

"I'll take you."

"If you think it's necessary."

"If Bonnie invited you, then yes, it is."

He chewed and she chewed, and other than chewing the silence was nothing less than profound. She should have left the TV on and at least they'd be able to watch actors in the background having a wonderful time.

"So um, Colton? You haven't told me anything about your life."

He set his fork down and sighed. "What do you want to know?"

"So much! Delores said you were never engaged before me."

"Nope."

"I never was, either, in case you were wondering. Also, this is my first fake engagement."

"Mine too." He almost smiled that time.

"How many girlfriends? Anyone serious?"

"Just once."

That was a loaded statement if there ever was one. Once. This was *huge*.

"Teenage sweetheart?"

"Yep."

Wow, that was just a shot in the dark on her part. A teenage sweetheart. She had to be the girl in the photo albums. Maybe she'd been waiting for him to come back and now here he was, pretend engaged.

"Young love. It's tough on everyone."

"I joined the service as I always said I would, so it should have come as no surprise. But Cherisse got tired of waiting for me."

Cherisse. What a name! Sounded like a cool stripper-name. She sounded blonde, buxom, and beautiful. Jennifer had always wished for a more imaginative name. She blamed her parents and their inability to think outside the box. In addition to choosing ordinary names, they wanted both their children to have the same first letter. Joseph and Jennifer. Yawn.

Why couldn't she have been a Jasmine, at least?

But back to the sweetheart. "For the love of God, she

wasn't tacky enough to break up with you via email? Please say no."

He met her eyes and quirked a brow. "As a matter of fact."

"Oh, *Colton*."

She reached for his hand across the table and squeezed it. His eyes jerked to her hand as if he'd just come up on a snake in the woods. Then he noticeably relaxed and she felt the warmth of his hand burning through her own. Solid and hard and…real.

"It was a long time ago and it's fine, alright? Don't feel *sorry* for me."

"I don't." She took her hand back. "I feel sorry for *her*. We're going to make her so jealous. She's going to rue the day she let you go. Oh, I'll make sure of it."

And there it was: Colton's lips were quirking in a half smile.

"You don't have to do that."

"It's a service I provide to all my bodyguards and fake fiancés. A package deal."

Later that night, after they'd both gone to their respective beds, Jennifer couldn't sleep. She tossed and turned thinking of young Colton and his first love. Cherisse and Colton. C and C. If he was the forgiving type, there might be a chance for the two of them once Jennifer was out of the picture. It might be unfair to discourage the woman, but it was nothing less than she deserved. She hadn't even thought to ask if Cherisse had married someone else and/or if they were already divorced. Women in this town had plenty of choices when it came to cowboys, but that kind of abject power might go to a lesser woman's head.

Just as she neared the utterly relaxing and ethereal moments between twilight and sleep, Jennifer smelled… chocolate. Either she was having a wonderful dream or Colton was cooking again. Turning over, she glanced at the digital clock on the nightstand. It was midnight. And he was cooking? Now? She climbed out of bed and threw on her bathrobe, padding into the hallway.

The ambient light from the kitchen spilled into the hall. She moved closer, peeking around the corner, and saw Colton. Shirtless again, he was stirring into a pan with a wooden spoon. On the counter he'd lined up ingredients: flour, butter, salt, sugar, eggs. He seemed completely caught up in the rhythmic sound of the spoon scraping against the metal of the pan, a little smile playing at the corners of his mouth. He looked…content. There was something so peaceful and calm about this big man bare-chested in the kitchen, finding joy in a small and unspectacular moment. The ordinary.

He was so…unexpected.

And in that quiet space of her own Jennifer realized she was in deep trouble.

If she didn't get out of Stone Ridge soon, she was going to fall completely and irretrievably in love.

CHAPTER 11

"What in the world do you think you're *doin'* here, Colton?"

Beulah Hayes stood in the doorway of the Trinity chapel's cellar, hands on her hips.

"I brought my fiancée." Colton stood with his hat tipped, aviator shades on, arms crossed. "We don't *like* to be apart."

"Isn't that lovely," Maybelle said from one of the chairs formed in a tight circle in the center of the room. "That's just how it was for me and Bonnie Lee's father. God rest his soul."

"It really is lovely," Winona said, balancing Mary on her lap. "And don't forget sexy."

"Nice and *lovely*, but it can't happen. Men are not allowed," said Beulah.

"Now, Miss Beulah, that sounds pretty sexist of you," Colton drawled.

"I vote for Colton to stay!" Delores stood indignantly. "What are rules if they're not meant to be broken every once in a while?"

"We are not voting to change any of our rules today as we don't have a quorum." Beulah sniffed.

"Aunt Beulah." Bonnie Lee tossed up her hands. "Good grief, let him stay. I don't mind if he does."

"Not when your intended isn't even here." Beulah twitched a finger. "It's just not *done*. We can't have a meeting about the men of Stone Ridge with one of them among us!"

Colton gave her an easy smile. "Why? You ladies discussing state secrets? Because I have a top-secret clearance."

"Not funny," Beulah said. "You will wait outside."

With a scowl, Colton relented after several seconds of lowering his shades and staring Beulah down. This woman would probably stare down a bear in the woods.

"I'll just be on the other side." He patted the door.

When Beulah shut the door, it almost hit his behind on the way out.

"Oh, c'mon!" Winona said. "They're in love, can't you see?"

Bonnie Lee rolled her eyes. "Y'all must have something against true love."

Jennifer had stayed silent, but here's where she wanted to tell them all that Colton just didn't want to look like exactly *what* he was: a bodyguard standing right outside the door. And now he most certainly did look like one, in case anyone was paying attention, in addition to sounding like a possessive man. Jennifer bit her lower lip. This whole thing did seem kind of ridiculous for anyone who had not read the latest emails. This morning after Colton read them, he'd forbidden Jennifer to ever be out of his sight whenever they left the ranch.

The decision had been made in seconds, right after coffee and breakfast. He would attend this weird ceremony with Jennifer because he didn't see a way out of it that didn't involve more lying.

Only now, he would wait outside.

Maybelle walked over to peek out the window. "He's still just standin' there, poor soul."

"Honestly!" Beulah shook her head. "It's like he doesn't trust the Ladies of SORROW."

"I'm not sure I trust y'all, either," Bonnie whispered in Jennifer's ear. "You're going to fill my head with all kinds of nonsense."

"Indeed they will," Winona said. "Just let it go in one ear and out the other one."

"Maybe poor Colton's afraid if he looks the other way, he'll lose this one, too," another of the ladies offered.

The words quieted the room with an uncomfortable stillness. Bonnie Lee wore a deer-in- headlights look. She was extremely protective of Colton, and even if she hadn't already told Jennifer, she'd sense it in the way her lips narrowed as if she'd just been insulted herself.

"Magnolia, that's not very kind. Cherisse had her head turned way too easily. That's not love." Bonnie shook her head. "Love is patient, love is kind. Love believes all things, endures all things. Sound familiar?"

"Sounds like Sean, a good man if there ever was one." Beulah nodded and took a seat in the circle of chairs.

Some of the ladies clucked and nodded vigorously. "That's right. Uh-huh."

"It's a good point," Maybelle said, shaking a finger. "Poor Sean was lonely for years and almost made a mistake with that Robyn. There are certainly enough lonely and available men, and they're bound to make a mistake choosing the wrong woman. Which is why we've been trying so *hard* to bring in some more women."

"Bless your heart, so true, because then no one will have to fight over a single woman. Plenty for all to go around!" Beulah clapped her hands.

"You make it sound like it's an adequate *water* supply, or

enough flour for everyone. No matter how many women we get here, there is always going to be unrequited love. More than one man might love the same woman and vice versa. Someone always loves a little more than the other. Sadly, love isn't a numbers equation, ladies."

Magnolia pursed her lips. "Spoken from someone who met her match when she was sixteen."

Jennifer found all this talk fascinating. She wished she'd brought her camera with her though Beulah looked like the kind of woman who wouldn't allow photos as if they were in some clandestine meeting. Since she'd been in Texas, there were so many opportunities for good visuals. Even this room was a throwback to older days, with its pine wood cabinets, daisy- patterned wallpaper, and uncomfortable folding chairs.

Bonnie sat in the center of the circle like a queen bee. She was beautiful, a fact Jennifer had known when she watched *Kavanaugh's Way*. But up close and personal, Bonnie's beauty wasn't in her alabaster skin, emerald eyes, and flaming red hair. A light seemed to shine from within her, a strong life force that radiated utter and serene contentment.

If only she could bottle it, Jennifer would buy it by the case. Recently she'd begun to realize a few things about her life so far. She thought she'd been happy with the podcast and all the listeners and fans she had accumulated, but she'd never been *content*.

It had always felt like there was something else to strive for, something new to reach for. What she'd had was never quite enough. Until Dan came along and blew up her life and career, she hadn't fully realized all she'd had in the first place. Because it hadn't ever felt like *enough*, and now she had to wonder why.

Maybe she was far more her father's daughter than she'd ever care to admit. To him, it seemed nothing was ever good enough. There was always another milestone to reach, another goal to slay.

A few minutes later, cookies and coffee had been passed out and Beulah started the meeting. She began by talking about the history of their group and Jennifer knew it must be for her benefit.

It turned out that the Society of Reasonable, Respectable Orderly Women (SORROW) was founded during World War II when women wanted to do something to help the war effort. They'd started by knitting baby blankets for expectant mothers and holding fundraisers to support widows.

The problem began when all the babies born that first year of the war were boys. Pink blankets went unused. Once the war was over and some of the more fortunate men returned, nine months later came more boys. And then more boys, with a lucky one or two girls in the mix born to amazed and grateful mothers.

Encouraged, and searching for another way to help, the first President of SORROW and the other founding members put together a primer: *The Men of Stone Ridge*. In it they described the loyal and hardworking cowboys who put family and faith first. They were determined to spread the word on how lucky the women of Stone Ridge were, with such handsome and plentiful men to choose from. And somehow, with promises of handsome cowboys and romance, lure women back into town.

Because it wasn't simply the fact that fewer girls were born. Stone Ridge wasn't exactly filled with modern conveniences much appreciated by the modern wife and mother. It was more, as Beulah carefully described it, "like a big man cave" and tended to chase some women straight out of town.

Before Winona had arrived, the ladies had plans to use the *Men of Stone Ridge* primer and start an email-order wife service. Sort of a pamphlet of "here's all you'll have to choose from." A bit worrisome to say the least. But then the brain-child of both Beulah and Winona, *Mr. Cowboy*, was born and Sean Henderson chosen to be the handsome cowboy to lure women into town for a chance to be his wife.

"It was a bit of false advertising there," Bonnie said. "Since you brought me to the contest to make up with Sean."

Beulah waved her hand dismissively. "Well, now, I didn't know for certain that you two would reconcile. I only hoped. And either way, I knew the women here would find another cowboy and stick around."

"Tabitha was the only other one of the final four that stayed," said a woman named Clementine.

"She's relentless, that one." Maybelle shook her head.

"But she's a nurse, too, and we needed one for the new clinic," Winona said.

"Colton and I met her, Angela, and Jessica when we went into Kerrville to go dress shopping." Jennifer spoke up for the first time.

Magnolia's hand covered her mouth, then lowered. "He went with you to shop for a dress?"

"For the wedding." Jennifer glanced around at the looks of the shocked women. "He took me there. We…"

"We *know*," Beulah said. "Don't like to be away from each other for long."

"And we went to get his tux, too," Jennifer added, feeling the need to defend Colton.

"We have some women, too, who were eliminated before the final four and still moved here. Not to mention ones that saw the show," Winona said, getting up to sway a fussy Mary in her arms. "They keep moving here. It's like Alaska but hotter."

"So, I guess I won't be making any new friends considering I'm from out of town and took one of the best men of Stone Ridge," Jennifer said.

"Not at all," Delores said. "The men reserve the right to choose who they want and we're always glad when they bring their own wife to town."

"It has happened a handful of times in the past." Bonnie Lee nodded.

"Leaves more choices for the rest of the men," Beulah said. "Very kind of you."

"Um, you're welcome…?" Jennifer shifted in her seat.

She couldn't help feeling surreal about this whole thing.

"Bonnie Lee was also very kind to come home," Maybelle said.

"Well, I wasn't going to let someone *else* have Sean. Please don't think of me as a martyr." Bonnie fanned herself and gave a wicked smile. "I mean, I have Sean. It's called winning."

Women tittered and giggled in the spirit of Bonnie's words and just when Jennifer thought this whole thing was nothing but a big throwback, the gifts were brought out. The height of them all was the quilt. Called a "marriage quilt," it looked like it had been hand stitched by Amish women. With bright rings of orange, red, yellow, and blue such as Jennifer had never seen on a quilt before, it still worked. In the center were Sean and Bonnie Lee's names, the date of their marriage, and a short verse. It read, "Love is patient" in beautiful cross-stitching.

"We couldn't decide on any one color for you, honey, so we went with all of them," Maybelle said. "I insisted on red, too, for your beautiful hair."

Bonnie Lee laughed and wiped away a tear. "I knew this day would be special, but gosh, the verse is just…perfect for us."

. . .

COLTON HEARD THE LADIES INSIDE, laughing and clucking away like hens. He felt like an idiot standing here but after reading those emails he'd been…let's face it, a bit spooked. This Dan dude sounded like he'd come unhinged. And if he wasn't just making false claims, and *could* find Jennifer, it was Colton's duty to be with her when he did.

Since he had reception downtown, he'd checked his phone for messages from Horace. Nothing. For now, Colton was going to hold back the disturbing news of the latest emails. He could handle things from here. But since he had a moment, he went through his podcasts and searched for Jennifer's. Finally finding *Truth Salad*, he went to the episode on returning soldiers.

The anonymous soldier she referred to was clearly her brother, Joe, who spoke only on the condition of privacy. Colton was impressed by the quality of her questions. They were probing, intuitive, and spoke of someone who'd done her research. Who understood there were no easy answers. Listening to Joe was like listening to himself. He understood, and God, it was good to know he wasn't the only one.

Jennifer's smooth and disembodied voice still sounded… well, throaty, sultry, and…sexy. He certainly could see the attraction even without laying eyes on her. The one-two punch to the gut was pretty much what he'd felt the moment he saw her.

He was so caught up in listening that he nearly missed the person several feet away on the stairway of the building adjacent to the church. The woman had stopped halfway up and stared down at Colton.

"I can't believe this. Is that really you?"

He'd known, of course, that he would eventually run into her again.

He pulled out his earbud. "Hey, Cherisse."

She rushed back down the steps and made her way

around to the back of the church to the door he stood guarding.

She was still beautiful. Still blonde, and hadn't lost any of her figure even though he'd heard about the three children. He was prepared for her to still be pretty, but he had also worried he might feel...something. Regret. It seemed that he should feel more, based on nostalgia alone. At one time, he'd loved her enough to consider marriage to her someday. She'd been his high school sweetheart and now she was a complete stranger. It was just one more acknowledgement to this soldier: we're not in Kansas anymore.

How strange that he felt nothing at all for her. He considered he might be closed up due to bitterness and the blocking of any feeling or vulnerability. His therapist, who'd known about the abandonment simply because it was something for Colton to talk about instead of bombs, had opinions. He was supposed to confront her at some point because otherwise he'd never get past it.

But the space where he'd loved her was empty now.

"What are *you* doing here?" Cherisse said.

"You didn't know I was back?"

"I was in San Antonio for a few days."

That explained the lull in information spreading. She would have known by tonight if she hadn't run into him.

"What I really mean is why are you standing in front of that door like a guard?"

"I'm not a bodyguard. What makes you say *that*?" Aw, damn it. Bad choice of word.

"I didn't say *bodyguard*." She laughed and tossed her hair back. "But now that you mention it, you do look like you're guarding the church and the ladies. I'm sure the biddies are in there having another one of their ridiculous SORROW meetings."

"They are. It's for Bonnie Lee. She and Sean are finally getting hitched."

"I heard all about it. Is that the only reason you're back?" She came closer and it was as if she'd forgotten what had happened between them.

Like she'd forgotten she dumped him for his best friend when he was thousands of miles away in the desert missing home and family. When he'd felt abandoned for the countless time in his life.

"Not the only reason, but yeah."

"I always hoped you'd come home."

Colton snorted. "Yeah. Well, my *fiancée* sure likes it here."

He'd never taken such pleasure in lying. Had he been more calculating about all this, he would have realized that coming home with a beautiful wife, one ten times more appealing than Cherisse, would let her know he'd clearly moved on. Was it shallow and childish? Yeah, maybe. But he couldn't wait for her to see Jennifer.

Cherisse blinked and registered utter surprise. "Your *fiancée*?"

"That's right. She's inside right now with Bonnie Lee and Winona and the rest of them."

"Isn't this rather sudden? When did you have time to get yourself a fiancée? Can she speak English?"

"Yep." Colton lowered his shades and smirked. "She's fluent."

"That's nice. I'm sure even a foreigner could settle into Stone Ridge. Eventually."

"Yeah, she's from Los Angeles."

"Oh." Cherisse crossed her arms, meeting his own defensive stance. "You'll probably hear about this sooner or later, but Taylor and I are recently separated."

"Sorry to hear it."

"That's why I was in San Antonio. He's moved there and it's his weekend with the boys."

Colton couldn't imagine how difficult it would be to handle a divorce with children. Given their town's unique situation, it wasn't too surprising that Taylor was the one to relocate. At least Colton wouldn't have to deal with him.

He didn't say anything, so Cherisse continued. "It was never going to work between us. We tried because I got pregnant with Dallas."

"You named your kid *Dallas?*"

Colton always had the impression this was something people not *from* Texas did.

"Yes, why?"

He shrugged. "Austin is better, or maybe Tyler. Both great names and equally great cities."

She frowned a little. "I also have an Austin and a Tyler, my youngest."

"Of course, you do."

So, Colton had once been in love with the least imaginative woman in all of Texas, apparently. The thought his children could have been named after cities sent a shiver through him.

"Anyway, we tried to make it work. But Taylor...he just never believed I loved him. You know? Never believed he could take your place in my heart. First love and all. Finally, he got fed up and left."

"Did you cheat on him?" Colton appreciated the thought. No one would have deserved it more.

"No, I didn't!" She sighed and batted her eyelashes. "I don't know, I guess one doesn't ever really get over their first love."

"A common misconception. Some people do just fine with that. Try a little harder."

She smiled, that conniving evil one that reminded him of

Cruella DeVille. The one that said: *nice try, but I'm not convinced.*

"You look good, Colton. Very good."

The door flew open, and Colton stepped aside.

"Yep, he's still here," Maybelle called out, then noticed Cherisse. "Oh, hey there, Cher."

"Howdy." She finger waved.

Colton stepped toward the door. "May I see my fiancée now?"

"You'll be glad to know we've taken pity on you, child." She waved him inside. "Come in now and have some cake and punch. Your *fiancée* is waiting for you."

"With pleasure."

Colton stepped inside and shut the door to his past. And if he had the key to this door, he would lock it.

CHAPTER 12

The punch was definitely spiked.

Unfortunately, Jennifer didn't realize this until she was three cups in. No one had warned her, in fact even now no one raised a single eyebrow. It tasted so good, a cherry sweet flavor but with a nice bite to keeping it from being too syrupy. And before she knew it, everyone was super nice and Jennifer was so, *so* happy. She didn't want to stop indulging in the delicious drink. Ever.

Conversations were held all around her as everyone dived into the cookies, cake, and punch. It was tough to think of anything to contribute so Jennifer stayed near the punch bowl.

When they'd allowed him in, Colton ate a piece of cake, didn't touch the punch, and generally scowled the entire time. He chatted with Bonnie Lee, admiring the quilt when she held it up for him.

"That was Cherisse outside talking with Colton," Maybelle whispered from behind Jennifer. "Can you just imagine the nerve."

"*Talking* to Colton? Acting like she hasn't done anything wrong?" Clementine said. "For shame!"

"What happened with Cherisse?" Jennifer turned toward the ladies.

She knew about the email breakup but maybe there was more. Instinct told her someone was about to spill the tea on everything Colton.

"Oh honey, don't you know she ran off with Colton's best friend, that's what!" Maybelle said. "It broke his poor little heart. Here he is off fighting a *war* for his *country*, and she takes up with his friend, that Taylor."

Poor, poor, sweet little Colton. Okay, he wasn't little anymore but still.

"Don't worry." Maybelle patted Jennifer's back. "Colton barely gave her the time of day. I'm sure he was just speaking with her to be kind. You're the best thing to ever happen to him."

"Oh. Thank you."

Jennifer helped herself to another glass of punch and took a seat. She swayed a little bit, and it was hard not to cry because Colton had been betrayed and abandoned by not one but two people. Oh, damn. And she thought she had problems.

"How many of these have you had?"

The voice was sharp and brisk and startled her. Colton stood above her, arms crossed, looking handsome and hot and...sad. Or mad. Hard to tell.

"Um..."

Colton turned away. "Ladies, who spiked the punch and why didn't you tell Jennifer?"

Beulah ran over, followed by Winona and Bonnie Lee close behind.

"It's usually fine and there's barely any rum in there."

Jennifer nodded. "It's *so* good."

Bonnie Lee poured a glass and took a sip. "Good grief, Clementine, did you follow the recipe?"

"Yes, I started with pineapple juice, orange, added the rums, both light and dark and grenadine."

No wonder Jennifer found this punch dangerously easy to drink.

"But did you get the right ratio of juice to rum?" Beulah said. "It's there in the recipe book."

After some discussion between the ladies, it became clear that Clementine had put too much rum in the mix. About *three times* too much.

"Oh dear." Clementine raised a hand to her throat, grimacing.

"That's it, Clementine! You will never make the punch for the Ladies of SORROW meetings again." Beulah shook a finger.

Jennifer heard many voices then, all arguing over who should make the punch next time.

"This is what happens when we veer from our rules. First, we let a man of Stone Ridge inside our quarters. And next we get his fiancée drunk," Beulah said.

"You can't blame this on Colton!" Delores shouted.

Colton took the empty cup from Jennifer's hand and hauled her up. "I'm taking her home. Looks like you've done your damage."

"Oh, Colton, we're so sorry," Beulah said. "Clementine didn't mean it. She's got to have her eyes checked again. When was your last exam at the optometrist?"

"I guess I'm due," Clementine said, sounding miserable.

"Please don't feel bad," Jennifer said, reaching to hug Clementine. "It was a simple mistake to make. And the punch was really, really, really good."

Bonnie Lee opened the door for them. "We'll see you two

soon. Get her home and pump her with plenty of water and she'll be fine within a few hours or so."

"You're so pretty," Jennifer said, hugging Bonnie Lee. "And I love you."

"Oh, honey. I love you, too," Bonnie said. "I can't wait for you to be my sister-in-law."

"That's right!" Jennifer swayed and pointed to Bonnie. "But not really because I'm—"

"We have to go." Colton pulled on her arm and walked her to the truck. "You don't want to get sick here."

Jennifer's hand flew up over her mouth. She'd almost blown their cover. Colton would be mad after all this work. They were in deep now. Plus, now she wanted to make Chernobyl or Cheryl or whatever her name was feel super bad about what she'd done to Colton. It was bad enough to break up via email but then she went off with his best friend?

On the ride home, Colton drove slowly, looking concerned about the interior of his truck (leather) and kept asking her if he should pull over. He obviously thought she might puke. But Jennifer didn't feel sick in the slightest. She was, however, highly emotional, which was how alcohol tended to affect her. Her inhibitions lowered, she could no longer bite down on the tears threatening.

Colton was being so nice, and he deserved all the happiness in the world after what he'd been through. Some people really sucked. Like Cherywinkle, or whatever her name was.

"You're so nice. I'm sorry about your girlfriend and your best friend. That's horrible."

He quickly glanced from the road to her. "Who told you about that?"

"I overheard them talking about how she dumped you for your best friend. You didn't mention that part."

"It's ancient history." He scowled.

"Friends should never do that to friends. He was a shitty friend."

"Yeah, he was. An opportunist."

"Now I *really* want to make her jealous."

"You will, without even trying." Colton chuckled, shaking his head.

She didn't know what that meant, but she was definitely going to put an effort into this one way or another. Poor, poor Colton.

"Do me a favor? Don't feel sorry for me."

They were quiet for most of the ride back to the ranch. Colton slowly went up the bumpy dirt road and pulled up to their cabin.

He shut off the truck. "Okay, let's have you take it easy for the rest of the day. Drink some water, eat some food, and take a nap. The wedding is tomorrow, then Sean and Bonnie Lee will be married and off to their honeymoon."

"And then what? You're going to get rid of me?"

His lips quirked in that half smile of his. She couldn't see his eyes because of those aviator shades but she saw his eyebrows wiggling again. They were very expressive eyebrows.

He turned and faced her. "Why would I want to do that?"

"I'm cramping your style?"

"You're cramping nothing."

"Of course, you would say that. You're so kind. Colton? I really want to give you a huggle."

"What's a *huggle*?"

"I mean a hug. Like a snuggle."

Jennifer closed her eyes and the spinning stopped. For long seconds, there was utter silence.

Then she looked over to the driver's seat and poor Colton was bent over the steering wheel crying. Covering his face and crying. That's how sad he was over Chernobyl, or

Cherywinkle...what was her name again? And his best friend! They honestly sounded like horrible people. She was definitely going to do a shitty-best-friend special on her podcast when and if she ever got back to it.

His shoulders were still shaking when she heard a snort and realized he wasn't crying. He was...laughing. Laughing so hard he wiped away a tear. All she'd wanted was a full-on smile, but she got laughter. That was even better, and she joined him because laughter was catching, same as yawns. And it was liberating to let it out, a combination of sobs and laughter. Sobs for the life she'd left behind. Laughter and a delight she couldn't quite wrap her mind around.

She was strangely...happy. Content.

She stopped laughing when she realized she hadn't heard the punch line. "Hey, what's so funny?"

"Oh, nothing. You're a cute drunk, that's all."

He went around to open her door. Most of the time it annoyed her when men did this because she could open her own doors, thank you. However, she was having a little bit of trouble at the moment. The handle wasn't working too well. Good grief. She hadn't had this much to drink since that one time in college when her roommate had a kegger and Jennifer had literally crawled to bed. The next day she'd felt like a building had fallen on her head. From then on, she'd been dry except for the occasional piña colada or mojito. Hmm. Guess she did have a thing for rum.

Colton opened the passenger side door and offered his hand. She took it, but her arm went out before her leg did, which was not the right order of things, so she fell into his arms. The thing about it was, well, she was not a small woman. Not that she was fat, but she hadn't ever been exactly petite. She'd lost stress weight during the last few weeks but even so was still not small. Tall, with long legs and arms, only a handful of men towered over her. Like Colton.

He caught her easily, holding her up in the circle of his arms. "Okay?"

"Yes."

She stared up at him, her thoughts and feelings spinning almost equally. He had the most expressive eyes, shimmering with warmth and intelligence. She didn't know what to do with these powerful feelings of attraction. He wasn't at all what she'd pictured, a buttoned-up soldier who sat up late cleaning his guns. Shouting out orders. Insisting on absolute compliance.

Instead, he loved to cook. He loved his horse and his family.

He found her funny.

And he'd already given her so much, taken her along with him simply as a favor to her father. She'd interfered with his plans, caused utter commotion in his life, and on top of all this was now a sloppy drunk.

"I'm not much of a drinker because I can't handle my alcohol too well."

"You're kidding." There went the quirked eyebrows again.

She couldn't tell whether he believed her and was surprised or was simply teasing.

"No, *really*." She steadied herself by plunking a hand on that solid wall of chest. "I didn't even drink much in college. Except for that one time. But, wow, the punch was so good. Guess I like rum."

"Apparently." He held the front door open and helped her inside, a hand low on her back. "I'll be sure to hide the rum."

"Ahoy, Captain Sparrow!" She saluted him and walked inside.

This time she caught the glimmer of a smile in his eyes. Thank goodness he wasn't angry with her. If she had to elicit any emotion out of him, let it be lighthearted humor even if at her expense. She could work with that.

"Sit down, wench." He pointed to the couch nearby and continued with the pirate references. "I'll make you something to eat."

"You really are going above and beyond in taking care of me. I think pretty soon it will be my turn. Just give me a chance."

"I'll consider it." He threw off his hat and it landed on the couch neatly beside her.

While she wickedly considered all the many and varied ways she could "take care of him" he was innocently making her lunch in the kitchen. Poor man didn't recognize when a woman was deliciously attracted to him. If she wasn't so drunk, she'd take him to bed right now. Rip off his clothes and have her way with him. She could be persuasive when she wanted to be, which admittedly wasn't often.

When he set the plate in front of her, it wasn't just a sandwich. This thing was a work of art. Cut in four perfect triangles, he'd added a sliced tomato decorated with a sprig of green.

"Egg salad," he said. "I had some hard-boiled eggs."

"Yummy. It's so pretty."

He shrugged and settled beside her, turning on the ancient TV and adjusting the bunny ears.

"I tried that," Jennifer said. "It doesn't help."

Colton eventually flipped to the celebrity entertainment "news" show that seemed to be the only thing they could get around here practically twenty-four-seven. That, and old black-and- white movies. They sat quietly while she tried to eat, and he watched TV.

"I should probably look into getting satellite. Delores didn't watch much TV and she was definitely a penny pincher."

Just as he said the words, the reporters began to chat about the return of *Kavanaugh's Way* and the imminent marriage of its star, Bonnie Lee Wheeler, to her teenage sweetheart, Sean Henderson.

Colton sat up straighter and turned up the volume. "Jesus. What *now*?"

"Ratings of the return of Kavanaugh's Way exceeded anyone's expectations," the male anchor said.

"All thanks to Bonnie Lee Wheeler reprising her portrayal of the youngest sister of the Irish mafia family, now heading up the crime syndicate. It's about time we get older actors portraying strong and powerful female characters, wouldn't you say?" the woman seated next to him said. "But the best thing about all this is her upcoming marriage as a result of Mr. Cowboy. Roger, did you watch the show?"

"I can't say that I did," Roger joked. "But looks like I missed out."

They flashed a posed photo of Sean and Bonnie Lee clearly taken after the wedding proposal.

"Oh, they look so happy," Jennifer said because she'd never seen two people look quite so content to be together.

And after listening to Bonnie talk about Sean today, practically with hearts in her eyes, it was the real thing.

Colton clicked the TV off and ran a hand through his hair. "Listen, I don't want you to worry."

"Why would *I* worry?"

"Sean assures me anyone who gets on this property will be fully vetted."

The pinched and worried gaze in his dark eyes left no doubt he was talking about her stalker.

"I don't see how anyone could possibly make the connection between me and the show." She attempted to assure Colton. "And as long as the photographers only take photos of Sean and Bonnie, we're golden."

"You're right. I shouldn't worry about this, either." He hung his arms between his long legs and clasped his hands together. "But if I'd known this wedding was such a big deal, maybe I wouldn't have allowed you to come along. This is too dangerous, too filled with the unknown."

Her father would have assigned her a snooty bodyguard despite her protests, and she'd have been forced to either live in her father's military complex like home or stayed in the condo under lock and key.

"You let me come along because my father said 'please.'"

It was the moment Colton had relented and she'd seen it with her own eyes. Right then and there she should have recognized the kindness and compassion still streaming through this stoic soldier. He was better adjusted than many of the vets she'd met. Far better than Joe had been, thank God.

"I can't be responsible for anything happening to you." He took her hand in his and squeezed it.

The warmth in the gesture surprised her. They were alone with no need to fake an intimate relationship.

"I didn't want a bodyguard, but this is different. Being with you is *different*. This is more like, well, being on a vacation."

"Maybe the lies we've told everyone helps with that."

It was true. No one realized Colton was guarding her from a stalker and that helped her to feel normal again. But she couldn't deny she had begun to feel like there was something between them, something unlike anything she'd experienced before. Granted, he was far more experienced and probably understood this to be nothing more than a pure and magnetic sexual attraction. Maybe a little crush on her part but purely situational. Kind of like Stockholm syndrome.

For her, it seemed deeper than that. It felt…bigger. Wider. Like she'd dipped her toe in the middle of the ocean without any real understanding of its depth.

And Colton was that ocean.

"Why were you baking late last night?"

"You heard me? Sorry I woke you."

"I couldn't help noticing it was *midnight*. Mostly, I smelled the chocolate. It was delicious."

"Yeah, I baked a cake." He motioned toward the kitchen.

"But *why?*"

"Why at midnight? I forgot to make it earlier. Baking relaxes me. Cooking does, generally. I think it's the routine, getting lost in the process."

"That's how I always felt about photography."

"Why did you give it up?"

"I got tired of weddings and Bar Mitzvahs. No one wanted my lovely scenic photos of Yosemite and Joshua Tree. Making a living with art is tough. Maybe I should have tried harder but the podcast just kind of happened. I did it for fun to see what would happen. If I might be able to get people interested in my photos from there. I had no clue what I was doing but I felt a passion to help people. Before I knew it, sponsors were paying me to advertise, and I started making money. It was hard to walk away from that."

"You should try photography again, as a backup."

"You mean in case I can *never* go back to my podcast?"

There. She'd said the words out loud. Maybe it was too dangerous. She'd never know, even if she got rid of Dan, whether he might someday resurface again. Or some other person would.

"You can't let one delusional person alter your plans. It might take time. You could move—"

"But I love my condo."

Colton nodded as if he understood. "Then maybe photography under a pen name. And never post your photo. Facial recognition software has come leaps and bounds."

Yes, she'd heard. And yes, her personal photo had been on her podcast page. Not even an avatar. Live and learn.

"All good ideas."

He squeezed her hand again. "Hey, I'm sorry this happened to you."

It sounded as if he meant far more than simply sorry. She swallowed hard, recovering from the feel of his warm hand.

"Joe thinks it may have been for the best."

"Your brother?"

"He's wrong, of course. It isn't for the best. But he didn't handle civilian life as well as you have."

"Who says *I* have?"

"Everything about you. You have a hobby, you're not completely withdrawn."

"My family does that for me."

"I can see. You're lucky."

He cleared his throat. "I also went through therapy for about three months before I let my family know I was coming home. I let them believe I was still overseas because I…needed that time."

She nearly dropped her sandwich halfway to her mouth. "You've had therapy?"

"Why the shock? Do I not seem that enlightened?"

"No, it's just so many soldiers like Joe hate to admit they need help."

"My family thought I was still serving, but I was debriefing and getting counseling. I wanted to be whole for them when I came back. Otherwise, they'd worry and hover, and that's the last thing I need."

"You love your family."

"Doesn't everyone?" He lifted a shoulder.

"*Your* family? Yes. I love your family, too. But no, not everyone's family is quite like yours." She thought of her own rather fractured family. "I'm close with my brother. But my father? You've met my father, the lieutenant. He ran a tight ship at home, too. As a child, he'd wake me up with: Good morning, Jennifer. Here's your first order of the day."

Colton blinked. "That's…interesting."

"Yeah, most of my friends thought so when they'd spend the night and hear the lieutenant's orders through the closed bedroom door."

"You must be like your mother."

It was true what they said about losing a parent. The pain never dulled.

"I lost her when I was twelve. Cancer." She took a deep breath. "But yes, I was like her. Very much. She was an artist. I still have some of her work on canvas. For her it was a hobby. Her children were her life."

"Your father never mentioned she was an artist. Then again, he didn't talk about her much. Too painful, I imagine." He rubbed at his temple. "I know what it's like to lose someone."

He probably meant his parents and not Cherisse. Or maybe he meant both.

"I know you do."

Jennifer finished the delicious sandwich. The feeling was starting to come back to her limbs, inhibitions creeping back in, and she wondered how big of a fool she'd made out of herself in front of Colton and the ladies.

"I listened to your podcast while I was banished from the meeting."

She cared too much what he thought. It shouldn't matter but it did. "What did you think?"

"You're very good at talking to people. I should have realized that from our road trip, but I didn't know how well it would translate into your work." He smiled and she read all manner of nuances into that half smile.

I see you.

I understand.

I accept you.

Maybe she was imagining it, but Colton understood her in a way she wasn't even sure Joe did.

"It was nice to find something where I could be a success. You probably know my grandfather was army, too. Highly decorated. Did you know even my aunt was in the service at one time? But me, I think I've tried for most of my life to fit in…somewhere else."

This was a truth she'd only recently come to fully understand in all its ramifications. She forgave herself, too, for being too kind to Dan.

It was all part of the journey to understanding she didn't need everyone in the world to like her. Some people never would, some would like her a little too much.

It was out of her control. And that was okay.

CHAPTER 13

On the day of the wedding, Jennifer primped like she hadn't done in years. The straightening, then curling, of her wavy hair brought back memories of prom night years ago. Prom night, when her father had interrogated her date, and she did not use that term lightly. Prom night, when her aunt chose the dress Jennifer would wear. Not the one she'd wanted because the yellow gown was "far too bright."

"You'll look like the *sun*. Do you *want* to look like Big Bird? A tall girl needs to wear more subdued colors so as not to appear even larger. You should look delicate. Like the petal of a flower. Think pink pastels and blues."

No, thanks!

Petal of a flower? She was far more like the stem.

That's probably why Jennifer went a little "girls gone wild" at university. But after that one unfortunate kegger, she kept her boldness and adventure confined to her clothes. It was nothing unusual to see her wearing cut-off overalls, and she rarely wore anything but yellow, orange, and red. "Here comes Jennifer! You can't miss her," her friends said. One fellow student had affectionately called her a walking stop sign. She'd gotten it out of her system that first year, but it had been her choice.

Aunt Betty probably wouldn't approve of the floor-length royal-blue gown she'd be wearing today, either, but at least it wasn't yellow.

Today, she wanted to impress, for Colton's sake more than her own. This was her part in their ruse. He'd taken such good care of her, even feeding her fantastic meals when that wasn't part of the deal. The least she could do is look drop-dead gorgeous. She'd never looked drop-dead gorgeous in her life but there was always a first time. Hope sprang eternal. After all, she'd been gifted with all the proper, um, equipment. Generous-sized breasts and long legs.

The gown was tight around the bodice and flared out a little, somewhat camouflaging her wide hips. She was sensitive about her rather ample behind, even if a former boyfriend had said she had a butt like *the* famous Jennifer. *This* Jennifer would have preferred to be model-thin and svelte. She had the height, but no amount of dieting or exercise made her butt any smaller. It would probably require surgery and she wasn't willing to go *that* far.

All the dieting made her rear end appear even more pronounced when the rest of her was too thin. So, back to potato chips she went, so the rest of her would match her behind. Oh well.

First world problems.

Today she'd watch two of her favorite new people vow their love for each other, followed by a huge party at the ranch thrown by a Hollywood production company. Who knew? Maybe she'd even make some contacts and find a way to revitalize her photography career. Colton made a good point. It could be a backup plan, because truth be told, she didn't miss the podcast like she'd thought she would.

Last night, she'd chatted with Mallory for over an hour

before bed. It was strange to no longer text, that impersonal way of chatting with friends that kept a distance between them. She could text while watching TV, for instance, and no one complained that she wasn't listening. Because she'd "listen" when she had a minute and then respond when she wanted. But texting was a dim memory now.

After assuring Mallory she was fine and still in one piece, Jennifer answered all pressing questions about her current situation.

"What is this bodyguard cowboy like? Is he anything like the bouncer types in bars? Big and hairy?"

"No, probably because he's *not* a bodyguard. He's just someone my father asked to look out for me until Dan stops the madness. We're staying in the same house, and he just follows me around when I go anywhere off the ranch."

"Sounds like a bodyguard to me. And what does his family think about all this? Did you explain what happened with your podcast?"

"This one is a little tougher to explain."

Jennifer told her about the fake engagement and how happy his family was about him appearing settled.

"I can't believe this," Mallory said. "You're like…living a romantic comedy."

"Except it's not that funny."

"Tell me about it. Nothing about Dan is funny."

"Has he been bothering you?"

Jennifer's second biggest fear was that he'd go after her friends. But at least he didn't know where they lived. He did, however, know that Mallory worked at the restaurant where they'd had their one and only date.

"He's been in a couple of times alone. Keeps asking about you. I told him we had a falling out and are no longer friends."

"Smart."

"I also told him he needs to stop bothering you before he gets arrested. He says that he never violates the restraining order and always stays the appropriate distance away. What's wrong with that guy? By all accounts he's handsome, seems perfectly normal, and should have to beat the women off with a stick."

"He's possibly done this before, and I can't see that anyone would put up with it for long."

"At least he's never been violent," Mallory said.

Yet.

Maybe her father had ripped her from her life out of love and not control the way she'd initially believed.

A love he didn't easily show.

"When will you come home?"

"I... I think my father was right. I might actually have to move."

"You love that condo! Don't let Dan do this to you. I thought we agreed you couldn't let him win."

"I'm not winning when I'm a prisoner in my home. When I don't have any real peace of mind. When I won't even go swimming because he might see me. When my family and friends fear for my life. Here, I feel like I'm on a vacation in the countryside. You should see it."

"Hey, let's not forget that place is temporary. Whether or not you sell the condo, you can't stay there."

"Oh, I know. But listen. There are horses and cattle here, and a cute dog named Beer. There's a lake I'm probably going to swim in, and you know how long it's been since I went swimming. And the people. They're the best."

"Okay, I'm going to let the dog named Beer go for now. I just hope you're aware that sooner or later, you are going to have to get back to work."

"I've been thinking maybe it's time to end the show. I'm just tired."

"Are you tired of being *successful*?"

When she put it that way…

"No. Of course not. But this isn't at all how I *wanted* to be successful."

"Cry me a river, Jen. We can't all do *exactly* what we want, or I would be Chris Hemsworth's personal assistant."

"You're right, I know. The money has been nice and actually making a living as an investigative journalist impressed my dad. But I only make enough to pay my bills with most of it being my ridiculous rent."

The subject of rent in California was another one they exhausted before they finally hung up and promised to check in again later.

Now, Jennifer applied one last wave of mascara over her eyelashes and red color to her lips. She stood back and admired her efforts. Not too bad for a girl who didn't normally wear makeup.

"Jennifer! Aren't you ready yet?" Colton pounded on the bathroom door, startling her. "We're going to be late."

"We are not going to be late. By my calculations, I still have…um, five seconds."

"Five, four, three…"

"Stop it!"

She took one last look in the mirror, fluffed her hair, and licked her lips. There.

"Two, one. Blast off. Open this door right now or I go to this wedding without you."

He knew where to hit below the belt. No way was she going to wait inside this cottage while outside everyone was having fun. Not to mention that his entire family would wonder how she could miss this monumental event.

She threw open the door.

Oh my. She shouldn't have been surprised but Colton looked incredible in black tie and matching black western hat. She'd been with him when he picked it up, but he hadn't even tried it on. He'd shaved, too, and was clean-cut again.

She stared…and stared…and stared some more. It took her a minute to realize he was also staring as his gaze raked down her body and back up again. A little open-mouthed, actually. *Oh God.* She'd overdone it with the gown. One of the worst things any wedding guest could do was to outshine the bride. In her quest to be the spiciest thing since Hot Cheetos for Colton's sake, she might have overshot. But surely not because Bonnie Lee was so preternaturally beautiful no one could even hope to compare. And blue was not anywhere near white. Or yellow.

She glanced down at her dress, feeling a wave of insecurity hit her. "Is this okay? It's royal blue, not even close to white. I know that's a huge no-no. But maybe…I don't know…"

Colton swallowed, then held up both palms. "No, no. You're fine, you're *perfect.*"

"Thank you. You look pretty good, too."

Pretty good? He looked amazing. She had no idea the man could clean up like this.

When he held out his arm she took it, grabbing her little wrist purse with her other hand, and followed him out the door.

Colton watched Sean and Bonnie Lee finally exchange their sacred vows, and marveled that his brother finally had the woman he'd always loved. It had been a long and circuitous route to their happy ending, but here they were, still with a lot of good years ahead of them. He couldn't be happier for his brother. At one time, Colton had also pictured winding up on that altar with his first love. It hadn't happened and now he couldn't be happier. As the Garth Brooks song went, sometimes God's greatest gifts were unanswered prayers.

He could barely remember the boy/young man who'd thought he loved Cherisse. Could barely remember what he found appealing about her at all. It seemed like an entirely different man had loved her, if he could even call it love. More likely it had been lust. Maybe true love was something that never died, like with Sean and Bonnie. Even with time and distance they still couldn't stop loving each other. Colton once had his doubts it would ever happen for Sean, but the look on his brother's face now was proof some things were worth waiting for.

Pastor June's sermon focused on Sean and Bonnie Lee's past, mentioning Corinthians and the true meaning of love.

"Sean Henderson, do you take Bonnie Lee Wheeler to be your lawfully wedded wife, to have and to hold in sickness and in health from this day forward until death do you part?" Pastor June recited.

"I do," said Sean.

"You better," whispered Bonnie Lee, and their small group of family and close friends in the pews tittered.

The vows were repeated for Bonnie Lee, who loudly declared, "I do," and then added, more softly, "I always have, I always will."

At that point, Maybelle, Delores, and Beulah brought out the tissues and began to quietly sob.

"This is so beautiful. I think I'm going to cry." From next to him, Jennifer sniffed and wiped away a tear.

"Here." He handed her a handkerchief, the kind he never

carried except to weddings and funerals since someone inevitably cried and Colton was always prepared.

He wasn't surprised by Jennifer's emotion. She was full of a range of feelings he'd witnessed since the day they were thrown together, neither one of them thrilled by the arrangement. He'd seen anger from her, desperation, fear, joy and now tears. His own emotions were ranging from tenderness to confusion to lust.

He'd nearly swallowed his tongue when he had a look at her today. She reminded him of a brunette Jessica Rabbit in that dress, all curves and scrumptious behind. Her sweet alabaster skin glowed pink, showing just enough cleavage to make him beg for more. At that moment he wondered how he'd keep his hands to himself and then remembered he didn't have to. At least, not in public. Everyone believed they were in love, about to be married, and no one would blame him for wanting to be near her every moment.

The vows and pronunciation over, everyone filed out for the ride back to the ranch. Colton steered Jennifer ahead of him down the steps of the chapel, scanning his surroundings, grateful he had a reason to be on high alert. He didn't just have to write it off to PTSD and the sense that something could go wrong at any time, no matter how careful a soldier was. In this case, he suspected it to be true. Jennifer was the kind of woman who drew a man in and if that man happened to be obsessed, anything could happen. He was ready for it.

Seeing Riggs leaving the church with Winona and all three kids in tow reminded Colton that he still needed to have "the talk" with his older brother. Once Riggs saw that Colton was staying, regardless of his relationship situation, once he was assured, it would go down easier when all this… ended. He realized with a start it wasn't the talk with Riggs he dreaded but the moment when Jennifer left. The moment he no longer had someone to talk to every morning and night, to cook and bake for, or commiserate with over bad TV reception.

She'd be gone soon, and he supposed the biddies would be after him to get hitched next. The last one standing. He could tell them his heart was broken and he needed some time, but that would only get him six months tops. The thing was, he wasn't interested in getting married. First, he had to get his own act together and he wasn't foolish enough to think three months of therapy and picking up a relaxing hobby meant he was good to go. He would sign up for more therapy at some point, even if the nightmares weren't coming as frequently. The other night when he'd gotten up in the middle of the night to bake, he'd had the first real nightmare since his arrival in Stone Ridge. But he had his coping mechanisms in place and kept reminding himself someday it would get a little bit easier.

Their ranch was barely recognizable due to a large white tent in the middle of the field, with an open area that had been converted to a dance floor. An eight-piece band was setting up on risers, and caterers were rushing back and forth.

"Colton, I've made a big mistake." Jennifer tugged on him.

"What is it?" If she was going to change her mind about the reception now, excuses might be even more awkward to make.

"I'm having a shoe moment."

He followed her gaze to her legs. She stuck out a foot wearing a shoe with a heel that made every man stop thinking coherent thoughts.

"I mean…? You know?"

He swallowed hard and then had the epiphany right along with Jennifer. These were certainly not the type of shoes to wear on a ranch. And wedding or not, they were on a ranch.

"They were great for the chapel, but I can't wear these here. I've already sunk into the ground a few times."

"You should have said something."

"I'm saying something now."

They went back to the house so she could change. He stood near the door, glancing at his watch, and waited several minutes hearing frustrated and agonized sighs from her. One pair of shoes flew out the door and sailed into the hallway landing with a thud.

"You okay in there?"

He moved to her bedroom to find her bent over the suitcase on her bed. The sight of her bent, her generously shaped behind poised in the air, was the kind of temptation he didn't need at the moment.

"I'm afraid this is all I have." She held up a pair of red and white Chuck Taylors.

He smiled. "No boots?"

"I'm from *Los Angeles*, Colton."

"I'll have to buy you a pair of shit kickers."

"A…what now?" She cocked her head, studying him.

"That's what I call substantially made boots with thick soles."

"Ugh, they sound ugly."

"Well, I won't get you the type with steel reinforced toes, then." He motioned to the chucks. "Slip those on, no one is going to care."

"You're right. Everyone is going to be looking at Bonnie Lee." She laced the high-top shoes.

Damn if he didn't get turned on watching her hike up the dress.

They got to the tent just as more people were arriving.

"Hello, who are you?" A small woman came up to him and Jennifer. "Oh my gawd. Did you know you look just like Sean?"

"I'm taller," Colton said, feeling like a jackass for pointing that out. As if it mattered.

"I'm Lori, the award-winning director of *Mr. Cowboy*. And this is Elton, he's with me."

"How you doing?" A beefy man holding a camera the size of a suitcase held out his hand.

Colton shook the man's hand. "This is my fiancée, Jennifer."

"Hi there," Jennifer said, still holding on to his arm.

"Welcome to our ranch. I'm Colton, Sean's brother."

"I should have figured that," Lori said. "Seeing as you could pass for his double."

Colton wanted to protest but what was the point? These were people from Hollywood, and they only focused on a person's looks. He looked like his brother. Somebody stop the presses.

"Thank you for your service," Elton said.

The remark always made Colton tense and it was the first time he'd heard it since he'd come home. Next to him, he felt Jennifer squeeze his hand.

"Oh, yeah!" Lori said. "Thank you so much for your service."

Again. What was he supposed to say? *You're welcome, it was my pleasure?*

It had most definitely not been his *pleasure*.

"Yeah," Colton said, and Jennifer squeezed his hand again.

It struck him that she *knew*. He had begun to realize that she somehow always understood when something had become tough for him emotionally.

A couple of days ago, he'd zoned out watching the horses and remembering some of the dead carcasses he'd seen in the desert. She'd pulled him out of that memory with a touch of her hand.

"Lori!" a throng of women squealed, coming fast in their direction. "Omigod, omigod!"

Colton stepped aside, taking Jennifer with him. He recognized three of them from the dress store, but there were more, and he counted. Seven, eight…he stopped at ten.

All fully vetted and no men with them. He scanned the crowd, reminding himself that even if the media had heavily advertised this event, the point was no one could possibly make the connection between *Mr. Cowboy* and Jennifer.

CHAPTER 14

"*H*ere comes our cast." Lori clapped her hands. "I never thought I'd say this, but I missed them."

The bevy of women descended on them, having arrived in a separate limo provided by the production company. Elton snapped away with his camera.

"Hello, hello, ladies!" Lori said. "Isn't this exciting? I hope everyone is thrilled! A little reunion of our sleeper reality show that became so popular with online viewers."

Colton took Jennifer's hand and started to lead them away but stopped when someone said, "Hey, Sean 2.0!"

Irritated, he turned to scowl and noted they were all taking selfies with each other. All except for the woman who had called him. Tabitha, or whatever her name was.

"Can I get a selfie for my Instagram followers?"

"No," he said.

"Oh, c'mon! I'm a local," Tabitha said. "We're going to be seeing each other around especially if you have to go to the clinic. I'm the nurse there."

"I won't be going to the clinic. I never get sick."

Everyone gaped at him.

"Never?" said one woman, holding a hand to her neck.

"How about you, Jennifer? Can we get a selfie?" the other woman asked. "Just us gals."

"Absolutely not," Colton said. "You will not take photos of my fiancée."

Jennifer squeezed his hand, obviously communicating he might be going over the top with his protection mode. No one had any idea of why he didn't want photos of her taken, and it certainly wasn't because he was an ogre. Though he might sound like one.

"Sorry," Colton said. "The thing is, I want this day to be about Sean and Bonnie Lee. Let's focus on them."

"He's right, ladies," Jennifer said. "I really don't want to take any attention away from the beautiful bride. Just wait until you see her."

"I'm sure she looks gorgeous," Lori said. "We have an entire photo shoot setting up right now for when they arrive. It's going to be in *People* magazine. *People!* I finally hit the big time."

Guests were arriving slowly, both from the church, and others who hadn't been to the private ceremony. The large Carver family was grabbing seats at a table together. Hank and Brenda, Lincoln, Sadie, Jackson, Eve, and Daisy with… was that *Wild Wade Cruz* holding her hand? And speaking of which, didn't Eve leave Jackson at the *altar*? Colton remembered that well. Seemed all was forgiven there. And Sadie, with Lincoln, the rodeo champion roper and town Casanova. They couldn't keep their hands off each other. Colton had missed…a lot.

And since arriving he'd had little time for anything other than getting ready for this wedding and worrying about how all the publicity and attention would affect his job. No, not job. Favor. He'd never been a bodyguard before in the civilian world, and he honestly had no idea if he was doing any of this right. But as long as he met his primary objective, keeping his principle safe, that's all that mattered to him.

He walked around with Jennifer at his side, waving to people he hadn't seen in a while, talking to a few, and hearing far too many "thank you for your service" greetings.

"There you are!" Jolette Marie Truehart, youngest daughter of the man who owned the largest horse ranch in the area, called out. "Welcome home, cowboy."

"Hey there, Jo." She was an old friend, and Colton didn't hesitate to open up his arms and accept her hug. Both he and Sean thought of her as the little sister they'd never had. She was beautiful but made bad choices when it came to men.

"Hi, I'm Colton's fiancée." Jennifer stuck her hand out and announced herself faster than he'd ever seen her do before other than the day they'd all been in the dress shop. "Jennifer."

"Fiancée? C'mere!" Jo grabbed her in a hug. "I'm Jolette Marie and we hug in these parts."

"It's really good to see you, Jo." Colton meant every word. "You look…happy."

Jo had been through a lot of heartache when she ran out on her last fiancé. It had been the third, count them, *third* time she'd run out on a man. No one was willing to take the chance on her anymore. Colton had been around to witness that carnage. The Ladies of SORROW didn't take it easy on her, either, accusing her of running perfectly good men right out of town. Though, if Colton recalled, it had been their choice to leave.

"Thank you, I am happy. Especially to see Bonnie Lee and Sean back together." She waved her hand between Colton and Jennifer. "When did *this* happen?"

Colton exchanged a glance with Jennifer, who smiled up

at him and nodded, as if indicating he should take this one. Right.

"We met through her father, who was my mentor." He kept it short and simple so that if their stories varied it wouldn't be quite as noticeable.

"Actually, we haven't known each other for long," Jennifer added. "We fell in love super fast."

"Yeah, that too," Colton added.

"I heard Cherisse is about to spit nails." Jo laughed. "Did you know she's here?"

"No."

Colton wondered how in the hell *she'd* scored an invite. Then again, it seemed that half the town's residents were here, and they sure wouldn't turn a woman away from the party. Not every man had a plus one as it didn't usually work that way around here. In years past, they'd actually had a service called the "rented ladies" who'd come from out of town to round out a party.

"Fair warning. First, three kids in three years. All boys. Next, Taylor cheats on her and moves out of town. She's been in a bad mood for *years*."

"Oh, how awful." Jennifer squeezed his hand.

"That's…sad."

Jolette Marie laughed. "You two are hilarious."

"I like to think so," Jennifer said, batting her eyelashes. "Aren't we funny, babe?"

He bit back a laugh. "Let's go find a seat."

JENNIFER THOUGHT that Jolette Marie was not only beautiful and sweet, but also petite. Her teensy waist matched an equally teensy weensy behind and she briefly reminded Jennifer of a flower petal. She'd come dressed in decidedly western-style glam and Jolette Marie rocked the look. She wore the western version of a little black dress: a V neckline with fringe detail throughout. She'd paired the dress with a matching black hat and boots with turquoise blue inlay. Jennifer wanted boots like that. Suddenly she felt out of place here, like the former contestants from the show most of whom were clearly out of towners. Around her, she saw plenty of similar western chic and amazing boots in all colors and designs.

Again, Jennifer didn't fit in. She was trying too hard, and everyone would notice.

Colton led her to a family table where they were seated next to Delores, Riggs, and Winona. But Winona and Riggs were getting up every few seconds, taking turns chasing their twin boys.

The dinner was a sit-down affair and catered. For now, waiters were walking around the tables carrying hors d'oeuvres and goblets of drinks.

"No, thank you." Jennifer held up a hand when the waiter bent toward her with the tray of wine glasses.

Colton smirked. "Want me to see if they have rum?"

"Ha, ha. I need 100 percent of my faculties today. I want to be prepared and alert in case your ex comes at me." She shadowboxed back and forth. "I'm ready."

He stood. "Stay here with Delores. I'm going to go talk to Riggs for a minute."

Delores pulled on Jennifer's elbow once Colton took off in that direction. "Those two really need to chat. Surely Colton has told you about the tension between him and Riggs."

This sounded like something she should know more about so Jennifer faked it. "Sure, but I just thought it was over with."

"I'd like to think so, too, but there's been years of disagreements between the oldest and the youngest brothers.

Sean, of course, played the proverbial middle child brokering the peace between them. He kept the lines of communication open with Colton no matter how long he was gone. Those two have always been close. But see, Riggs didn't want Colton to enlist in the service. He didn't think he could serve two masters and he turned out to be right. Colton basically gave up the ranch and pretty much his family while he was in the service. But the military was important to him, too. Now, it looks like he's home to stay, and I'm not sure Riggs is buying it."

"He should. Colton is serious about staying."

Delores smiled, then glanced down at the ring on Jennifer's finger. She'd almost forgotten.

"It looks good on you."

"Thank you, I love it."

"How did he put it on you? Did he make a big production or just slip it on your finger? I imagine the proposal itself was the big deal. If I know Colton, he goes all out with the woman he loves."

Jennifer didn't know why this made her feel bad. Maybe because she pictured some other lucky lady getting the full treatment. But she couldn't expect anything at all when this was all pretend.

"Yes, well, he is *so*...romantic, right? But he'd already made the big production when he asked me, so he made sure I liked the ring and just slipped it on my finger." She cleared her throat. "And then he kissed me, of course."

Jennifer briefly wondered if Delores was referring to Cherisse with the reference to 'woman he loves.' Maybe he'd been trying to spare Jennifer's feelings, and he *had* asked Cherisse to marry him. Maybe he'd made a big deal out of it, going down on one knee, or writing it in icing on a cupcake. Jennifer decided then and there that Delores would be her conduit to all things Colton. There were certain parts of his past it made sense he would not discuss with her.

This shouldn't matter to Jennifer because she wasn't actually Colton's fiancée. She couldn't quite figure out why it made a difference, but it did. There was a thirst inside of her to know all things, maybe the casualties of the investigative reporter side of her. She was curious, that was all.

"Why did he never propose to Cherisse?"

Delores shook her head. "He was too smart to do that. But he must have promised her something because for a while she waited for him."

He must have promised her something. Of course he had.

"My brother is a soldier, and he had a girl back home. They weren't engaged but very much in love. Thank God, she waited for him."

Unfortunately, that hadn't lasted long after he'd come home, full of anger and hostility, ready to start a fight with anyone who even looked at him the wrong way.

Her gaze followed Colton and found him a few feet away from Riggs, who was chasing one of his boys, taking a fork away from him.

And then, a woman intercepted Colton, tugging on his arm. He turned and a scowl formed on his face.

"Oh, good Lord. There she is, that *Cherisse*." Delores shook her head and patted Jennifer's arm. "I bet she came with one of her brothers, who probably couldn't get a date. Don't you worry about Colton, now. He's true-blue. When he loves you, he loves you."

Except he didn't love Jennifer. Maybe true-blue Colton could find a way to forgive his first love. After all, Sean had forgiven Bonnie Lee for leaving him to go to Hollywood.

"He's never been one to go after bright and shiny. Single-minded, that one."

"I'm sure it's why he made a good soldier. Better than average."

It was in the way her father had referred to him in quiet serious tones. *I'd trust this man with my life.* Colton was an above-average soldier, a Green Beret, and now he'd be an above-average cowboy.

Cherisse was beautiful, too. And blonde, though tall, and definitely *not* petite. Yet another woman wearing a hat and matching boots. Hers were red with black piping. She had a presence about her, too, one that said, "I know I'm beautiful and you'd be lucky to have me."

Were there any women in this town who weren't blonde and beautiful? There *was* Bonnie Lee, of course, a redhead though that hardly counted. It was even rarer.

Behind her, and frankly all around her, the former contestants on the show were taking selfies with each other. With Lori and the cameraman. With one of the caterers. Jennifer's gaze roamed to those in attendance and landed on a pretty brunette flirting with a man who looked vaguely familiar. He could be another actor, perhaps, but he did seem to be a resident as he sat at a table with a group of others. Perhaps they were also from the show. But yeah, at last, another brunette!

"Who is that?" Jennifer pointed to the familiar man sitting with the brunette. "He looks familiar."

"That's Jackson Carver. He's a country western musician you've probably seen on TV and he and Winona were married for about a minute." Delores chuckled. "But Eve, that's his wife sitting there with him, she was his first love and they got back together when he came home for his brother's wedding."

Which was *exactly* what Colton had done.

Was she the only one who saw the pattern? It made her

uncomfortable, as if she was the only person standing between Colton and a reunion with his first love. Of course, she was hardly between them other than for appearances' sake. But she didn't want to be the reason Colton didn't get everything he wanted. She'd leave here sooner rather than later, and he'd be alone. She pictured the Ladies of SORROW and every single woman in town bringing him casseroles, cakes, and pies, making sure he understood that *Jennifer* was the villain for leaving him. Then, along would come Cherisse, and with Jennifer fake-priming Colton for marriage, she'd swoop right in and have their first sweethearts' reunion. Piece of cake.

"Oh now, don't be upset, honey." Delores patted Jennifer's arm like she'd read her mind. "Not everyone winds up with their first love. I didn't marry mine. He was an idiot."

That made Jennifer snort-laugh. "Mine was, too."

She pictured Ethan, a man/boy that had been as different from her father as humanly possible. He was white but wore dreadlocks, hated the government, was a vegan, and smoked marijuana. Jennifer thought he was perfection. He thought gun ownership should be illegalized and the military complex wiped out. Ethan was also super cute, looked like a young Jude Law, and Jennifer fell for him. Hard. She'd hoped they'd graduate from college, and he'd sweep her away to a secluded island where they would live a bohemian lifestyle. They'd make macrame to sell to the villagers and he'd fish for their dinner every night. Yeah, she was an idiot.

Instead, in their senior year he'd been arrested for dealing drugs on campus. Last she heard he was an accountant in New Jersey.

"I married my second love, the great love of my life. This may be the only time when it doesn't matter if you're the first. Only that you're the last," Delores said. "It's not a race."

She had a point. But Jennifer wasn't going to be last with

Colton, either. She wasn't going to be anything at all but a favor he'd done for her father.

Colton seemed engaged in a heated conversation with Cherisse. It didn't look to be pleasant for Cherisse. However, the discussion looked passionate.

Passion was generally preceded by strong emotions like…love.

The opposite of love wasn't hate. It was indifference.

Sadly, he did not look even slightly indifferent.

CHAPTER 15

"This is not the time or the place," Colton said.

He was trying to be a gentleman but every time he tried to extricate himself from Cherisse to get to Riggs, she put herself in his way. And Riggs, whose son apparently had a fascination with forks, kept following the boy from table to table, bending down to take one away.

"When else am I going to be able to talk to you? You're not going to have anything to do with me. But if I do nothing else, I want us to be friends again."

"Don't bother."

It was the height of hubris for Cherisse to think he would take any time to listen to a word she said.

"You're still angry, aren't you?" She crossed her arms. "I broke your heart, and you'll never forgive me."

He snorted. "Don't make this all about you."

"Then what's it about if not the way Taylor and I hurt you?"

"It didn't occur to you that I have a few other things on my mind today and you're not the center of the universe?"

"I know I'm not. I'm guessing that would be your fiancée."

He threw a glance in Jennifer's direction as he'd been doing every few seconds in addition to scanning the crowd for anyone who looked out of place.

This time, she met his eyes then quickly looked away.

"Please, Colton. Please forgive me. I'm *really* sorry."

Allow yourself to be vulnerable, the therapist had said.

Not with her. Hell, he'd forgotten that part of treatment and assimilating back into society. He still had his walls strong and high, and he hadn't eased them down an inch. Not a centimeter, not even with Riggs. Only Delores, of course, and Sean because, well…he was *Sean*.

And then there was Jennifer.

Jennifer, who stood out here today, so beautiful, and almost regal in the midst of all these small-town country folks. Jennifer, who'd drank too much rum, who wanted to give him a huggle, and who made pirate references to one of his favorite movies. It seemed he'd opened himself up to her because he felt…invested. There was no other word for it. This favor had stopped being a job almost from the moment he'd laid eyes on her. He cared probably more than he should about what happened to her. He wanted to protect her because she'd somehow vaulted over the high walls he'd constructed. She understood him, warts and all.

"Fine, I forgive you." Colton sidestepped her and finally made eye contact with Riggs.

He seemed overwhelmed and already exhausted. He'd come to parenthood later in life than some, so it was no surprise. Wonder what on earth Riggs would do if one of his kids wanted nothing to do with the cattle ranch.

"Hey, Riggs."

He looked up briefly. "Yeah?"

"I've been meaning to schedule a time to talk with you."

"About *what?*" The words were short and choppy, and anyone could hear the anger laced through them.

"My place at the ranch."

"There's nothing to schedule or talk about. You have a place as long as you're here."

As long as you're here. Colton reminded himself that Riggs didn't know how difficult this was for Colton. He had no idea that Colton was feeling awkward and vulnerable and trying to work with that.

Riggs picked up his son, Colton didn't really know which one this was. They both looked like carbon copies of a smaller Riggs. The kid squirmed in his arms.

"I know you're busy so maybe we can set aside some time. I have some ideas."

"Great," Riggs said, sounding as if Colton had just told him the price of a head of cattle had been decimated.

Then he did something so shocking that Colton might never forgive him.

"Here." He handed his son over to Colton. "Hold him. I'll be right back."

Colton had to take the kid, or he'd have fallen to the floor. That's how fast Riggs moved.

The boy looked at him. He looked at the boy. His nephew.

"Hi, I'm Colton. Your uncle."

He stood there, the most uncomfortable he'd ever been, holding the kid at a safe distance. At least for now, he seemed fascinated with Colton and reached with a wet and gummy finger for his hat.

"Um, no. Not my *hat.*" Colton winced and jerked his neck back.

The kid gave him the full bottom lip.

Riggs returned in the nick of time with a wet cloth, and he cleaned his son's sticky fingers one by one. "Okay, that's better."

"Which one is this?" Colton looked at the boy, as if discussing cattle before they were tagged.

"This is Cal." Riggs finally took his son back then met Colton's eyes. "Okay, look. Come by the house tomorrow and we'll talk about your ideas."

Colton was about to say thanks when the crowd erupted because Sean and Bonnie Lee had arrived.

"We better get back to our seats," Riggs said.

Colton found his seat between Jennifer and Delores, who were both wearing big grins.

"What?"

"You looked so good holding little Cal," Delores said. "You're going to be a great uncle. Probably an even better dad."

Colton cleared his throat and tugged at his tie. He wasn't even thinking about a *wife*, much less kids. For the love of God, he just got back and was trying to get his bearings. He hadn't even made it home before he'd offered to help someone.

"When do you two think you'll have children?" Delores, relentless, continued chipping away at the subject.

"I...I..." Jennifer picked up her napkin and folded it on her lap.

"Well, let's have the wedding first," Colton said, taking Jennifer's hand in his.

"You were holding him like toxic waste." Jennifer smiled at him. "*That's* why I was smiling."

"What?" He pushed back a laugh. "*You* didn't think I looked good holding him?"

"You just need a little practice, Uncle Colton."

Sean and Bonnie Lee arrived at the white-tented area and were seated at a table together that was on a slight rise and faced everyone else.

"They decided not to have bridesmaids and groomsmen since the wedding in the chapel was small and intimate," Delores said. "And as Bonnie Lee said, 'I'm not an ingenue.'

Besides, don't you know those producers tried to talk her into having some of the former contestants as bridesmaids!"

"Tacky," Jennifer said.

"But yet they're still here," Colton said, and glanced at the table filled with women taking photos of everything in sight. Sean and Bonnie. The food. Cake. Each other. Because nothing was real anymore unless captured with a photo and then uploaded to social media. Presumably they'd be posting them when they got to Wi-Fi.

Toasts were made by both Riggs and Colton. Delores cried when Sean stood to thank her for being like a mother to him and warned he expected babysitting for his children, too. Bonnie gave a little speech in which she thanked both her mother and Aunt Beulah for helping to bring her back to her one and only love. More tears. Even Jennifer wiped away a tear and pulled out the hanky he'd given her.

He turned to her. *"Really?"*

"What? This is an emotional time." Her lower lip quivered.

She was a soft touch, but this didn't bother him because it was real. Honest emotion glittered in her blue eyes, and he used his thumb to catch one of her tears.

Dinner was served and dancing began, with Sean and Bonnie's first dance as a married couple. They danced obscenely close (if you wanted to take Delores's opinion) to the music of Ed Sheeran.

"This is '*Perfect*,'" Jennifer said as the song played with lyrics about two people who were kids when they met and fell in love.

"Think so?"

"I meant that's the name of the song."

"Very predictable. I would have chosen something a little less, I don't know—"

"Weepy?" Jennifer completed his thought with scary accuracy.

People cried too much at weddings. Leave that for the funerals.

"And a little more heavy metal."

Jennifer made a face. "Yikes."

After the first dance, it was a free-for-all and Sean danced with Delores. Bonnie danced with Riggs, then later Jackson Carver, Lincoln, and the rest of the men lined up for a chance. It was never difficult to find a man around these parts. Women were another story. But tonight, Sean had a line of them, too. All the former contestants, Jolette Marie, and even Cherisse.

"Want to dance?" Colton said to Jennifer.

"You don't want your turn with Bonnie?"

"I'll dance with her later." Colton stood and offered his hand. "For now, it would look weird if I didn't dance with my fiancée."

EVEN IF COLTON was simply putting on a show, Jennifer appreciated the way he'd held her hand and walked her to the faux dance floor. She enjoyed the way he held her close in his arms, one hand lowering to her back. With any luck, they would only dance with each other tonight. The whole newly engaged and in love thing played into that narrative.

It was a beautiful day, and the sun began to crest over the hills in impressive splashes of purple and pink. Whomever had put on this wedding, the producers of the show, or Bonnie's family, they'd knocked it out of the park. The white tent outside the main house gave a sense of seclusion and protection from the sun. Beautiful gardenias and blue hydrangeas filled the tent with color. The food had been a delicious mix of Tex-Mex and continental cuisines, the kind where one didn't have to eat with their hands.

And Sean and Bonnie Lee appeared so in love that every time Jennifer looked at them, she felt her eyes fill. How inspiring to see this kind of lasting love still existed. Bonnie had mentioned someone always loving a little bit more than the other but today seemed to be one of those times in which love was equal.

"Did I tell you that you're beautiful?" Colton said, lowering his chin so close to hers they almost rubbed together.

"You don't have to say that."

"Give me a break. I'm trying to be vulnerable here."

"You?" She glanced up at him. "Why?"

"My therapist said it's necessary for a full recovery."

"Oh, yes, true."

That was somewhat disappointing, as she would have rather heard about his undying devotion to her, but that was unnecessary, not to mention unrealistic. And she couldn't argue with a soldier working toward full mental health. She certainly hadn't witnessed any of the hostile behaviors she used to see in Joe before he'd gone through rehabilitation for drug treatment. Colton seemed well adjusted but the fact he'd even had to mention becoming vulnerable told her maybe she wasn't seeing everything. Maybe he was struggling and she'd been too busy with her own problems to notice, pining away for this handsome man she was spending time with.

"Thank you for saying that," Jennifer said. "In case I never told you, I find you ridiculously handsome."

"I accept the compliment. Look at me, being all vulnerable and stuff."

"Are you, though?"

"Yeah. With you, it's easy. You see me as I am, and not

someone you have to repeatedly thank. You know who and what I am and I'm grateful for that. This is a job." His lips quirked in the hint of a smile. "How's that for vulnerable?"

"That's…good."

She was with him every second until the moment he said, "This is a job." She had hoped he meant the service but couldn't miss the clear facts here. They wouldn't be here together had her father not asked him for a favor. He wanted someone to keep his daughter safe and Colton was a man he trusted.

Now, she understood why. He was strong and honorable and took any duty handed to him with serious intent. She was certain he would take love with the same amount of intensity, too, and imagined how much it had hurt to be dumped when he was off fighting a war.

And if she understood Colton, she had to believe it was all because of Joe. Because of her father. Because she understood the mindset of a soldier and how difficult it was to hear simple and well-meant words like "thank you for your service."

"Joe said he understands why people thank him, but every time they do, he remembers. He remembers…things he did for which no one should be thanking him."

Colton nodded. "Exactly. And whatever happened to your brother? You never said, although I figured out that was him on your podcast. Anonymous Joe, not to be confused with G.I. Joe. He sounded good."

"It's a happy ending. He got the help he needed, no thanks to my father. Now he and a girlfriend have joined the Peace Corp and he's doing good overseas. I think. I haven't heard from him in a while."

"You will."

"He didn't have the same kind of welcome and support

that you have here." Jennifer glanced around. "I'm proud of him for getting to the other side of all that pain."

The song ended and Sean approached them.

"Can I cut in?" Sean asked sheepishly. "I've danced with every woman here and Bonnie is starting to give Tabitha the evil eye every time she tries to dance with me again."

Colton laughed. "Sure, brother."

Sean took over, dancing with a healthy distance between them. "Tabitha was the runner-up in *Mr. Cowboy*."

"I heard. She's pretty."

"Bonnie knows that, too, which is where the jealousy comes in. She has no reason to be, of course, but old habits die hard. She's always been in a competitive field."

"Well, they *were* in competition with one another over you."

"Yeah, hard to get past that. But for me the contest was over when Bonnie arrived. I've never been able to love anyone else and believe me, I tried."

"Something about first love, I guess."

Sean shrugged. "Guess so."

Jennifer turned to see that Colton was dancing with Cherisse and there didn't seem to be the healthiest of distances between them.

Sean caught Jennifer looking. "Don't worry about her. Colton has been trained to be a gentleman, as we all have, to the women in Stone Ridge. From birth to eighty."

"Well, Cherisse is a lot younger than eighty."

"Don't worry. When Colton loves you, he loves you hard. And he doesn't easily change his mind."

"I have heard." She tried a smile.

Except he didn't love her.

CHAPTER 16

*I*t was close to midnight when the party ended, and Jennifer followed Colton to their cottage. The production company would be cleaning up for hours.

"It's nice that the show offered to do all this for Bonnie and Sean."

"I personally think it's nice they *allowed* them to. Don't forget they agreed to an exclusive photo shoot of the bride and groom they're going to sell to *People* magazine." Colton held the door open for Jennifer. "I'm getting up early tomorrow because I'll be taking over for Sean while he's gone on his honeymoon. And I have a talk scheduled with Riggs, too."

"Okay. So, I guess I'll just stay in all day?"

"You could take a walk around the property. And if you're up to it, I'll take you to the swimming hole around here."

"I would love that." Jennifer plopped on the couch and slipped off her chucks. "And I'll bring my camera along."

Colton shrugged off his jacket and hung it on the hanger still on the doorknob. If she thought he looked good in the tux, he looked even better in the fitted white button-up tight against his torso. She continued to stare as he undid the first few buttons and unspooled his tie, making a sound between a growl and a grunt of relief.

"*What?*" he demanded when he noticed her openly staring. "Did I get the shirt dirty? Oh, shitfire. Where?"

She muffled a laugh as he turned in a half circle and tried to find the stain.

"No, no. You're fine, I don't see anything. And I was *really* looking."

Did he really not understand how attractive he was to every woman with a heartbeat and good eyesight? Birth to eighty, more than likely. And Jennifer was hands down one of those women. Holy *cowboy*.

That time, she couldn't muffle the laugh and it came spewing out of her like a firehose.

"What's so funny?" Colton narrowed his eyes.

Oh God. She was losing it. Pretty soon she couldn't catch her breath as she was overcome with the giggles. What a terrible time to lose control. If she didn't stop soon, she'd pee all over herself and wouldn't that be wonderful. She tried to breathe but then she looked at Colton. Big mistake. Now he was laughing, too.

While he continued with his manly and appropriate laugh Jennifer began to wheeze. "It's just…I…you know, 'holy cow?' I…just…thought holy cowboy! *Holy cowboy!*"

She bent, *literally* doubling up in laughter. So that's where the expression came from. The joke wasn't even that funny, but she still couldn't stop. She hadn't laughed in weeks, and it was as if all the laughter, all the joy, came rushing out in one fell swoop.

She'd once done a podcast on happiness and the choice to be happy, talking to an expert on the subject. It was about how true happiness was often a conscious decision, and it suddenly occurred to her she hadn't chosen to be happy in a long time.

Colton plopped on the couch beside her, still laughing. His was a more controlled kind of laughter coming out of a normal person instead of a geek.

Get a hold of yourself.

Finally, the laughter slowed somewhat spurred on by Colton sitting so close to her, something which inspired anything but laughter.

"You mean like holy cow, but instead holy cowboy?" He smiled.

They both glanced at each other, and the laughter began all over again.

"I know," she wheezed. "It's not even that funny."

She slowed again, putting her hand on Colton's thigh maybe on some level to remind her of truly unfunny things. His presence grounded her. Steadied her. She was able to breathe normally again but refused to look at him in fear the smile on his face would inspire yet another round of the giggles.

"Thank you," he said after a moment. "I haven't laughed like that in a long time."

"Me either."

They were both breathing hard, as one does after a bout of uncontrolled hilarity such as theirs. But nobody laughed when Colton finally noticed her hand on his thigh. No, she hadn't removed it. His gaze lowered then raised to meet her eyes. She'd touched him, again, but this time in private with absolutely no good reason other than she simply wanted to. In that moment, she should have moved her hand. She should have stood to say good night and thanked him for a nice time.

She *should* have done a whole lot of things that would

make far more sense than moving her hand only to climb sideways into his lap.

"Hey," she said, two inches from his mouth. His gorgeous, beautiful sensual mouth.

"Hey." His hands skimmed down her legs and then back up again, settling on her hip.

She studied him another long moment, without words, and then she kissed him. Just lowered her head, pressed her lips against that full mouth and hoped for the best. The surprise was that he tasted like the chocolate wedding cake they'd had not long ago. She'd jokingly remarked that his midnight cake was better, but even if that were true, tonight's cake tasted divine now. The kiss was slow and simmering with heat that, although she initiated, he took over and controlled. One hand on the nape of her neck, he tugged her closer, his fingers sunk into her hair. When he tugged on a lock of her hair, he went deeper with the kiss. He was making this last, and last, and she found that she was breathing hard after a few minutes, relishing the absolute passion of his kiss. No one had kissed her like this. No one gave like this.

And then it was over as quickly as it started.

Colton broke the kiss, releasing her. "Okay, no. I'm not doing this. We…we can't."

Humiliation pulsed through her. He was right. They couldn't do this. No matter the attraction she desperately felt for him, she was leaving, and he was staying. They didn't make any sense as a couple, either. He was like her father, a man she didn't particularly admire or respect even if she loved him. And Colton had an opportunity to reunite with his first love. Just like Sean, and Jackson, and God only knew how many people in this small town. She needed to put herself out of the equation entirely.

She didn't belong here.

Jennifer couldn't risk his future happiness. It would be wrong and selfish of her. All she really wanted was his happiness. She wanted to see him smile and laugh more, ride Freya, hang out with his brothers, cook delicious meals.

Live the rest of his life in peace, not with a woman who came with her very own stalker.

"You're right." She climbed off his lap. "I've been thinking. Even though we don't want to tell your family the truth about us, you could tell Cherisse."

His famously quirky eyebrows did their thing. "Why would I want to do that?"

He hadn't moved from where he'd been sitting but instead shoved a pillow on his lap. She could guess why. Dear God, she was a harlot! This poor man. He'd vowed to protect her, had rearranged his plans and entire life to do so, and she was mauling him.

She waved an arm in the air. "She's your first love. And it's like Sean and Bonnie, and this Jackson Carver dude I heard about today and his wife, Eve. Do you know he came back for his *brother's wedding*? And he and Eve got back together, worked out their problems. A second chance. Maybe you two could find a way past all the pain. And…I just want you to be happy."

He made another frustrated male sound, ran a hand through his hair, and might have cursed under his breath. "Yeah."

Yeah? Yeah *what?*

Yes, he should get his second chance, or yes, he understood she wanted him to be happy? Yes, he understood this thing between them was hopeless?

Or yes, he heard, but didn't necessarily agree with her?

Not surprisingly, he didn't elaborate.

. . .

Colton was awake before his alarm went off the next morning and this time not due to a nightmare.

Instead, he'd tossed and turned all night, sexual frustration burning a hole in his brain. Last night, he'd been about to get very, very stupid and he couldn't let that happen again. Still, just the memory of her sweet soft body so close to his, revving him up like he hadn't been in years, sent him spinning.

She was vulnerable and having been pulled out of her real life saw him as the only person she could rely on. Depend on. Maybe he was an escape for her. All he knew was that he couldn't start something with her now, when she was reeling from a man who'd obsessed about her. He was going to be the very opposite of that man, so she could relax and feel assured of her safety with him.

But he had no clue where the hell this idea about Cherisse had come from. The obsession with first love was odd to him. Maybe because he didn't have a romantic bone in his body, but hell, he had zero interest in going backward. The plan was to move forward not revisit old relationships that didn't work out in the first place.

There was often a damn good reason for breakups. Lack of commitment, maturity, loyalty, love. But he didn't want to argue with Jennifer, so he'd simply gone to bed and tried to push down his more basic thoughts about her. Thoughts of ravaging her and going a lot further than a simple kiss. He hadn't been with a woman in a long time and had a feeling when he did, it might wind up being a bit disappointing for the woman.

And he sure in the hell didn't want the woman he disappointed to be *Jennifer*.

Just before sunrise, he took a shower, dressed, then made coffee. He peeked into Jennifer's room, finding her dead to rights on her stomach, her long hair covering half of her face.

She'd apparently had no trouble getting to sleep after nearly giving *him* an aneurysm.

He made a quick breakfast burrito, leaving one for Jennifer and taking his with him. With Sean and Bonnie Lee off to their honeymoon, Colton was ready to pick up the slack. His day began in the stables, feeding Freya and the other horses, then leading them out two at a time to graze in the pasture. By then the sun had risen and he saw movement inside the main house where Riggs and Winona lived.

Riggs hadn't set a time, just told him to come by in the morning, so Colton headed over.

Delores swung open the front door, holding Mary in her arms. "Colton! Hi, sweetheart. Come in, come in. You've missed breakfast, unfortunately."

Beer came toward Colton, jumped up to greet and smell him, then ran back to the dog bed and settled down. He'd be staying with Riggs, Winona, and the kids while Bonnie and Sean were gone.

"Already had breakfast. Riggs told me to meet him here. I've been out there for a few hours, but it would be good to know exactly where he needs me now that Sean is gone for a bit."

"Our routine is a bit off the rails today," Delores said, carrying Mary on her hip into the kitchen. "Joey threw up during the night, and then Cal did. We think they had a little too much fun yesterday. Overstimulated and all that."

"Yeah. All those forks everywhere." He chuckled.

"Anyway, poor Winona was up all night. So was Riggs. She's sleeping now because the boys are finally sleeping."

"Oh, damn. Anything I can do to help?"

"I'm sure Riggs will want you to do everything on the ranch today." Delores laughed. "But that's impossible. With Sean gone, things are going to be tough around here for a while."

It irritated the hell out of Colton that no one thought he could step in easily enough. The military wasn't exactly a paid vacation and he'd worked harder than he ever had in his life. Ranch work was going to be easy after some of the things he'd done.

"Morning," Riggs said, coming into the kitchen with a mug that read "World's Best Dad." He proceeded to fill it up with more coffee. "Want some?"

"Nah, I've been up early and already had enough."

"C'mon, sweetie, let's get you a bottle," Delores said to Mary, who'd been wriggling to get to Riggs since he'd walked in the room.

Riggs took a step toward them and planted a kiss on Mary's head. "Hey, Princess."

Mary responded with a smile that lit up her entire face. She looked a lot like Winona. "Da-da!"

"You're the best one, and don't let anyone tell you otherwise," Riggs said, blowing her a kiss.

If he hadn't seen it with his own eyes, Colton might have thought someone had body-snatched his surly older brother and replaced him with a different family-friendly version.

"Oh, Riggs. You know you love your boys." Delores swatted him.

"I can still have a favorite." He winked at Mary then turned to Delores. "Colton and I will be in my office."

Riggs's office turned out to be their father's old office. Colton didn't know why he should be surprised. As the oldest, Riggs took over operations the minute he'd obtained his law degree, so it made sense he would have the office. And the main house. Speaking of their original home, Colton would have been lost down here without a guide. The ranch-style house had been expanded with hallways leading down long corridors. He almost didn't recognize the original hallway that led to the office at the back of the house.

"Winona did all this." Riggs waved his hand around as if he was embarrassed by the large and ostentatious nature of their remodeled home. "And she made sure the office was at the very back. She wanted to separate family from cattle ranching operations."

"Makes sense."

Riggs shrugged. "Happy wife, happy life. You'll learn."

Colton cleared his throat. "In time, I will. I'm sure."

"You're not going to have a long *engagement,* are you?"

Colton wanted to ask why the hell not, but Riggs had made a long engagement sound like a terrible thing. Like it was not much dumber than lighting your house on fire. Colton wasn't here to butt heads with his older brother. He was here to find a way to fit back into the fold. Contribute.

"No, guess not. Why wait."

Um, because she isn't actually your fiancée, genius?

"Just give us a little time between weddings."

Colton nodded. "We just had one."

"Exactly." Riggs leaned back in his chair and cradled his mug. "Does she want a big deal? Huge wedding? I figure her folks from Los Angeles might have a say in this."

"It's just her father and her brother. And an aunt that helped raise her."

"Maybe we can have it here, then."

Colton steered the conversation away from his big fat lie and toward more pressing matters. "I didn't come here to talk about weddings."

"Yeah, sorry about that. Winona was wondering. But you said you had some ideas." Riggs set his mug down and leaned forward, clasping his hands.

Colton appreciated the interest in what he had to say. His body language said he was open to suggestions, even if Colton realized he was about to make a radical one.

"Bison." Now Colton leaned back, letting Riggs digest the word.

"Bison," Riggs repeated. "We raise cows here."

"I know, and I'm suggesting we add a specialty market. Do you know how much folks pay for organic beef?"

"Organic bison," Riggs repeated.

"Yes, and before you say anything, I've got my own money to invest in this operation. I've saved for years, and I've done the research."

"Yeah, I figured you were saving since you never sent any money home all those years you were gone."

The words sliced through Colton with their bitterness. "It's not like I made a hell of a lot of money as a soldier, even in Special Forces."

"I'm aware, but for a while there, we were struggling."

"And you don't seem to be struggling any longer."

Colton glanced around the room at all the leather and classic furniture like the desk Riggs sat behind. Window treatments. Framed photos—obviously professionally taken —of Riggs, Winona, and the children covered the walls.

"That's my wife's doing. I just happened to marry a wealthy woman, but we were doing okay before I met her. For years, though, we struggled. After Dad died, it was rough."

"I know."

"I'm not saying we needed your salary. What we needed was *you*. Instead, I had to hire help. Help at the time we could barely afford. It was just me and Sean running this ranch while you were gone."

While it was refreshing for once not to have someone thank him for his service, in this particular case he'd appreciate a little gratitude from his brother.

"Riggs, I wasn't out of the country having *fun*."

"I know, I know!" He tossed up his hands. "And maybe I

sound like a jerk, like I'm ungrateful for your contribution to our country, but damn it, I worried every day you'd be killed over there. So did Sean. It killed me to watch him twisted up in knots every time we heard of another bomb going off. It's just that you've been gone for years, and this operation has been self-sustaining for all that time. We're doing okay except for drought years."

"Is okay good enough?"

"We don't need to change anything or reinvent the wheel. I don't want you trying to rearrange everything when..." Riggs stared off into space as if he'd just come upon a bear in the woods.

"When I'm leaving anyway?"

"I didn't *say* that."

"Well, you were thinking it. But I didn't just come home for Sean's wedding. I came home to stay."

But clearly no matter what Colton said or did, even pretending to be engaged, Riggs expected he'd leave. Expected he'd get itchy feet and want to see the world. Colton hadn't given him any reason to believe otherwise and based on past experience, he understood Riggs's point. He didn't know what he could do to convince him, other than *show* him. And showing would take time. Colton simply had to be patient. It was a lesson the army had taught him well.

Colton stood. "Have it your way."

He strode out of the house, nearly getting lost in the process. Going out the way he came in, he crossed the kitchen and went out the front door, noting Riggs hadn't said a word. He was also not following Colton. It was fine. He didn't expect his set-in-his-ways, traditional cowboy of a brother to understand why it might be good to expand their operation. To think ahead and not simply cling to the old ways but move forward toward the future.

He understood, too, why Riggs doubted Colton. A

fiancée, especially one from *Los Angeles*, didn't inspire enough confidence either. So, Colton would find another way, by making himself indispensable around here, by patiently contributing and waiting for the right moment. Eventually, given time, it would become evident he wasn't going anywhere.

Colton had closed the front door when it opened again and Riggs stood there, looking tired and angry. His big brother now had salt-and-pepper sideburns and wrinkles that he hadn't owned a few years ago lining his face. Colton wondered how many of those worry lines he'd given him, and regret pulsed through him.

Why hadn't he listened to Riggs in the first place? Why had he had this burning need to be a hero?

"If it helps any, I regret every day I left this ranch and signed up. But once I made that commitment, I couldn't back away. *That's* what service taught me and it's what I'm going to give you now and for the rest of my life. Loyalty and devotion. I'm committed and I don't walk away when things get tough. And I know they will."

Riggs didn't say another word. He just took two steps toward Colton and hauled him into his arms.

"Forget everything I said. Whatever you want. Let's do it."

CHAPTER 17

The morning passed quickly because Jennifer sought ways to keep busy and contribute. She needed distractions from last night and the mortification she'd felt at being turned down. Colton didn't want to have sex with her because he was obviously still pining away for his ex. His loyalty was inspiring even if he'd appeared to be at least a little tempted. Or a lot. His body, let's just say, had responded. But he definitely had a type and facts were, Jennifer couldn't look any more different from Cherisse if she tried. Cherisse was the petal; Jennifer was the stem. But that was okay because Lord knew some men found her attractive. Including obsessive ones, apparently. Just her luck.

Trying to find things to do and ways to take her mind off Colton, she realized this place could use a deep cleaning. She went back to her roots. Her father, among other things, taught his children how to keep a clean house.

"Make that bed again. Tight corners. There's no excuse for your barrac—your *bedroom*— to be in any kind of disarray."

For him, disarray meant leaving a book on her bed that

she was *still reading*. Said book belonged in the bookcase when not in her hands. Also, did she really need that many books? Not that her father was a fanatic about orderliness but um, hello, yes he *was*. And she and Joe were his very own platoon. Once a month, Jennifer and Joe took turns cleaning floors with a toothbrush. Old school. Every day she told herself it would be different were her mother still around. She'd remind her father the children and house were *her* command, as she had been fond of saying.

But the experience of living with her father served Jennifer well now, staying in the home of a former military man, and knowing just how they liked things. Clean and sparkly. Orderly.

She went through the kitchen first, cleaning floors till they shined, wiping down counters and scouring sinks and the stove range. At lunchtime, she ate the breakfast burrito Colton had so thoughtfully left for her. Another thing she would do while here is cook…something. Ironically, it was the one thing her father hadn't insisted she learn to do. It was probably too feminine of a skill in his opinion. Besides, he knew how to cook three things: a grilled cheese sandwich, canned soup, and hot dogs. Not surprisingly those were the only things Jennifer could cook.

But now, thanks to Delores, she knew how to make a succulent pot roast. She thought about the cut of meat she'd need, then looked out the window to see cattle roaming in the distant fields. This made her sad and guilty, so she ate her third piece of chocolate cake.

She showered after cleaning, dressed, and took her camera outside to wander the fields and take photos. Maybe she'd come across this river Colton said was good for swimming. Outside the day was clear and beautiful with only a scattering of white cotton-candy clouds dotting the heavens. Green pastures surrounded her as far as the eye could see. Cattle bayed in the distance and birds chirped.

She viewed everything better behind the lens, so she zoomed in on blue and yellow wildflowers, a black bird perched on the corral, the beautiful classic red barn. Walking farther past the cottage and Sean and Bonnie's house, she noticed a sprawling ranch-style home in the distance and realized at once that this was the main house. The house where Colton had grown up with his brothers.

The metal clang of a fence startled her, and she turned to see Colton and Riggs behind her. Without realizing it, she'd walked so far that their cabin was like a dot in the distance. She'd wound up at the cattle operations. Colton and Riggs were talking, side by side, their backs to her, and they made a nice picture through her lens. There were several cows who were separated from the rest in a steel-looking contraption.

Riggs pointed in one direction and made motions with his arm. He then stuck one boot in the gated fenced rail while Colton, astride a horse, continued to separate cattle by herding down one enclosed aisle into another while Jennifer snapped away. The feeling of anonymity returned to her again, the pleasant rush of privacy with freedom to create.

Way before she'd been concerned with paying her bills and having a career to support herself, she'd wanted to document a life in pictures. It hadn't worked out that way, but photography could still be a hobby. True, she didn't make time for hobbies anymore since the podcast had become her everything. Social media and her phone had been her constant companions, and she would have thought she'd miss them more.

But the relaxation and complete detachment she felt at being allowed to let all of it go, of in fact being ordered to let it go, was freeing. In the past, she would have taken these photos and immediately posted them because why make the effort in the first place if it couldn't be used for content. If you take a photo and don't post it online, does it even exist?

Now, she made the effort for herself. For beauty.

These photos belonged to her and her alone, not for public consumption. For her eyes only as she watched the brothers work together, the definition of cowboys. Hard-working, rugged, and loyal to each other and the land. Great, she sounded like a commercial for a pickup truck. But hey, this was Americana at its finest and she snapped away.

Then, through her lens, she noted Colton turn in her direction. His hat partially shaded his face, and he still wore those aviator shades. But damn if she didn't catch an eyebrow quirk through the zoom lens. Him and those eyebrows. She lowered the camera, then caught him tipping his hat to her. Like an invitation. She could already almost read cowboy code. The tip of a cowboy hat meant "hello" and also "please come here." Unless she was reading into things. At first, she thought maybe she'd better let the men have their brotherly time but when Riggs also turned in her direction and gave a slight wave, she walked toward them.

She carried her camera in front of her like a shield. This whole country-vibe thing was cool, but she was so out of her element here. The smells were, well, not ideal and the closer she got the worse they became. She fought the desire to fan her hand in front of her face like she did when a friend's dog farted. God, this was *so* much worse. It was like a thousand dogs had passed wind all at once.

"Hi," she said to Riggs.

He gave her a smile that showed her in one split second exactly how he'd managed to woo a Nashville celebrity to give up everything and come live with him in the country. The man was devastatingly handsome.

"Hey, there. We're separating cattle."

By the looks of it, Colton was doing the work and Riggs

was supervising. "How do you separate them? By color? Size? Sex?"

Riggs gave her a look. "These calves are being separated from their mothers for vaccination."

"Oh, yeah. That makes way more sense." After all, she watched *Yellowstone*, too.

Wonder if they also had a "train station" around here for the bad men.

"Sean was a bit behind on these so Colton is finishing up. I would help but he insisted he wanted to handle this. My wife and I had a rough night with sick kids." He turned back to the gate, spreading his arms out. "How are you settling in? I hope you're comfortable."

"Absolutely. It's wonderful. Except, well, the smell if I'm being honest."

He chuckled. "Honesty is the best policy. Listen, if Winona could adjust to this lifestyle, I have no doubt you will, too. Even if you are from Los Angeles."

He made this sound like, "Even if you are from Mars, you will grow accustomed to our ways."

"Mm-hmm," Jennifer said, holding up her camera to take a shot of Colton and his horse leading a calf. "You know, Los Angeles is still part of the United States."

"So I've heard." Riggs snorted.

The sound of a truck coming up the dirt road made them both turn in that direction. "There's Eve now. She's our veterinarian, just off maternity leave."

It was the same brunette she'd seen with Jackson Carver at the wedding reception.

"Isn't she the one married to Jackson Carver?"

"Yep, the one and the same."

"Weren't he and your wife married at one time?"

"In what had to be one of the shortest marriages in history. But I'm lucky because if she hadn't come to Stone

Ridge to visit Jackson, I may never have met the love of my life."

That was sweet and certainly not what Jennifer expected to hear from a rugged cowboy. Refreshing. Riggs led them to the area where Eve would be vaccinating. He introduced Jennifer as Colton's fiancée.

"Hi, there!" Eve said with a wave. "Y'all are my first visit since my long break."

"How did Annabeth do without you all these weeks? She had to come out here for a colicky horse last month and looked pretty fed up," Riggs said.

"She's fine, but in answer to your question, she was a bit overwhelmed. She's gone to Austin for a couple of weeks. Anything that happens, I'm your person, day, or night."

"We'll try not to bother you much what with a newborn," Riggs said. "I know what that's like."

"It's fine. Jackson is great, really stepping up to take care of our baby girl."

"Oh, you have a daughter," Jennifer said.

Eve smiled as she set up her station, pulling out vials, syringes, and plastic gloves. "Lillian Pearl after Jackson's grandmother. We call her Lily."

"Do you mind if I take some photos as you work?" Jennifer tapped her camera. "I'm just trying to keep busy."

"Jennifer is from *Los Angeles*," Riggs said, as though he still hadn't quite forgiven her for that faux pau.

"Sorry," Jennifer said under her breath.

Eve answered, holding up a syringe. "Flash away."

Jennifer snapped photo after photo for the next hour as Eve, Colton and Riggs worked with her to get the calves all vaccinated and then led to another area. It was an impressive operation from the perspective of someone who'd never seen this before. Eve was a true professional, great with the animals, at ease with what she did.

As she was wrapping up, Eve asked to see some of the photos and Jennifer showed her the shots she'd taken through her digital camera window.

"These are great," Eve said. "You're really good."

"Oh, I'm just an amateur." Jennifer shrugged. "But it's fun."

"No, you captured the angles and lighting so perfectly. We actually need some updated photos for our website. Annabeth was complaining about that a few days ago. I'm going to make an executive decision. Would you come down to the clinic and maybe take a few more of our office so we can put them on the website? I'll pay you."

When Jennifer stared blankly, Eve said, "Oh, we have Wi-Fi at the office. It's downtown."

Jennifer suspected Eve was just trying to be nice. And Colton might not be okay with this because he'd want to come with her. With Sean gone, he'd be busy every day.

"Well…I'll have to ask Colton. He's going to be so busy I doubt he can take me for a while. Maybe when Sean comes back."

"I can take you," Riggs said. "Or you can take one of our trucks."

Great. Should she pretend she couldn't drive one of those "big, manly trucks"? Nope, Jennifer couldn't bring herself to give him one more lie.

"No rush," Eve said. "We probably don't get much business from the website, mostly from word of mouth. But I've been told to keep up appearances. We want to join the new millennium."

"Yes, that's smart."

Jennifer wished she could rush downtown with Eve right now and do a special podcast for their clinic. In case people were still listening to her or waiting for her return. But no, that part of her life might be over. Forever. The emptiness that realization had conjured up a month ago, the utter sense of hopelessness and loss, didn't seem as wide and deep anymore.

COLTON HADN'T PLANNED for the chores to take him this long, but once he knocked off around five o'clock, he headed to the cottage sweaty and filthy. He should probably take a shower even before he took Jennifer to the river's creek to swim.

He found her sitting at the table with her camera and laptop opened.

"Hey, sorry it took me so long."

"Not at all, you have a job to do. And you do it well." She pressed something on her keyboard. "I also used to have a job and I was pretty good at it, too."

"I have no doubt."

"Eve liked my photos. She wants me to take some more photos of her clinic for their website."

"Great idea."

"I'll have to go downtown and I'm going to assume I can't go without you." She seemed a bit disgusted by this fact, shaking her head.

"You're assuming correctly."

"We can wait until Sean comes back from his honeymoon."

"Not necessary. I'll find the time."

"Really?" Her eyes lit up, a swift softness and warmth filling them.

She was truly beautiful, and he'd known that from the moment he first laid eyes on her. But now he also understood that she was fierce, funny, strong, and loyal. And for purely personal reasons he didn't want to believe she was this unhappy hanging out on the ranch. Sure, it wasn't his job to entertain her or help her feel good about herself. Only to keep her safe. But still.

He sat beside her. "You're bored."

"Well, even when I couldn't work or leave my house, I had Netflix and Wi-Fi and I could sit in my condo and randomly watch videos of people falling down. Or dogs trying to talk to their owners. Those were my favorites." She sighed.

He chuckled because those were his favorites, too. "Look, I promised to take you swimming. So, let's go before dinner."

"And I brought a swimsuit!"

No questions or hesitation. She was up and changing faster than he'd thought possible.

Within a few minutes he was leading her down to the riverbed hoping this, too, hadn't changed while he was gone. The number of changes were unnerving, and he clung to those landmarks and people he recognized to still be the same. The familiar and comforting. So far, it mostly seemed to be the land. Because even the home he'd grown up in had changed, if for the better, and looked barely recognizable.

Thankfully, a river tributary didn't suddenly decide to pick up stakes and move. But Texas had gone through periods of drought and the part of the river that ended and streamed through their property had been unbearably low in the past. He'd been out here once with Sean and Bonnie, years ago, and turned back when there wasn't enough water for them to reasonably swim.

Gratefully, he heard the trickling sounds of the water as they neared on foot. He'd made Jennifer wear a pair of his old boots, warning her of snakes, scorpions and fire ants until she nearly changed her mind about coming with him. He grabbed her hand now, tugging her along. A sense of gratification pulsed through him upon hearing her swift intake of breath. The river that he'd always considered his own slice of heaven was still shaded by a leafy black willow tree, some of its green and lush branches nearly hitting the water.

"Oh, this is beautiful," Jennifer said and let go of his hand, walking forward. "I bet you spent a lot of time here as a kid."

"Fair amount. You can't dive here, it might be too shallow."

She was already moving toward the rushing bank of cool clear water, throwing off the boots, and slipping off her jeans.

And holy God, here came the longing and desire again, bursting out of him like an unspooled coil. He had to get a handle on this. Push these feelings underneath and keep them down.

She wore a red bikini that wiped out several hundred brain cells in one fell swoop. Then she whipped her shirt off and he lost the rest of them.

Brainless, he followed her, watching as she plunged into the water without a second thought. She swam several feet down and back again, her strokes sure and practiced. Clearly, she loved the water. It was a damn shame some idiot had frightened her enough to keep her restricted indoors, the only place she felt safe.

But I'm doing the same thing.

Trapping her here on the ranch.

Even if for her safety it was unfair that she should have to be the one punished. She wasn't in Los Angeles anymore, was it necessary to keep her in hiding? He determined at that moment he'd let her see more of Stone Ridge in whatever time they had left here together. He'd show her more of downtown besides the veterinary clinic, even if there wasn't much to see.

The Shady Grind was always a good place to get a burger and Jackson performed from time to time, according to Eve.

She'd called it a great place for "date night" in case he was looking for a nice place to take his "fiancée."

Earlier today, after Riggs had settled up with Eve, he'd met Colton in the tack room.

"Is Eve the new veterinarian? I remember her back from where she ran out on Jackson on their wedding day. All seems to be forgiven."

"Yep, though I'm sure it wasn't easy. Those two have been through a lot. I guess I can say it now, because pretty much everyone in town knows, and Eve is no longer hiding it. In fact, last I heard she's done a few talks to local domestic violence groups. Felt it was the least she could do after what she'd survived."

Worry pressed down on Colton, hard and tight. "What the hell happened to her?"

"While she was away at college, she was attacked. Her roommate interrupted or she might have lost more than her hearing in one ear."

"What the…I…I had no idea."

"She wears a hearing aid in that ear but it's not always noticeable. Still the best vet in the area."

"Damn. Some random attack?"

"Not exactly. The guy was obsessed with her."

Colton felt himself go stock still. He thought he heard the sound of blood rushing through his veins. For certain, he heard the thud of his own heartbeat. In his *ears*. His throat was suddenly dry and parched.

"How did this happen?"

"I don't know all the details, but she dated the guy once or twice, I guess, and didn't want any more to do with him. But he wouldn't take no for an answer. After the attack, coming home was exactly what she needed. We all looked out for her. And she's been safe here, even before Jackson came home. It took some work to get past the trauma but she's well on the other side of it now."

"And…the guy?"

"Prison, where he belongs."

Which was exactly where Dan would wind up if he ever hurt Jennifer. Colton would make sure of it.

Maybe Jennifer could talk with Eve about her experience. Only another woman would truly understand. Or maybe it would be too frightening to hear how badly it could have ended for her if her father hadn't pulled her out of the situation. He didn't know.

"Colton." Jennifer's voice snapped him back to the moment. "Aren't you coming in?"

Her dark hair was wet and gleaming, her skin soft and pink in the glow of the sunshine.

It would take a tank and a few good men to keep him away from her.

"Try and stop me."

CHAPTER 18

The water was cool and clear and everything she loved about swimming came back to Jennifer. The trickling sounds of the stream as it rushed through the rocky and hilly land gave her the calm she craved. Water washed over her skin and the peace that had been robbed returned.

Colton had brought her here, to his private swimming hole as he'd promised, but for several minutes he seemed to be lost in his thoughts as he watched her. She noticed he did this occasionally, zoning out, in another place. Whether it was a flashback or a memory, she wouldn't know.

Maybe due to her sensitivity on the subject and at seeing Eve once again today, a reminder of first loves, she couldn't stop imagining Colton and Cherisse. Had he brought her here to make out, or to have teenage sex for the first time? And why couldn't she get the image of Colton and another woman out of her mind? It shouldn't concern her. He was attractive, sure, and he'd kissed her back. That didn't mean anything other than the fact he was a red-blooded male who didn't mind the attention of a woman. Especially when they were both stuck together, and he was possibly…bored.

However, he was also the man who'd practically shoved her off his lap.

Considering she'd been dealing with Dan, who'd been tone-deaf about *her* rejection, she certainly wanted to respect Colton's feelings. No meant no. She understood, and maybe there was a chance for him to reunite with Cherisse after Jennifer was gone. Her heart snagged on the thought because Colton deserved better than the way his ex had discarded him. He deserved someone who would love him with her whole heart.

For a while they swam several feet away from each other as though they might be strangers who happened upon the same watering hole and were giving each other space. He dove underwater, and she lost track of him for several seconds in which she tipped her head to study the tree's willowy branches. A bird tittered above as if watching them then flew to another branch. The day was just the right kind of warm, the kind that cocoons instead of smothering. Perfect, Texas. Perfect, and thank you.

But suddenly something under the water wrapped around her ankle.

She screamed, shook it off, and a second later Colton came up inches from her.

"What's wrong? All I did was touch your leg."

"Oh my God, what are you, *twelve*?" She splashed water at him.

He ran a hand down his face, grinning, wiping away rivulets of water. "Yes, when it comes to you, I am."

Well, that sounded kind of sweet actually. She made him feel like a kid. Maybe that wasn't a bad thing.

"You *are* far too serious most of the time."

"Let that be a warning to you. But I also forgot to tell you about the snakes here."

"Snakes that *swim*? Wh-what kind of snakes?"

"Water snakes." He made a sound like, *duh, city girl.*

"Do…t-they like to swim? In *this* river? Is—is that what you're telling me?"

"No, they like to *hike.* What do you think?"

"Don't make fun of me, Colton! You and Riggs can make all the jokes you want about Los Angeles, but we don't have water snakes in *my* city! And that's the way I like it."

Close to terrified, she wrapped her legs around Colton's torso, surprising them both.

He quirked his now famous (to her) brow. "This is going far better than I had planned."

Even in this cool water, a warm rush of heat pierced her. He'd moved his hands to her behind and slid her a decidedly devilish smile.

"What do you mean?"

"All I wanted was to tease you but now you're in my arms through no fault of my own. I've told you that I'm not going to try anything with you and if you want to touch me, you better be the one to do it."

"Funny. That's what I did last night, and you turned me down."

"Yeah, well. Things were moving too quickly, and I needed to slow myself down."

"Why?" And then suddenly she remembered what had stopped him. "It's because you still have some underlying loyalty to Cherisse. You can tell her we're not actually engaged. When I'm gone maybe you two can get back together."

He swore. "I don't want that. She and I are *history.*"

"Are you sure? She was your first love and I know how powerful that can be."

"Not for me, it isn't. And it wasn't."

"Jackson came back for his brother's wedding too, and he and Eve reunited."

"So what? That's not going to happen for me."

"How do you know?"

"Because it's the last thing I want. I don't love her, okay? Someone wise once told me, 'when people show you who they are, believe them.' She doesn't know the first thing about real love *or* loyalty. We were never a good match. You've heard there's a lack of women in my town. Maybe it's because she was available to me that we were even together in the first place. Did you ever consider that? Don't make us into some romantic Romeo and Juliet from a romance book."

"Well, that's a tragedy not a romance."

"Whatever."

But Jennifer let the knowledge settle. Maybe two people who were thrown together due to circumstance might confuse love with a simple fondness. They were quiet for several minutes.

Colton was tall enough to stand in the water and for the next few minutes they floated together, her in his arms. She leaned her body and head back to study the blanket of sunshine dappling through leafy trees, giving them cover from the sun.

Then she worked up her nerve and faced him, hands plunked on his shoulders.

"Sometimes I feel like you're stuck here with me and just trying to make the best of it."

"Not even close. Why? Is that what you're doing here? Is that why you crawled into my lap last night?"

"No! I don't…well, maybe I'm missing my work but not much else. And being around you is far from boring."

"That's exactly what I think about you. You're not boring."

He said this like it should mean something and her heart nearly tripped over itself trying not to laugh at the way he mixed sincerity with unremarkable words.

"Wow. High praise."

"Shut up, I'm not any good at this."

"Clearly." She chuckled. "So, you're not a romantic?"

"Nope. I wish. I seem to be missing that gene."

"Luckily, you're not missing any other ones." She allowed her gaze to slid down his powerful chest and the arms sinewy with strength.

He hadn't earned those with a gym membership.

At least her ogling seemed to please him, given his heated gaze.

"I just know what it's like to have someone obsess over you, even when you don't want them."

He smirked with something that looked like satisfaction. "You're obsessed with me?"

"No." A single finger trailed a drop of water on his shoulder. "But I could be. I don't want to hold you back, if I'm not what you need. God knows I come with an entire luggage rack."

"Look, I don't want to be anywhere else, or *with* anyone else. What the hell can I possibly do to convince you?" Frustration seemed to bubble out of him, and he let her go.

She found her footing on the riverbed in front of him, feeling the smooth ground below her toes, studying the rocky man in front of her. Most days he was like a big boulder she had to emotionally climb. Challenging, and unlike anyone she'd ever been with because he was like her father.

But yet Colton was different, too, in every way. There was a kindness to him, a warmth that showed in everything he did. In every move he made. With his brothers. With Delores.

Even with people who'd wronged him.

"What can I do to convince you that you're not holding me back? Tell me." His deep voice was as smooth as a river pebble, his eyes soft. "I'm right here."

"Don't back off because I'm complicated, or you think I'm too vulnerable. Please don't think I'm this fragile flower, this...this *petal* that's going to fall off and crumble. I'm the stem."

"Yeah?"

More quirking from the eyebrow whisperer. He threw in a scowl for good measure. But at least he didn't seem to think she'd lost her mind.

"Funny, you look like a woman to me."

Aw. And that's exactly what she was, damn it, a woman and not a girl. She may have made mistakes in the past, wanting everyone to like her, trying hard to please, but no more. No longer would she fear confrontation of any kind. Life wasn't always going to go according to plan. Not everyone would or even had to like her.

"Yes. A grown woman and I'm *not* fragile. I could probably knock some men on their asses if I had to. You don't need to worry. Okay, worry a little because of my situation but not because I can't take care of myself. Right?"

"Right."

"Now kiss me." And as if he needed direction, she put a finger to her lips giving him a tentative smile.

He didn't hesitate as he drew her into his arms again, lifting her body to his, pressing his mouth to hers and kissing like he'd waited forever to do it. They slid against each other, bodies wet and slippery. She clung to him, wanting him so badly. This. She wanted him even if they didn't make sense. Even if this was crazy or risky or scary. She wanted him and now it seemed he wanted her, too.

Maybe he'd been waiting for this, waiting for an invitation. Waiting to prove that he wasn't going to obsess over her if this didn't work out between them. Or if she stopped him midkiss, or even midcoitus. She believed him. It hadn't ever been a thought that crossed her mind.

Colton was the kind of man who listened. Who had respect for a woman's choices and desires. She'd known this, of course, from the moment her father put her in his care. But he'd proved it to her, again and again. If he kept her close, if he called the shots, her safety was the only reason. Not a need to control her.

She broke the kiss, out of breath.

"From now on, you don't need to ask. Just kiss me anytime you want. I'm here, and you're here and we—"

He covered her mouth, swallowing her words. She could possibly be thinking too much and definitely talking too much. She wanted to enjoy this, enjoy *him*. She wanted to luxuriate in his hard body pressed against hers, the hard rough feel of his beard stubble as he lowered his head to her neck and kissed her there. Then skimming down the column of her neck, too, down to the cup of her bikini top. He tugged her hips flush against his so she could feel how hard she'd made him. When he gently sank his teeth into her earlobe she moaned.

"Sorry. I'm going too fast," he breathed.

"No, you're not. Not fast at all."

"It's just you drive me insane. I'm crazy about you."

"Same, cowboy. And this is the healthy kind of crazy."

"You better believe it." He brought her face inches from his, hauling her by the nape of her neck. "Have you had enough swimming for now?"

"Oh, yes. Yes."

She chased him from the river back to the house, where once inside they each peeled off what little clothes they had on and tried to make it to the bedroom. *Tried* being the operative word. Because just inside the front door, Colton pressed her up against the wall.

He pinned her there and for the next few minutes sent her straight to orgasm heaven. If he was going too fast, so was she. This happened to be exactly what she needed now. Hard and fast.

They didn't quite make it to the bedroom.

Jennifer lay naked and quite slayed over an equally bare-skinned Colton, thinking that she'd never in her life felt this safe, or this…wanted. Adored. Today, he'd searched her eyes with such tenderness it made her ache. She might be the stem but he treated her like a precious petal and in this case she would go along with it.

Colton had whispered sweet and filthy words of how beautiful she was, how much he wanted her, how good he was going to make this for her. He'd delivered every time, making her skin tight and bones elastic. She was spent but couldn't wait to do this all over again.

"Okay?" Colton murmured against her temple.

"Oh, yeah. I just wish we'd been doing *this* since day one."

He snorted. "You and me both."

"I want to do it every day, three times a day if we can." She buried her face in his warm neck.

"I'll see if I can keep up with your insatiable demands, woman. You are a lot younger than me."

Funny, she didn't feel much younger. "Only ten years and I'm sure you can more than keep up."

"If not, just know that I'll die trying."

It was way past time for dinner, the sun had set a while ago, but she wasn't even hungry. Colton had been notorious about cooking and feeding her on a regular schedule but even he hadn't noticed. The knowledge filled her with more than a small amount of satisfaction. She'd been a good distraction from his regular routine and the thought brought about a warm and heavy pulse of delight.

"Hey," Colton said, his hand gliding up and down her

spine. "When you take photos of Eve's clinic, you should take some time and talk to her."

"Sure, I will. She's easy to talk to. About what? Anything in particular?"

"About Dan."

"*What?*" Jennifer's head whipped up and she met Colton's eyes. "Why? That's the last thing I want to do."

"I think it would be good."

"No! I said I didn't want anyone to know about my situation. We agreed."

"I know. We agreed, and we can still keep it that way. You know you can trust me. But you can trust her, too, and if you confide in Eve, it might help. No one else has to know."

"Why would I even do that?"

"Because you have nothing to be ashamed of and you need to stop believing any of what happened was your fault."

"I *know* it's not my fault."

"I'm not sure you do. There's still some small part of you that takes on some of the blame. And wrong as it is, I don't think that's uncommon."

"Oh, now you know everything. You're an expert?" A small spark of anger surged and spread.

He didn't take the bait and pulled her back into his arms. "No, I'm not, sweetheart. But I know someone who might be."

"Eve?"

"Riggs told me that she's been giving talks to domestic violence groups. She went through something similar. I figured it couldn't hurt to talk to her and she will keep your confidence. I know Eve and her family. They've been in Stone Ridge forever and are people you can count on."

"Something similar?" Jennifer was now intrigued.

The confident, self-assured veterinarian had been stalked at one time? She carried herself without a hint of fear. It was inspiring to believe Jennifer could also stop blaming herself for having wanted people to like her.

"I'd rather her tell you but for what it's worth, it sounds worse than what happened to you. She didn't manage to get away from her stalker in time."

"Oh no. Poor Eve."

"I thought it might be good for you to have someone to talk to that understands what you've been through. Unlike me."

No, he'd been through far *worse* and was now trying to help her. God, she was an idiot sometimes.

"I'm sorry I got angry. I know you mean well."

He brought her fingers to his lips and spoke through them. "I know what it's like to have people all around who want to help but who have no idea what you've been through. They do the best they can, given the circumstances. But even though I doubted it would make a difference, I found it helped for someone to listen without judgement."

"What if I told *you* everything that happened?"

Maybe he could be a trial run before she shared with Eve. Colton was this solid presence in her life. If she couldn't tell him, she couldn't tell *anyone*. And yeah, maybe it would be good to talk to Eve if she'd been through something similar and was now such a confident woman, good at her occupation. A wife and new mother.

"You can tell me anything you want."

And so, while he held her, she told him everything. Every last detail of the reason she'd been torn away from her life. She told him about the first time she'd run into Dan in a coffee shop, all handsome and well dressed. Successful. How she'd only later learned, on their one and only date, that he was a huge fan of the podcast. How she really hadn't put together until later that he'd been stalking her before they'd even met, knowing where she liked to grab a coffee, shop for groceries, go out to dinner.

How little by little he eroded her self-esteem and security about the world, texting and emailing her. A restraining order had only worked to a point. Then he watched her from a distance, never crossing the line, but still called and emailed. She changed her phone. She eventually stopped leaving the condo. She'd lost friends who didn't understand how she'd allowed this kind of a man into her life. Who, whether they'd meant to or not, had put some of the blame on her.

Colton slid his hand up and down her back in a soothing motion. He didn't say a word. Just listened.

She ended by wetting his chest with big, sloppy tears over the life she'd lost.

Over the career that had supported her financially and that she'd probably never get back.

The apartment that had once been her safe haven and now only reminded her of how she'd been trapped inside it.

The peace of mind he'd robbed which she secretly worried she'd *never* get back.

"You *are* going to get it back. Everything you want."

Then he rolled her under him, threading his fingers through hers, kissing her slow and sweet. And then again, not as sweet, and not nearly as slow. Urgent, needy. Desperate. And she matched him in every way, clutching him to her, urging him closer and deeper. He pulled her knee to his hip and entered her in one feverish thrust.

It was a long while before either of them spoke.

CHAPTER 19

*J*ennifer might be using him, but Colton found that he didn't care.

He would be whatever Jennifer needed. A distraction, and the release of the sexual tension sparking between them. He'd be anything she wanted him to be because he was falling in love, or maybe he'd already been there from the very first time he laid eyes on her. In that moment, he had been thunderstruck.

Not enough of a romantic to believe in first love lasting forever, he wasn't sure it made sense to believe in love at first sight, either. But this was different, and if there was anything to that term, if it ever existed, it would have to be something like this. Similar to this sensation that she knew him inside and out and possibly understood him almost better than he understood himself. It didn't quite make sense logically, but yet felt real.

If this was true love, then he understood all those sappy love songs for the first time. He suddenly appreciated Ed Sheeran songs. He understood why people got tied up in knots over the future. Because his own prospects didn't look as bright when he pictured Jennifer walking away. Funny how that worked. He'd come home to start over, with a fresh new plan that had never included a woman.

Hours later, he disentangled himself from Jennifer, pressing a kiss to her temple. He hadn't eaten, or even noticed they'd missed dinner, until his stomach became a hollow cavern.

"Wait. Where are you going?"

He slipped on his black boxer briefs. "We need to eat."

"Right. But then after that, back to bed with you."

"Yes, ma'am."

She rolled over, twisting the sheets, showing him her bare bottom. He was almost sure she hadn't intended that but he licked his lips anyway. Her insatiability was gratifying. More gratification had come in the way she cried out his name when she came to her own release. She was incredibly responsive and, like her, he wondered why they weren't doing this all along.

Because, genius, this is supposed to be fake. Pretend. You're not supposed to fall for her.

Yeah, the only problem was this farce had become real, at least for him. He hadn't expected this to happen at all, even with the initial gobsmacked feeling. He'd hoped that was lust and nothing more. Something temporary. Not the case. This thing with her, whatever he wanted to call it, was far more. She was everything he'd ever wanted in a woman, in a partner, in a best friend to grow old with.

But she was *young*. He couldn't ignore that fact. Maybe too young to be ready to settle down with anyone, least of all this cowboy. With a hint of despair, he wondered how in the world he was going to be able to say goodbye to her. He couldn't think about that now, not when she was in his bed bare naked, waiting for him.

Enjoy this. Stay in the moment. No regrets.

Cooking always relieved him of stress and it was a godsend when it came to the nightmares. He hadn't had one of those in a few days. It might be the clean air, or all the coping strategies he'd learned, but he saw himself on the other side of the bad times. One day the memories wouldn't rise as close to the surface but be buried below along with other painful ones.

He chopped onions and threw some butter in the pan, knowing the scents would entice her. Then he found some ground beef and made two thick patties. Nothing smelled better than a fried burger.

"Don't think I can't see you over there," Colton said.

He'd heard and then spied her sneaking into the kitchen from down the dim hallway, carrying her camera.

"This is so much better when my subject is unaware he's in the limelight." She snapped and moved closer.

He groaned to see that she wore his blue chambray shirt, falling to her luscious thighs.

"Please. Go on, chef. Pretend I'm not here."

"That's going to be pretty impossible." But he flipped the burger and tried his best not to smile.

She didn't lower the camera but kept playing with the lens, taking a photo, then looking in the digital window to admire her work.

"Oh my, look at you. I could sell these to some porno site and be like, a multigazillionaire."

"Don't even think about it."

She laughed. "God, you're so sexy when you cook naked."

"I'm not *naked*."

"Close enough. Seriously, you could have your own cooking show on YouTube. We could call it *Raw and Naked*."

"Where I cook raw food while naked? Not interested. Don't forget, I'm a cowboy. This is just for fun."

"But it would be a shame to deny the public your unique mix of food and naked."

"Stop." But he laughed.

"Oh! Maybe we should call it *The Naked Cowboy*!"

"I think that one's taken."

She dissolved into loud peals of laughter.

This was another thing he hadn't done in a long while. Laugh, and laugh loudly. She brought it out of him. And he'd like to think he'd helped her too. She still talked more than anyone he'd ever met but there was also a playful quality to her.

He didn't think she was quite as concerned with what others thought about her as she'd been before. She didn't seem to have the blazing need for everyone to like her. Hopefully she'd come to understand only what she thought mattered.

Unfortunately, she was a kind and loyal person who some idiot guy had seen as a mark.

If he did nothing else while she was here, he'd convince her one bad experience shouldn't change who she was. He didn't want her to shrivel up and let fear rule her actions. She had a huge heart, and a great deal of talent she should be able to share with the world. But the truth was when he looked at the stalker situation, he wasn't sure there was any good resolution here.

He agreed with her father that she'd at the very least have to move permanently. But she might not have to move out of Los Angeles since in a city that large she could become anonymous again. *If* she stayed off the podcast. Her best bet might be to start over, and she wouldn't like that. Not that he could blame her. She'd accomplished a lot and had the kind of success that took some people decades to achieve. But at least she was still young and had time to start over.

"Colton, where'd you go? Come back to me."

Ah, she was behind him now, arms wrapped around his waist, mouth pressed against his back. This time, the reason he'd zoned out had nothing to do with a bad memory or a flashback.

"I'm right here."

He turned to grab plates, and she showed him several pictures. In each one he was the epitome of stony concentration, attending to the task at hand like nothing else in the world mattered.

"Look at you," she said. "You're so relaxed, in your own little world."

His brow furrowed, he wore the hint of a smile on his lips. The picture expressed everything he felt. She'd perfectly captured him. At home, and at ease with everything around him. It was strange to think now that he'd ever worried about coming home again and fitting in. Strange he'd feared he wouldn't be the same person he'd been when he left, and that he'd be the jagged piece of a puzzle who didn't fit anymore.

"That's the same way you look at me when we make love. Like it's everything you need. Everything you want." Her smile was sweet and almost a little…shy.

"It *is* everything."

She set the camera down and went into his arms, reaching up to bury her face in his neck.

"Hmm. You smell so good."

He drew her closer, instinctively knowing he should count every second of his time with her from this point forward. Every single moment before she left him.

He kissed her deeply and then slapped her behind. "Now, let's eat these burgers so we can hurry up and go back to bed like you wanted."

"Like *I* wanted?"

"Like we both want."

"Want to see how fast I can eat a burger?" She grinned.

They ate in companionable silence for a few minutes, until she decided to finish eating her burger...in his lap. It was an interesting dynamic and a change from the early days of eating across from each other like an old married couple.

"Here," she said, offering him a bite. "You're always feeding me."

He narrowed his eyes, chewed, and swallowed. "Not sure that counts. I still made this meal."

"I feel guilty I haven't cooked anything, but you banned me from the kitchen."

"I wasn't serious about that."

"I don't think you'd much like what I know how to cook. I can make a toasty grilled cheese and I'm excellent at heating cans of soup and chili." She lowered her gaze and her voice hushed. "My mother was the real cook in our family. All kinds of delicious casseroles and cakes. Too bad she didn't leave behind a book of recipes, but she probably didn't think she'd die at forty-two."

The quivering tone in her voice made him hold her tighter. "Did you know she was dying? Were you prepared?"

"I don't think so. My incredibly sunny nature wouldn't allow me to believe it, and by the time I did it was a little too late. It happened fast. A year from the time she was diagnosed with colon cancer. It spread to her liver."

"If it helps, I don't think you can ever be prepared." He lowered his head to her shoulder, kissed her neck.

"No, you can't." She ruffled his hair, lightening the mood.

"So, what you're telling me is I'll be the cook in this family?" He wasn't able to catch himself in time to stop the incredible assumption that they were a *family*.

But even if for a little while, it sure felt that way.

She didn't seem shocked or upset by the statement but nodded in agreement. "I'm afraid so, Captain Sparrow."

"Yarr!" He did his best imitation of a frustrated pirate, picking her up in his arms and carrying her toward the bedroom. "Hide the rum! Hide the rum!"

She kicked her legs and laughed all the way to the bedroom where they both stopped laughing for a long while.

THE NEXT FEW days went by like a blur, Colton working long hours but coming home for lunch. They'd have amazing wall-banging sex, he'd take a shower and then go back out. She wandered the ranch, getting acquainted with the horses and livestock. She took photos of Freya and the wild horses as they galloped chasing the wind and Beer. She visited with Delores, Winona, and the children in the afternoons, taking photos of them running, their little chubby legs working double time to catch Beer. They played fetched and tumbled in the grass head over behind.

But no matter what time Colton walked in the door, Jennifer jumped him. His hat would fall off, and he'd pretend to stagger to the couch where he'd kiss her into next week.

Evenings became longer sessions of sex, making (she helped) and eating dinner, showering together, then sexy times again because they were both insatiable. They watched the *Hollywood Entertainment* show and Colton swore he'd get satellite TV next time he was in town. But for now, they enjoyed making fun of all the actors while they ate whatever delicious dinner Colton had created.

One lazy sex-filled afternoon, Colton had just gone back outside when the landline rang.

It was Mallory. "How are you enjoying your vacation in the country? I see your socials are still completely dead. It's like you fell off the face of the Earth."

"Well, that was the plan."

"What do you do all day long? You must be climbing the walls."

Or climbing a certain cowboy.

"Believe it or not, I'm used to this now. Funny thing, without all the distractions I'm *forced* to relax. You should try it sometime. I'm no longer worried about who's doing what and whether or not they're having more fun that I am. No more fear of missing out. I don't really have any idea what everyone else is doing but I *know* I'm having more fun."

"Oh, really? Well, this sounds like the start of new podcast series. *Unwind and Unplug.*"

Funny, Jennifer hadn't even considered it. It would defeat the purpose. She was going to get listeners to plug in just so she could tell them to unplug?

"Actually, I think my father might have been right after all. I'll have to give up the podcast. Or he'll find me again because I'm a public figure."

"Well, you can't just hide away forever!"

"Can't I?"

"I haven't even told you the best part about my call. For the past few days, Dan has been a no-show at the restaurant. After coming in every night for dinner and asking about you, I thought that was unusual. I asked around, and someone told me he moved to the East Coast where he had a better job opportunity."

"Are you kidding me? Why didn't you say so in the first place?"

"Well, who knows if it's true? I don't think you can trust a word coming out of Dan's mouth. But it's at least encouraging that he hasn't been coming by. Has he stopped emailing?"

Jennifer had checked early today and there had been no more emails. That made a few days now, which was a definite break in his routine.

"No more emails. It's been days."

"It sounds like he's moved on. When are you coming home?"

Dan had stopped torturing her and obsessing. He'd finally gotten the message and given up. The sense of relief was almost a palpable swelling in her chest. She'd get her life back. Swim in her condo's pool without fear he'd be watching. Go out with her friends to restaurants and clubs without worrying he might be following. She could resume her podcast and do the work that meant something to her.

But she'd have to leave Colton.

"I don't know. I'll have to see about flights."

"Thank God you don't have to drive back! I still can't believe you did that."

"I can't, either."

But she'd never forget that road trip. The way Colton had quietly listened to her without once interrupting. It wasn't that he didn't have anything to say, he just wanted to listen to her. He'd bought her a coffee at the rest stop and let her sleep while he drove all night. She was so glad to have been a bit of a distraction for him and help him ease back into his old life.

It was time to leave now and go back to her little corner of the world. Maybe he could visit her in LA. She'd seen where he lived and worked, and now he could come see her. But of course, even if he did, that wouldn't last. He wouldn't stay and she couldn't blame him. No one would trade these golden hills, horses, trees, and river streams for smog, congestion, and ridiculous rent.

She'd tell Colton tonight that she could go home. Maybe he'd even be glad to be alone again. Now he'd have the little cottage to himself. He was the type to crave solitude and she'd been one loud pain in his behind since day one.

When Colton walked in the door, early, he appeared to have been drug through the mud naked. He had dirt caked on his face, hat, his shirt, his jeans. And he…smelled. Not his usual delicious smell of leather, soap, and musk.

She covered her nose. "Oh my God, what happened?"

But he was grinning ear to ear. "The most fun I've had in years. We had to pull a cow out of a ditch."

"That sounds really…hard."

"You have no idea. I had a great time. There was a rope and a truck involved. And look at all this mud! Isn't this fantastic?" He took a step toward her, and she took a step back. "What's wrong?"

"Umm…" She waved her hand up and down his body, demonstrating.

"What? You don't want to give me a kiss?" He wore a big grin, his arms stretched out wide.

"Well, it's just…" She smiled, shook her head, and took a step back, holding up both palms. "Later."

He studied her. "Not ready for mud wrestling. Check."

"Why? Is that a thing?"

"Sure, all the women here love to roll around in the mud with their cowboys. There's even an annual contest. I plan to win this year, so you better get ready to practice."

She was about to make excuses that since she was from LA. such a thing shouldn't be held against her when he burst into loud peals of laughter. He was teasing her again.

"I'll go shower and drive you to the clinic."

"That wasn't funny, Colton!" She said to his retreating back. "Hey, is there really a *contest*?"

He laughed even harder. "No, but there should be!"

Eve's veterinary clinic was truly impressive. While the outside was an ordinary and functional office building with suites, walking inside felt like being transported to the wild west. The walls were papered in green and gold and there were artist renderings of horses, cattle, goats and pigs. Every kind of domestic dog breed was showcased on another wall. The receptionist desk was L-shaped and a lady with silver hair, coiffed perfectly, rose to greet them.

For a second, Colton, who had been leading her inside, froze. It was Jennifer who extended her hand to the receptionist first.

"I'm Jennifer. Eve is expecting me. I'm here to take photos of the clinic for the website."

The woman, whose name tag read, "Regina" and had a drawing of a cute puppy on it, ran from behind the desk straight to Colton, and threw her arms wide open.

"You sure are a sight for sore eyes! C'mon over here and give us a hug! Oh, aren't you handsome. Always were."

Colton accepted the hug but looked less than thrilled. "This is my fiancée, Jennifer Walker."

"Hi," Jennifer said.

The woman took the news like someone might take the announcement of a loved one's death. Her face fell, her jaw gaped, and her eyes might have teared up a little.

"Oh. Well, congratulations, I guess." She pointed to Colton. "I was almost going to be his mother-in-law."

"Cherisse and I were never engaged," Colton said with a tight-lipped smile.

She recognized this now as the smile he flashed when extremely irritated but trying to be kind. Over the twenty-four hours of their drive to Texas, she'd witnessed the look numerous times. Proud to say she hadn't seen it in over a week, at least not directed at her.

"Well, you would have been had Cherisse not turned into an idiot overnight. Honestly, it pains me to say she's my kin some days. But the boys are awfully cute." She held a hand to her chest and took a breath. "And I'm sorry about *that Taylor*. I never did like him."

"Regina?" Eve called out. "Please send my guests to the back."

"Sorry, I'm chatting too much as usual. I took this job when Earl retired because he's home all day and drives me up a clear wall. Anyway, I've adopted three cats since I've been here so beware. Eve takes them all in. Some folks abandon them here when they can't pay the bill." She made a valiant effort at a smile and led them toward the back. "Right this way."

"Do you mind if I take a few photos?" Jennifer didn't wait for an answer and pointed her camera to the vibrant colorful walls.

Colton waited for her to come along, which wasn't necessary, but did make her feel pretty special. Regina, however, was frowning as she backtracked to rejoin them. Maybe she expected Colton would leave Jennifer behind, follow Regina, and secretly ask for Cherisse's phone number. How irritating.

"Hey, guys!" Eve greeted them from inside a room labeled "X-rays" in bold black letters above the entrance. Next to it, another room said "Surgery."

Eve spread her arms. "So, this is it. I see you've already met our receptionist. Thank you, Regina, I've got it from here."

Regina reluctantly went back to the front desk.

"How about a tour?" Eve led the way. "We remodeled last year and we're pretty happy with how it all came out. Our website still has all the old photos. With all this effort, the least we can do is also remodel our website, too. But neither one of us is very good with all that, nor do we have the time."

"I'm happy to do it for you." Jennifer snapped away as she went down the hall.

There were framed photos of black-and-white sketches

of different dog breeds along one long hallway. Chihuahuas, Labradors, Spaniels, Terriers.

"From a local artist," Eve pointed.

Jennifer took a photo of Eve pointing to the artwork. The best stills were spontaneous ones where the light and aperture worked together. Eve looked pretty and natural, wearing very little makeup, her long dark hair in a single braid. Natural light poured through the windows, making her almost glow.

Eve walked them through the building, telling them how and when she and Annabeth had taken over the business from the previous owner. She explained they were both a small and large animal service and took them through the kennels in the back. Some of the dogs and cats were recovering from surgeries and others had simply been abandoned.

"Sean brought Beer in here after he found the pups on the side of the road in a Miller crate." Eve laughed. "Did he tell you that? They were in fairly good shape, especially Beer, who was mostly just dehydrated."

"Ironic." Colton snorted. "What, he didn't get enough beer?"

Jennifer elbowed him but bit back a laugh.

"Our mission statement is that every animal will get the care they need whether or not their owner can afford to pay us."

"That's generous," Jennifer said.

"We raise funds. It's one of the Ladies of SORROW's pet projects." Eve made air quotes. "Pun intended."

She went on to talk about her education and how she'd decided to come back home instead of setting up practice in a bigger city. It seemed like the perfect moment to bring up the difficult subject.

As though sensing the timing, too, Colton slid a hand down Jennifer's back. "I'm going to go get a drink of water."

"Next to Regina." Eve pointed. "There's a little refrigerator with some bottled water."

He nodded and was off.

"I heard that you also do some talks on domestic violence in your spare time."

"Yes." Eve nodded. "But that doesn't go on the website. I like to keep them separate. Everyone in town knows my experience by now but making it so public doesn't feel right, either. Anyone could see the website and I'm protective of Jackson and Lily."

"That makes a lot of sense." Jennifer lowered her camera. "I had a bad experience, too."

Eve quirked a brow. "Yeah?"

"Yes, I…well, Colton thought maybe I should talk to you about this. I really don't know why or where to start. It's not easy to talk about and—"

"It's never easy. But if you're talking to someone who understands, it can make all the difference."

"Yes." Jennifer swallowed the golf ball in her throat. "I had a stalker."

She chose to go with the past tense because she wanted to believe Dan had given up on her since he could no longer find and terrorize her. It no longer fed into his need to control.

"I'm sorry. An ex-boyfriend of yours?"

"He wasn't even a relationship."

And then Jennifer explained it all, how obsessed Dan became after only one date because he'd somehow fooled himself into a deeper relationship as a fan of her podcast.

"This was…all before I met Colton, of course." She might confide in Eve, but Jennifer would stop short of confessing he was actually her bodyguard.

Eve nodded. "And did the man hurt you?"

"I was lucky. He didn't lay a hand on me. But he hurt my

sense of peace, my self-esteem, my freedom. He may have robbed me of a successful career. I may never go back to my podcast. It's too public and I can't risk him finding me again."

"There's more than one way to hurt someone. Before my stalker hurt me, he wouldn't stop calling or texting. He couldn't accept that I no longer wanted to see him."

It sounded far too familiar.

Eve went on. "I made the mistake of not realizing quite how desperate he'd become for my attention. And coming from where I did, in Stone Ridge, I was accustomed to men who respected me. Who listened when I said no. This man didn't."

"Did you…did you blame yourself?" The words were low and almost hushed.

"For a long time. But because he nearly killed me, I suddenly had a lot of support. It shouldn't come to that, but it did. The police, the prosecutors, my family, and friends all explained that I'd done nothing wrong. For a while, I kept thinking: maybe if I'd just been less polite to him. If I'd shut him down immediately and been more straightforward. Or, if I'd never gone out with him in the first place. That was the tough one. It was a choice I'd made so it was easy to take part of the blame. I made a snap decision I lived to regret." She tapped on her ear. "I lost the hearing in this ear, but I came out with my life. It took a few years to get past all the trauma because the attack left me feeling isolated emotionally. But my friends, like Sadie, wouldn't give up. Then Jackson came back to town, and we got our second chance. I don't like that any of it happened, but it took me on a journey. I grew and changed and feel stronger for it. Still, of course, I wish it had never happened."

Here was a woman who'd almost lost her life and had come to a sense of peace about her ordeal. Now, she helped others, in the same way she was helping Jennifer.

"Please." Eve's hand went softly on Jennifer's shoulder. "Don't blame yourself."

"I'm trying not to but…"

"Don't."

"Okay, I won't." Her eyes wet, she wiped them with the heels of her hands.

Eve gave her a gentle and understanding smile. "Easier said than done, I know. But work on it."

And then Eve put her arms around Jennifer and hugged her for a long time.

CHAPTER 20

"And then, finally she kicked him out of the house." Regina completed the long, winding sad story of Cherisse and Taylor. "I know she regrets every day that she sent you that awful email. Just in case it doesn't work out with your fiancée, Cherisse's still got feelings for you. Not that I hope it doesn't work out because Jennifer seems like a lovely girl."

"Thank you, she is."

He decided to take the opportunity of having a good phone signal to give Horace a call. They hadn't checked in since Jennifer told him about the emails and Colton had reported back late one night when Jennifer was sound asleep.

Before they'd started sleeping together.

"Excuse me. I'll be right back."

Colton stepped just outside the front door for some privacy and phoned Horace, who picked up immediately.

"Looks like he left town. He told his landlord and a few other people that he'd found a job opportunity back East. Left quite suddenly. I had a feeling this would work. Out of sight, out of mind. The idiot has moved on. He'll find another easy mark. It looks like Jennifer can finally come home. Is she anxious to get back?"

"I believe so. She's been worried about the podcast."

Colton swallowed at the thought of Jennifer leaving him. But he should have been ready for this all along. This also meant it would soon be time to tell his family the truth if he didn't want them to think he'd been abandoned. And he didn't. It seemed too cruel. By now hopefully he'd convinced Riggs he'd stay with or without Jennifer. This was his home, and he wouldn't ever leave here again.

Horace muttered, "I'm still not sure she should continue, because it's so public. Even from a distance, what if he continues to harass her? She'll have no peace of mind."

"If the podcast is what she wants to do, she can't let him stop her. Safety measures can be put in place."

"Maybe you're right. I can't thank you enough. I've had nightmares of what could have happened if she'd stayed in that apartment. Alone. Eventually, he would have gotten inside. The stories…well, I'm sure you've heard them, too."

"Should I put her on a plane back to LA?" The thought made his stomach roil and pitch, but it needed to be asked.

Her life was waiting for her in the city. Even if she'd made the best of everything here with him, he couldn't fool himself into thinking this was the kind of life she wanted. Far from it. Her family, her friends, her fans, and the life she'd built were in LA and not here. The dreams she had were there and not in his small town. He couldn't and wouldn't ask her to give anything up. If she wanted to stay, she'd have to get to that realization on her own with no pressure from him.

"Anytime you're both ready," Horace said.

"I'll talk to her tonight."

"Thank you again, son. I'll never be able to properly repay you."

"You don't have to. It was my honor to help you both."

Colton hung up and, in order to give Jennifer and Eve more time, he crossed Main Street to the Shady Grind. He hadn't been inside in ages. Way before Jackson owned it, this place used to be a haunt for him, his brothers, and friends. Friends like Taylor. Truth be told, Colton missed him far more than he ever missed Cherisse. He and Taylor had been friends since third grade, and it was difficult to acknowledge they'd let a woman come between them. This, of course, happened far too often in their town. With Colton's long absences, he could almost understand what Taylor had done. He and Cherisse had both been lonely. But it also meant Cherisse had never loved Colton. That's not how love worked.

He understood real love now.

Jennifer knew how to love and she'd taught him how.

Colton knew without a doubt that he wouldn't be seeking comfort for *his* loneliness anytime soon. What he'd want to do after Jennifer left is simply be alone for a long while. Stew in his own misery. Keep busy with the ranch and his horse. He couldn't even think about letting anyone else into his heart again. His heart already felt too raw and whipped.

He stood, hands in his pockets, staring at the announcement outside the door.

JACKSON CARVER and the Outlaws
Performing live tonight
Debuting new single
"Texas Time"

How about that.

Sounded like a date night.

Colton would take Jennifer to dinner at the Shady Grind and throw in a concert. Dancing. After that, maybe later tonight, he'd tell her it was safe to go home. But first he'd talk up the town, sell it hard with all the progress they were making, and mention that he was going to miss the hell out of her.

He wouldn't talk about love. He wouldn't ask for anything more than what they already had. A good friendship and a smokin'-hot sex life.

Then, he could only hope she wouldn't be in any hurry to get back to LA.

An hour later, as they both sat inside the Shady Grind, Jennifer said, "These are almost as good as *your* burgers."

Colton smiled, remembering the night they'd raced each other to finish eating so they could get back to bed.

"The Shady Burger isn't bad, especially with the sweet potato fries on the side."

Jennifer dabbed at her mouth and reached for his hand. "Thank you for suggesting I talk to Eve."

"Did it help?"

"It made all the difference to talk to someone who'd been through something similar. She had it so much worse and she's such a survivor. It's strange to feel grateful about what happened to me, but I am in some ways. I had someone in my life who took this seriously enough to intervene and get me away. And I had you, the man who took me out of the hot mess. Without you, I don't think I'd have enjoyed these past two weeks quite as much as I have."

"You've had fun."

"I had a good time even *before* you exercised your conjugal rights." She winked and took a bite of the sweet potato fry.

He loved that she didn't pick at her food and pretend to eat like a rabbit. She was a woman who enjoyed a meal that consisted of more than lettuce and carrots.

"I don't think they're technically called conjugal rights

before marriage, but I get your point. Although I'm not sure who *exercised* those rights first." He smirked.

"We'll call it even."

He made a motion in the direction of the risers toward the back of the bar. "You probably noticed there's a concert tonight."

An area was being cleared for a dance floor, meaning there were fewer tables available. They were sitting at one where Colton could face the door, his back to the wall as he preferred.

"Eve told me."

"Would you like to stay for it?"

"Really? Can we?"

"Sure we can."

"I assumed you'd have to get back to the Grange."

"The ranch isn't going to be my whole life. There has to be a balance, right?" He set his iced tea down, worrying he was already selling himself a bit too obviously.

She'd see right through this pitch, intelligent woman that she was. She didn't miss a thing.

Stay with me, Jennifer. Pick me. I'll make a good husband.

"I know what you mean better than most. Coming here made me realize how much of my work life was out of balance. It's so freeing not to have to worry about what's happening on social media. Not to have to make *everything* a story and content. Only a few weeks ago, I wouldn't go anywhere to eat without taking a photo of my food."

They'd left her camera in his truck. "Would you like my phone?"

"No," she said without hesitation. "I'm going to take a picture in my mind. For posterity."

She made a clicking sound and aimed toward the food. Then she turned the imaginary camera on him and clicked again.

She pointed to her temple. "That's going right here. Forever. I don't have to worry about a hard drive failure or a social media site suddenly closing my account and wiping out all my history."

"I haven't had an account in years. What did I miss?"

She blinked until it dawned on her he might be joking. "Nothing."

"Well, hello there, young Colt!" They were interrupted by Lenny, whom Colton had known his entire life.

Colton stood to shake the old man's hand, but he was pulled into a hug. Lenny was older now, thinner, balder, and grayer, but the man still had all the raw pulsating restlessness of the energizer bunny.

"I hear congrats are in order! You're the last brother standin'. Gettin' hitched, I hear."

"Uh-huh." Colton swiftly changed the subject. "You here for the concert?"

"I'm Jackson's head roadie, or didn't ya hear?"

"Doesn't that require a lot of heavy lifting? Amps? Speakers?"

He flexed a muscle. "Still got it. And after the show's over and we're all packed up, I have my car service available. For a small fee, I drive everyone home who shouldn't be behind the wheel, if ya catch my drift."

"Like Uber," Jennifer said.

"Sorry." Colton gestured to Jennifer. "Lenny, this is my... my fiancée, Jennifer."

Why is it harder to lie now? The lie had been perfectly harmless and useful but no longer. Now it felt like an invasion of privacy.

"Hello, Lenny." Jennifer finger waved.

"Nice to meet ya, young lady. I've known Colt since he was a little whippersnapper around yay high." He made a motion to his waist. "Later, I nicknamed him Colt 45 because he was rather handy with a gun."

Jennifer laughed. "Everyone should call him that."

"Excuse me. I see I'm needed. No one can figure out how to hook up that particular amp. Tell ya, they'd be lost without me." He strode off with a wave.

"Well, Colt 45, tell me truly. Are you packing heat?"

"What do *you* think?"

"Of course you are."

"And I wasn't exactly *born* a good shot. It took hours of practice with Sean, shooting empty cans off the fence line. Now, I can probably shoot the stink off a skunk at five hundred yards."

She might not yet know they didn't have anything to worry about with her stalker gone, but for him, carrying his weapon was a force of habit. He'd like very much for there to be a day when he didn't need his gun.

Maybe someday that sense of peace would come.

He could only hope.

JENNIFER WAS HAVING A GREAT NIGHT. She'd met all kinds of new people, including a quirky old guy named Lenny. In the crowd were some people she'd already met, like Tabitha the nurse, now dancing with the handsome Dr. Grant, the only one in town. Jennifer also met his midwife, Trixie, who seemed to be giving both of them the evil eye as they danced. So, there was a story there. Levi was a horse trainer Colton seemed to know quite well. He was very chatty and flirty with Jolette Marie, whom Jennifer had also met at the wedding. Then there was Beau Stephens, who had to be the biggest flirt in the bar. He was tall and recklessly handsome.

"Can I cut in?" Beau said. "I've danced with everyone but your fiancée. Don't worry I won't steal her."

"She's not a bag of money," Colton said with irritation, but he relented.

Within two seconds, he was dancing with Jolette Marie.

"I'm Beau. We haven't met. I own Stephens Construction and we're building all the new cabins by Lupine Lake."

"I've heard. Are you selling many of them?"

"Renting some, selling some. It all depends. They're going up fast." He spun her around.

Jennifer wondered if after she went back to LA she could come out here again and rent a cabin. Stay for a month or two and rekindle whatever she had with Colton.

Unless he moved on.

The thought made her stomach plunge and not because of all this spinning Beau was doing with her. Just the idea of leaving Colton was unbearable. She didn't want to tell him that Mallory had good news about Dan because this meant she could, and probably should, go home. He'd probably want to have his home back, grateful to no longer have to be the cook for two people.

She didn't believe he'd rekindle anything with Cherisse, but that didn't mean he'd stay single for long. Not a man like Colton. Not even in this town. The few women would be knocking his door down the moment news spread his "fiancée" had left him. Tabitha was already sending him sultry looks and that's when she believed him to be engaged. What would she do when she heard he was free? She'd have her chance at Sean 2.0 in her mind.

Stop it, Jennifer! Stop. Enjoy whatever time you have left with him.

Because she had to go home. Right? That was the deal, and nothing had changed other than the fact they happened to appreciate each other now. She liked him far more than she *should.*

Jackson gave an amazing performance. Apparently, this

Nashville celebrity always tried his new songs out on his home turf. He had a huge fan base not only here but in Nashville. His appearance on *Mr. Cowboy* had renewed his popularity after he'd taken a long break from performing. "Texas Time" was an anthem song, similar to Friends in Low Places by Garth Brooks. This latest song was sure to be a huge hit when it released. It was so catchy that Jennifer was still singing it by the end of the evening.

She and Colton were buckled up and he'd just started the truck when she remembered her takeout, having left it on their table. All that was left was the sweet potato fries, but they were delicious. Crunchy, with just the right amount of seasoning.

"I'll get it," Colton said. "Stay right here and I'll be right back."

She watched his retreating back as he disappeared into the place that reminded her of an old-time saloon. Everything in this little town was quaint and retro in the best of ways. Tonight, when they went home, she'd make love to him and then, if she got up her nerve, she'd tell him the God's honest truth. She'd never felt this way before. Never hung on a guy's every word like a lovesick city girl, never wanted anyone so much that her heart split open to make even more room. It was possible, entirely likely, she'd fallen in love with him.

Which might be a bad idea if he didn't feel the same way. But tonight, he'd searched her gaze with such a soft tenderness that she began to wonder...and hope. This was more than sex. More than two people who were wildly attracted to each other. This sudden rush of deep affection could only be called love. A love sudden and unexpected. Unplanned. And far sweeter than she could have ever imagined.

Maybe they could find a way to be together. Long distance worked for some people, right?

"That didn't take you very long."

She'd fully expected Colton to be held up again by one of the many adoring residents tonight who'd wanted to welcome him home and thank him for his service.

But when she turned, it wasn't Colton who'd just opened the driver's side door.

It was Dan.

CHAPTER 21

"Get out of the truck, Jennifer, nice and easy."

He had a *gun*. Dan had a gun, and he was pointing the thing at Jennifer. All she could see in that moment, all she could *hear*, was the long barrel. The cylindrical shape of the cold gray metal. The click it made when Dan cocked it. But he was supposed to be somewhere on the East Coast starting a new life and leaving her alone. How had he even *found* her? They'd been so careful. For one long moment, she couldn't speak. She wasn't even breathing.

"Hurry, we need to move." Not waiting for her, he pulled her by the elbow across the seat and out the driver's side. "Before your Neanderthal boyfriend gets back."

She slid across without meaning to, pulled along by his strong-arming. "I don't...I don't want to go with you."

"Too bad. I have a gun and you're going to listen. Besides, do you want *him* to get hurt?" He threw a look in the direction of the Shady Grind. "If he comes out before we leave, I'll have no choice but to shoot *him*. Is that what you want?"

"N-no, no. *Please* don't hurt him."

She could picture Colton, lying in a pool of blood after

coming home from a war overseas. Not even able to survive more than a couple of weeks back home.

All because of her.

Dan grabbed her by the hair and tugged. "You're coming with me and we're going to talk this out. Breakups happen. I get it. But we haven't had a chance to discuss what went wrong with us."

Dear God. What went *wrong*? The delusions were still intact, apparently.

Pulling her along, he opened a sedan driver's side door and shoved her inside, still pointing the gun.

"Don't even try to get out. You're going to drive us."

"Where? Wh-where are we going?"

"Eventually to Mexico. You're coming with me, of course. No hard feelings, we'll just start over."

He got in the back seat of the car, directly behind her, pointing the gun to her head.

"Go. Now!"

As she drove off, Jennifer cast a longing look at possibly the last place she'd ever see Colton. Funny how she wasn't thinking of whether she'd survive this. She was only thinking about him.

She spied the figure of a man in her rear view coming around the corner, wearing a dark cowboy hat. Not Colton, but *Beau*. She could only hope he'd seen her and recognize the back of her head leaving in a strange vehicle. Colton would be able to figure things out when he saw her missing from his truck. When he'd notice her purse, left behind. He'd know that she'd never purposely just take off on him. He'd know Dan was involved. Colton would feel so guilty. He'd blame himself when all he'd done was leave her alone for a few seconds.

As Dan ordered, she drove to the outskirts of town but not in the direction they usually took for the H Grange. They were going in the *opposite* direction. Her mind relentlessly spun its wheels, thinking of something, anything, she could do to leave clues behind to where they were going. But it wasn't anything like the movies. If she rolled down the window and casually threw an earring outside, Dan would notice. He'd get angrier than he already was and right now she had to talk him down. She had to make him believe she was on his side.

Yes, establish rapport. Cooperate.

"I wish you hadn't made such a big production out of this. You scared me but I'd have been happy to go with you. It's just the gun was…upsetting."

"Do you really think I like weapons? The gun was *necessary*. Your boyfriend is a soldier. He wasn't going to let you go that easy. Surely you realize that?"

How did he know all this? How long had he been spying on them, collecting information?

"My boyfriend? Oh, he's not my *boyfriend*," Jennifer tried lamely. "Just a friend. And you're overestimating him. He was a military *cook*. He didn't see any live combat, Dan," she lied. "He was simply a cook."

"Word in town is *that cook* is your fiancé. It would appear you work fast."

"That's just a lie we told everyone. Colton is my bodyguard."

"You don't need a bodyguard! You're not anyone vitally important to the rest of the country."

"It's because of you. You scared me."

"Wow, so you're telling me that you can't handle a little intensity, a little hot passion. But I would *never* hurt you." He waved the gun. "Can't you drive any faster than this? You're trying to give him time to catch up to us, aren't you?"

"Of course not. It's just these curvy and bumpy country

roads. I'm not used to them. Not like LA, right, Dan? We have *real* roads."

Establish a connection. Sympathize.

We're both from LA. Aren't these country bumpkins ridiculous? They call this a road?

"Pull over! You're not only unfaithful, but you're also a terrible driver!"

Jennifer stopped the car not far from a large field of Long Horns grazing. Maybe if she took off at a run she could get away. Run into the fields. She'd probably have a better chance than if she allowed Dan to take her to a second location, wherever that might be. Beau might have seen her, but he'd have no idea where they were headed.

She stopped the car, got out, and made her lame attempt at a run. She got about six feet away before Dan caught her and dragged her back to the car.

"I can't let you go *that* easily." He shoved her back in the car. "You see? I didn't shoot you. I don't want to hurt you and I won't as long as you cooperate."

He hadn't shot her, but he had hauled her in forcefully. *Twice.* This time, when he did, she'd gone to her knees and skinned her arms and elbows.

"I'll take care of that injury when we get back. I have to do everything, apparently." He climbed in the driver's seat, pointing the gun like a ruler to emphasize his point. "Sooner or later, you're going to have to start being a part of this relationship and carry your weight."

"I'm sorry."

"You should be. The things I do for love." He shook his head, sighed, and drove them further out into the country.

Jennifer began to despair that Colton would never find her. She considered throwing herself out of the car, but the gun still worried her. It was entirely possible Dan didn't actually want to hurt her, but he didn't look as comfortable wielding it as he might think. It could accidentally go off. Even if she managed to get away from Dan, her sense of direction was such that she'd probably get lost and wander Hill Country for days.

Salvation came in the form of a lake they were approaching on the right. A large, beautiful, blue lake. And all around, clusters of cabins. *Lupine Lake.* At least she knew where she was now. The cabins Beau and his family were building. And then the headlights shined on the sign:

Stephens Construction
Lakeside cabins for rent and sale.

There was a phone number listed to call for inquiries.

This might be easier than she could have hoped. As long as she managed to keep them here until Beau came back to work tomorrow, she'd somehow contact him. Maybe when Dan was asleep or went into the bathroom. She'd let Beau know she was being held against her will and to get word to Colton. Or she'd simply run for it and hope Dan was a super bad shot.

But her heart sunk when Dan headed to a cabin obviously still under partial construction. Beams and sheetrock were stacked on the outside perimeter. Dan parked his rented sedan under a group of leafy trees.

"It's not like I can't *afford* to stay here. But if I'd rented, I'd leave a paper trail. Your boyfriend would have figured it out before we could get to the airport. This way, I bought some time. No one is supposed to be staying in this unit. It's vacant."

"What a brilliant idea," she lied, despair mounting. "But, how am I supposed to travel without ID? You took me so fast I left my purse behind."

He snorted. "I'm a lot smarter than that. You think I'm

going to have you traveling as *Jennifer Walker*? You're going to have a brand-new identity. I've even got a wig inside. Get ready to find out whether blondes have more fun. New social security number, name, everything. All the paperwork is inside."

Jennifer gaped. God, the man was truly insane. He must have been planning this since before she'd left LA. Dan pulled her by the elbow into the cabin. It still smelled like fresh pine. In the middle of the open room was a sleeping bag. Clothes were strewn about, snacks, and toiletries.

"I didn't have a chance to clean up. Honestly, I have been watching you two for two days and this is the first time he left you alone for a minute. Idiot. Well, I had to act fast."

"You told Mallory you had a job opportunity back East."

"She told you." He smiled with satisfaction. "And you people think I'm stupid!"

"No one thinks you're stupid. You're as bright as they come."

Dan led her to a corner and forced her to sit. He finally set the gun down and reached for some duct tape.

Jennifer flinched. "No. Please, no."

"Sorry about this, but I can't trust you. This won't hurt, just slow you down if you try to leave." He wrapped her hands together and then her feet. "And don't try to leave."

"A-are you going to kill me, Dan? Because I think we could really have a bright future together if you give me another chance."

"Of *course* I'm not going to hurt you, Jennifer. I love you."

"Oh. Good, then."

Too bad she didn't believe him. A cold sliver of dread slid down her spine. Lucky her, loved by a man who probably had a murder kit in the trunk of his car.

"How did you find me? I'm just curious, that's all."

"How did I *find* you? It was way too easy. Call it the absolute vanity of some people. I have a suggestion for a new podcast: social media and its direct effect on the intellect of human beings and the death of society. One of those insipid bachelorettes posted her selfies at the wedding of the year" —at this Dan held up air quotes— "and it wound up on the show that loves to dumb down society in short five-minute segments. You were in the background. I wasn't sure at first, but I would recognize your long dark hair anywhere. A little research, and here you are."

"Right. I was at the wedding of the year."

But she wasn't supposed to have been in any photos. Colton had insisted. Had warned, coming close to sounding like an ogre. And she'd thought he was overreacting.

Most people would not have made the connection, but then again Dan wasn't most people.

"I'll take care of that skinned elbow now." He unzipped a red first aid kit nearby. "Never let it be said I don't take care of my woman."

Jennifer almost threw up in her mouth. "Thanks."

"How did you get involved with all these stupid country hicks? Were you really that desperate to get away from the city?"

Yes. But not from the city. From you.

Jennifer's hackles rose and she held back the spears of insults she wanted to throw at Dan. But she had to let him believe he could trust her, and then take the first moment he let down his guard to run.

"WHAT HAPPENED?" Beau Stephens said, catching Colton rushing out the door.

"What do you mean?" He carried the takeout container with him and headed toward his truck.

"Jennifer." Beau pointed. "I saw her get in the car with some other dude and drive off."

Panic seized Colton in short bursting waves. He dropped the container and ran toward the truck. She was *gone.* Gone. His mind was still trying to accept this, still trying to find another excuse. Maybe she'd run over to the veterinary clinic to see Eve again. Beau had seen some other woman drive off. Not Jennifer.

"You sure it was Jennifer?"

"I'm sure."

Then Colton noticed her purse still sitting on the floorboard of the passenger seat.

He cursed and kicked his truck.

"Calm down," Beau said, holding up his palms. "I'm sure y'all can work it out, whatever you've done wrong."

Colton picked up and waved her purse in front of Beau. "This isn't an argument. She wouldn't willingly get in someone's car without *this*. Someone kidnapped her."

And Colton knew exactly who that had to be. Dan was more of a criminal mastermind than anyone had ever given him credit. Apparently, he'd laid the groundwork and had everyone believing he was in the wind. Three thousand miles away on another coast. Instead, he'd snuck right into Colton's town. In military jargon, this development would be called Fubar. And this mission was in serious danger of going upside down.

"Jennifer has a stalker, and he must have found her."

"Jesus." Beau stared, comprehension of the seriousness dawning on him.

No lover's quarrel here. Nothing that simple.

"Tell me everything about the car."

"It was black, four doors, sedan, probably a BMW and..."

"Yeah? Go on. I don't have all day."

He rubbed the back of his neck. "And, come to think of it, I think maybe I've seen that car once before. At the lake."

"Lupine?"

"Yeah, so far, we've only rented or sold cabins to families and some of the single women who've moved here. No single men."

"Could he be working for you?"

"I mean…it's possible." Beau dragged a hand through his hair. "But I don't think so. All my guys drive trucks for obvious reasons."

Colton gave Beau a brief description of Dan as given to him by Horace.

"Doesn't sound familiar."

This still had to be the first place Colton would search and he was wasting valuable time. He may have already hurt her. Raw and pulsating fear rushed through him.

"I've got to look there first."

"I'm going with you." Beau went to his truck and grabbed a shotgun from the back.

A small crowd had gathered outside, and Levi yelled, "What the hell's going on out here?"

"Someone took Jennifer!" Beau yelled back. "C'mon, we're going to the lake, and we need some men."

Several men had spilled out of the restaurant, Jackson included, and they were hopping into trucks. Colton could hardly believe his eyes. He had a small platoon within minutes.

"Follow me!" Beau said, hopping into his truck.

Colton was right behind him, pealing out, kicking up dust. He thought about Jennifer, who must have been terrified that in the small time frame he'd left her alone her stalker had appeared. He wondered why she'd gone so willingly instead of putting up a fight as she should have.

He'd have heard her and taken seconds to get to her.

None of this would have happened. The issue of being taken to a second location was a dangerous one because there Dan would have the privacy he needed to do whatever he wanted to her.

Colton couldn't think beyond that one horrible thought.

245

In the time it took to drive to the lake, Colton spent every second berating himself and his own incompetence. He should have told Riggs. He should have told *Sean* even if he was busy with a wedding. Maybe if more people had known to look out for Dan, they would have reported a strange man in the area. In this case, privacy may have hurt them rather than helped. There were so many things he would have done differently, and his anxious brain now listed them all.

He should have never lied to his family.

He should have never trusted for a second Jennifer was safe until he'd confirmed the facts he'd been told. That was Security 101.

Lastly, he should have told Jennifer he'd fallen in love with her.

Because damn it, he wasn't scared of fighting and never had been. He was afraid to love someone with all his heart because it meant they'd also be taken from him, like his first parents. Like his "real" mother and father, the Hendersons. Like all the good friends he'd lost over the years. Too many.

He'd lost all the people he'd loved since he'd been a child. His entire life had been a series of losses. Some at home, most on the battlefield.

And now it might happen again.

Colton blamed himself.

Maybe it took a line of trucks following him to Lupine Lake, but it all came back to him now. He wasn't alone, and never had been. This was his *home*, not simply the place where his family and ranch were located. Everyone cared for each other, the residents looked out for one another. Even Beau, who Colton previously wrote off as a playboy who worked only to pay for his fun.

Instead, he was the one who'd noticed something unusual and was now leading the calvary. So, yeah, maybe Colton didn't always have to be the leader. Maybe, for once, he could let others help. Because if Jennifer didn't walk out of this situation safe and whole, he wasn't going to be good to anyone. For anything.

Beau pulled up just outside the single lane entrance to the lake and everyone followed suit behind him.

He walked up to Colton's truck. "We don't want a line of vehicles to come in at once and spook him if he's here. My truck is the only one he might expect."

"I've got to get in there, Beau. I can't just *sit* here."

Beau held up his palm. "No. I get it. Let's just all *walk* inside and try not to make it too obvious. Remember, there are people here. Families and *children*."

Right. Beau was probably terrified of collateral damage and suddenly so was Colton. When Dan had brought Jennifer here, he'd made it everyone's problem. Beau was correct. They had to protect the residents. Cooler heads and all that rot.

If only *his* head wasn't about to explode.

"Let me walk around first and see if I can spot the car." Beau tapped Colton's shoulder. "I'll be right back."

"Yeah, yeah."

Colton pinched the bridge of his nose. He hadn't seen the car because he'd been too busy inside thinking he didn't have a care in the world. Looking forward to exactly how he would slowly disrobe Jennifer the moment they got home.

With the others, Colton huddled and waited, gun loaded, holstered under his jacket.

Only a few minutes later, Riggs pulled up next to Colton and rolled down his window.

Colton met him. "What are you doing here?"

"I got a call there was trouble. You think someone took Jennifer? Why? How the hell did that happen?"

Colton dragged a hand down his face. "My own stupidity and hubris. I thought I could keep her safe without your help. Without anyone's help."

Riggs scowled. "Explain."

Colton told Riggs everything. How he was doing a favor for a friend, Jennifer's father. How her podcast had acquired a stalker and how her father had made an executive decision and sent her out of town. He finished by confessing Colton wasn't actually her fiancé, but her bodyguard. Riggs's guarded expression went from irritation to shock but landed square back on anger.

A familiar place for him when it came to Colton.

"Does Sean know?" Riggs spit out through a tight jaw.

Colton shook his head. "No. He was getting married and the last thing I wanted him to think is I'd come to his wedding with a job. It all happened very suddenly. I couldn't say no to her father, and Jennifer needed me. And, to tell the truth, I hoped having a fiancée might go a long way to help you finally believe I was here to stay."

"Damn it, Colton." Riggs climbed out of his truck, looking ready to give Colton hell.

He should have never brought trouble with him, should have never brought Jennifer here. He'd led a dangerous stalker right to their quiet little town.

"You *should* have asked for my help from day one."

"That's…not what I expected you to say."

"No, it never is, is it? What's it going to take for you to know that we're brothers and we stick together? We're blood, by both birth and choice. If I'd ever had a choice in the first place, I'd still choose you for a brother."

"I would choose you, too." Colton swallowed hard, the emotions running too deep for him now. "Every single time."

He was on the cusp of despair, anger, revenge, and Riggs had thrown in brotherly love. Riggs, the older brother who'd made sure to keep them together when they were all farmed out to foster care. He'd heard since then that it was unusual for all siblings to remain together, but Riggs was old enough to make the argument. It was probably the first time he'd made a persuasive argument worthy of his future law degree.

He swore to anyone who would listen that he would take care of his younger brothers if they could all remain together. Riggs had given up a lot for him and Sean. He'd been a teenager when their parents lost custody, but he became a father figure until Calvin Henderson came along and relieved him of that duty.

"I know," Riggs said, cracking a smile for the first time. "You would be lost without me. Now, let's make a plan."

"I don't have time for a plan. If she's not here, I need to move on. Fast. They could already be on their way to God knows where. Or maybe he already…" He couldn't even finish the sentence.

He'd seen too much violence and death and wanted more

than anything to leave that part of his life behind for good. And he believed he had.

"Don't worry, we'll find her, one way or another." Riggs clapped a hand on Colton's back.

Beau returned a few minutes later, his face drained of color.

"The car I saw leaving is parked behind a thicket near a house that's still under construction. We stopped a few days ago, waiting on a permit. Damn it all to hell, we got a squatter."

"And that's the least of your problems," Riggs said.

Within minutes, with Colton's help, Riggs had devised a plan worthy of a military operation. He organized the men. They would surround the house, and as soon as it was determined Jennifer was inside and under duress, they would get her out. But of course, it might not be that easy. It was as close to a hostage situation as any he'd been involved in. Jennifer was the hostage and if Dan wanted to walk away from this, he'd try to take her with him. Colton would die before he let that happen.

Stealthily, all five men approached the house on foot. Jackson and Levi went toward the back. Beau and Riggs took the front. Colton approached the side windows, keeping his body low to the ground, footsteps quiet, avoiding rocks and scattered twigs. Sheetrock and beams were stacked against the side of the house. Windows were installed but without trim. Ducking, he approached a window and glanced inside.

His heart slammed against his ribcage at the sight of her on the floor, hands and ankles bound with duct tape. She looked up as if she'd heard him or seen a shadow and met his eyes. They widened and she shook her head as if trying to discourage him from coming inside. She mouthed, "Don't."

Yeah, he got it. Colton was going to assume Dan was armed and dangerous. This wasn't a game they were playing, and he'd find out soon enough Colton had been here before. He put a finger to his lips to indicate she should be quiet and ignore him.

Colton watched from behind the bush as Dan walked in the room and knelt in front of Jennifer. He placed a blond wig on her head and made animated gestures. Jennifer, smart girl, didn't argue with him. He removed the duct tape from her hands and allowed her to adjust the wig.

Colton realized two things: this man foolishly thought he could take Jennifer out of the country under an assumed identity; and secondly, Colton *wasn't* going to kill him. This last realization hit him like a fist because it was so unexpected.

He'd killed enough people and he was done.

But Colton would find a way to get Dan away from Jennifer, get him into custody, where hopefully he would get the mental help he desperately needed.

His instincts had always been to act first and ask questions later. But he had to admit to himself, he'd changed. The soldier was no more. When he'd arrived, he'd still seen himself as a soldier more than a cowboy. But now, surrounded by his friends, and the lake where so many of them had spent time as children, he understood a few things. Some people needed the same kind of help he'd had. Some people were fighting their own wars daily with mental health. With their own personal demons. He'd met many of them, some of his closest friends.

Jennifer had a brother that had struggled.

There was a fine line between getting someone the help they needed and preventing them from hurting someone or even themselves. A line Colton was about to cross.

He now understood why Jennifer had been compassionate with Dan. How she hadn't shut him down until it was too late. She'd been far too kind because she had a big heart.

A heart she'd shown him and a heart he wanted to emulate every day of his life. He could do this. He could help Jennifer without seriously hurting anyone else. Cooler heads would prevail today.

Colton slowly walked back to Riggs and handed him his gun. "Here. I'm going in to go get her."

"What?" Riggs took the gun but grabbed Colton by the shoulders when he turned. "You can't go in there. What if he's armed?"

"I think he may well be armed, but that still doesn't change my plan."

Beau joined them. "No, Colt. Would you bring a knife to a gun battle? Think about it."

"Look, I'm not worried. I have y'all here to help me if things go really crazy. You're my backup. But, and hear me out, I…think I want to talk to him first." At the unhinged and gaping jaws, Colton continued to talk. "You said it, Beau. We can't have a gun battle here. There are families and children."

"Well, we could wait for the sheriff to get here. He's a few miles out." Beau pointed in the direction of Kerrville.

"Look, I've been where this man is. I've felt desperate and confused, angry and hostile. I had nightmares that wouldn't stop tormenting me and images I couldn't unsee."

"You were in a war. That's different," Riggs said.

"But we don't know what he's dealt with. People who struggle with mental health are in a war, too." He took a breath. "Daily."

"You're being too generous and that scares me."

A fear Colton hadn't ever seen in Riggs's eyes flashed clear and bright.

"I have to see if he'll talk to me. If he won't, then we have no other choice. But if he knows we're here, he might realize his initial plan is done."

"Exactly! And when he realizes he's backed up into a

corner, is he going to come out swinging?" Beau said. "With a gun?"

"I can take care of myself. I'll probably disarm him before he can even take his first shot."

"I don't like this," Riggs said. "It's too dangerous."

"The other option is we wait until law enforcement arrives. And when they arrive, that tends to escalate situations."

"Right," Beau said. "Speaking of being backed into a corner. He's trapped."

Colton turned but gave Riggs one last look. "I've got this. Don't worry."

CHAPTER 23

olton was here. Beau must have recognized her after all, told Colton what he'd seen, and he'd found her. Maybe they'd already called the police. This would be over with soon, because now Dan had crossed a line law enforcement could not ignore. Maybe now he'd get help. Or jail time.

He'd given her a wig as if that alone would make her look like a different person. She'd tried talking sense into him, telling him the wig didn't fit. She'd told him that people would be looking for her, wig or not. None of her arguments were working. The thing that scared her the most was how he was packing everything as though he expected to leave here within minutes. But he'd put the gun down, forgotten, and she allowed a sense of relief to flood through her. He didn't really want to hurt her. Maybe this part was genuinely true. He just mistakenly thought he could force her to love him.

When there was a knock on the front door, both of them jumped.

"Who could that be?" Dan said with narrowed eyes. "Are you expecting anyone?"

"Seriously?"

"Hey, Dan." Colton's voice, on the other side of the door. "Is that you in there? Can we talk?"

Fear gripped Jennifer suddenly, churning her insides.

"How does he know who I am?" Dan said.

"I told him all about you. You're…you're important to me."

Dan went to the door and spoke through it. "What do you want to talk about?"

"A few things. I would love to talk to my fiancée for a second, if you don't mind. You took her away so fast I didn't even get to say goodbye."

Jennifer shook her head. "No, no, he's not really my fiancé. It's like I told you, we were faking it."

Dan smirked. "She says you're not really her fiancé, dude. I'm sorry to be the one to break the bad news."

Colton groaned. "Well, we had a fight. I guess that makes sense. If you open the door maybe we could talk man to man. I mean, we both love the same woman. Right?"

Love. He *loved* her? Or wait. Hang on, this was hostage negotiations 101. Colton must have a script or something. At least, she *hoped* he knew what he was doing. Oh Lord. He was a soldier and a cowboy, not a hostage negotiator! He was going to get himself killed.

"Colton, go away!" she shouted.

She mentally telegraphed he should wait for the police to handle this.

Dan happily blew her a kiss. "You heard her, man."

"Right after I talk to Dan. I'll go away then. Promise."

Dan went back to get his gun, as if considering opening the door.

"No, don't let him in," Jennifer argued.

"Why *don't* you want me to let him in?" Dan narrowed his eyes.

"She's afraid I'll tell you everything that's wrong with her," Colton replied through the door. "And there's plenty."

"See? I'm *way* more supportive than this guy. What do you even see in him?"

"If you open the door, I'll tell you," Colton said.

For the love of a cowboy, he wasn't giving up!

"Colton, he has a *gun!*"

Dan gave her a disgusted look, like she'd outed him and betrayed his confidence. "You didn't have to *tell* him that. I bet he has his own."

"Actually, I left my weapon behind. Thought it might discourage conversation."

Was he being serious right now? The man who'd walked all over town with a holstered gun under his jacket decided *this* was the moment to leave it behind?

He was lying. Probably.

If he was smart.

"Maybe I want to find out what the hell you see in this guy that you don't see in me." Dan opened the door and brandished his gun. "Come on in. Join us."

"Hey, thanks." Colton walked in, hands in the air.

"Show me you don't have a weapon. I need proof."

Colton gave a half smile. He turned in a circle, quickly glanced in Jennifer's direction, and sent her a short wink. Then he opened his jacket, and the holster and gun were both missing.

Missing.

He wasn't lying.

"Do you want to put the gun down so we can talk?" Colton said.

"I better not. You might try to take her, and I don't want to have to shoot anyone."

"That's smart. The sound of a gun is far louder than most people realize. It's going to bring quite a bit of attention your way."

"Right," Dan said, but if she wasn't mistaken, he looked uncertain for the first time. "This is simply insurance. What did you want to talk about?"

Colton cocked his head toward her. "Could we untie Jennifer? I mean, she looks uncomfortable."

"Don't worry about that. She's fine." Dan glanced at her. "Right, sweetie? Tell your ex-fiancé you're fine."

"I'm *fine*," she repeated like a parrot.

She was still trying to figure out Colton's plan. He didn't have a gun, and a soldier in a situation like this one without a weapon was an anomaly. She thought of Joe. She thought of her father. They'd both come in weapons blazing. This is what she'd expected from Colton, too. But he'd surprised her. He was trying to *talk* to Dan instead, and God knew he was completely out of his element.

But in this moment, she loved him for trying. Loved him for stretching to be a better man. Maybe he now saw what she had. Dan was a man who needed help and maybe, *maybe* he was even somehow crying out for someone to stop him. And no one had. She hadn't been able to because her safety had to be the first consideration. But other than asking him to get help, she hadn't done more. She hadn't reached out to try to find members of his family who might help him. Who might intervene. No, that wasn't her place but it had been her plan until everything escalated so quickly and she let fear take over.

But if this were Joe, she'd want someone to help him.

Dan backed against the wall and appraised Colton from head to toe. "You're tall but nothing special."

"Don't I know it," Colton said. "I'm just a cowboy."

"Why the hell do all women love cowboys? I mean, seriously. Every woman I know is in love with the bad guy on *Yellowstone*. Is it because of the beard?" He turned to Jennifer and stroked his jawline. "Because I can grow a beard."

Jennifer gaped at him. Words failed her, particularly because she didn't want to say the wrong ones.

"I don't understand it, either," Colton said. "Now, look at you. You're a good-looking guy. Tall, thin, clean shaven and I bet you dress well."

"The best money can buy."

"My favorite flannel shirt has a hole in it." Colton shrugged. "Go figure."

"No accounting for taste." Dan eyed Colton suspiciously. "I'm sorry to be the one to tell you this but the woman we both love is unfaithful."

Colton covered his eyes with his hand. "Man, I had hoped that would never happen to me again."

Dan blinked. "*Again?*"

"Yeah, my last ex cheated on me while I was overseas. Broke my heart."

Dan scratched his temple with the gun's muzzle, making Jennifer cringe.

"How did she do it? Did she tell you she was too busy to see you and then found someone new right away?"

"She took up with my best friend." Colton cleared his throat. "*Former* best friend."

Now, Dan gaped. "That's just…evil."

"It was a tough way to lose a friend, that's for sure." Colton moved a little closer to Jennifer while Dan seemed distracted by the truth bomb.

Newsflash: even handsome cowboys got cheated on.

"It…it's happened to me before, too."

"Yeah?"

Dan stared off into space. "We were about to get married. Invitations were sent out, everything was perfect. She changed her mind. And that was the end of it. Nothing I could do to make it better. It isn't fair."

Jennifer's heart dropped to her feet. She should have known it might be something like this that sent Dan off the edge. It was even reasonable to assume he'd have a difficult time accepting this. It was so…human.

"I'm so sorry," Jennifer blurted out.

Colton sent her another sharp look. He had a plan that apparently didn't involve drawing any sympathy from her.

"Women." Colton snorted. "Can't make up their minds. They want to get married, then they don't want to get married."

But the distraction didn't work, and Dan zeroed in on Jennifer again. At that point he noticed how much closer Colton had moved in her direction.

"Hey, get away from her," Dan said, waving the gun. "*She's* just like my ex-fiancée. I started listening to podcasts to relax and what do you know I came upon one by a woman who sounded *just* like my ex. At first, I thought it really was her, messing with my head by taking on a new identity and trying to trick me. But I'd moved to LA after the break-up, so it seemed unlikely. Then I saw Jennifer's photo and I knew it couldn't be Rachel. Rachel has beautiful blonde hair. Long, down to her back."

The wig took on new significance and Jennifer bristled.

"Long hair is great. Blond, even better," Colton said, blocking Jennifer again.

He now stood between them.

Jennifer had to say something, however, and Colton wouldn't stop her. "You should have said something, Dan. I didn't know you were in such pain."

"Why?" He snorted. "Women don't like weak men."

"It's not weak to be hurting. It's real. Women love it when

men reveal they're hurting just like the rest of us are. Don't fall for that alpha macho crap. Don't do it!"

Dan ignored her and turned his focus back to Colton, his new best friend. "It's her voice that got to me. The smooth velvety sound. It used to put me to sleep every night. Then when she stopped the podcast, it was like she was *punishing* me."

"Yeah, she shouldn't have done that," Colton said. "You needed to hear her voice if nothing else. I mean, I get it."

"Do you? Because I'm really sick of women taking, taking, taking from me and never giving anything back. I thought Jennifer was *different*. She was nice to me. Kind. The next thing I know she stops taking my calls, stops answering my text messages, and one day…she's gone."

"That must have been difficult for you to accept."

Jennifer blinked. If she closed her eyes, she'd almost believe someone other than Colton stood right in front of her, blocking her from Dan. Talking to him. Distracting him with a great deal of emotional intelligence. Without a gun or show of force. Just…words. She really hadn't given Colton enough credit. He was completely unlike her father. Colton was his own man. He could have barreled his way in here and strong-armed Dan to the ground, with or without a weapon. Tall but wiry Dan would be no match for Colton's impressive physique.

"It's been nice talking to you, but I need you to go now," Dan said, pointing toward the door. "I don't want you to see the rest of this. This is just for me and Jennifer."

Colton went palms up. "Don't do anything stupid."

"Oh, I'm not going to hurt her. I meant it when I said I never would. But I want her to be here when I take myself out of this world. It was going to be in Mexico, at the beach, but this will do fine."

No, no, no. The irony was Dan knew exactly what this

would do to her. He had discovered exactly how to hurt her in the biggest and most life-changing way.

"Sorry, can't let you do that." Colton took a step toward him. "That's not going to happen."

"You don't know what it's like in my head every day." He pointed to his temple. "I'm tired."

"Dan, please," Jennifer begged. "You can't, you j-just c-can't."

"Oh, *now* you care!"

"I always cared."

As she panicked, Colton grew calmer but with every word, he inched closer to Dan. "I'm tired, too."

Jennifer was about to tell both of them that the whole world was tired.

Returning soldiers, people struggling with chronic or terminal illness, the ones who couldn't get past a breakup, and too many others who were simply desperately lonely and unloved. Theirs was a big round sphere filled with hurting and desperate people doing the best they could every day.

But she didn't get to say a word because Colton suddenly rushed Dan and grabbed him, wrenching the arm that held the gun.

And the loudest sound she'd ever heard came out of the gun going off in the little cabin by the lake.

CHAPTER 24

$\mathcal{E}$verything moved in a flash of chaos and confusion after that.

Beau burst through the front door carrying a huge rifle, and behind him were Riggs, Levi, and Jackson. Then they just kept coming, a line of men through the front and back doors. Some she'd never seen before, others she recognized, like Lenny, the old guy she'd met so recently.

In the commotion, Jennifer lost sight of Colton and Dan where they'd gone down to the floor.

"Colton," she whispered in the voice of a windpipe constricted and small, so similar to the sound she'd made when Sean burst through their cabin door that first morning.

Was that only two weeks ago? Why did it feel like two years ago?

Once again, her heart was frozen, just a thick block of ice in her chest. Terror spliced through her every raw nerve ending, leaving her arms and legs trembling.

While most of the men crowded around Colton and Dan, Lenny knelt beside her.

"Well, this ain't no way to treat a lady." He shook his head. "Some men just don't know any better, Imma guessing."

Jennifer crawled on her hands and knees toward Colton. It seemed faster that way. Between several long jean-clad legs, she saw Colton on the ground, holding Dan in a kind of chokehold. But neither of them appeared injured.

"Get off me!" Dan shouted, face beet red with exertion.

The gun had been kicked to the other end of the room, and when Jennifer followed Beau's gaze, she, too, noticed the hole in one end of the ceiling which the bullet had made.

Beau threw off his hat. "That's going to cost me even more time!"

"I brought the ambulance," Lenny said. "When I got the call from the phone tree, I didn't really know what we'd need so I came prepared."

"He doesn't need a hospital, he needs the Sheriff," said Jackson.

"*Nobody* needs the ambulance?" Lenny almost sounded disappointed. "What about you, Jennifer?"

Slowly, Dan rose from the ground, pulled up by Riggs and Jackson and hustled outside between them.

Dan cursed at them all as he walked by. "This is none of your business! I'm going to sue every single one of you for invasion of privacy and I've got a great lawyer."

"You're going to need one," said Riggs, the lawyer.

Jennifer was still kneeling on the ground watching as Dan was led away, unharmed, when she felt someone behind her take her by the waist and slowly pick her up off the ground.

Colton.

He turned her to him. "You're okay now. I'm sorry about all this. I know it's a lot."

Jennifer studied his handsome face, his earnest puppy dog eyes, and tentative smile. She both wanted to smack him and hug him tight for a trillion years.

She buried her face in his neck. "Don't ever do that again! Ever!"

"Okay."

"Why did you come in here?" She pulled back, fisting his shirt. "I *told* you he had a gun."

"I'm supposed to leave you in here with an armed man? Think about it." He cocked his head and tugged on a lock of her hair. "More importantly, why did you go *with* him? Haven't I taught you better than that?"

"I had to! He said he would hurt you. And then you talked your way in here without a gun. Imagine my shock and awe!"

"Well, I would rather it be me than you."

Her heart tripped over the words, and she ached with a deep longing. No one had ever loved her like this. He'd taken her in on day one and never once complained.

"Oh, Colton," she whispered.

"I mean, your father would kill me."

Those words were like the screech of metal and squeal of brakes when a car came to a sudden stop.

Had she somehow forgotten taking care of her was first and foremost a favor to her father? His mentor? Had she somehow let the past two weeks of closeness and together-ness in their very fake engagement fool her into thinking this was more? *They* were more?

Answer: yes, apparently, she had. She wasn't much better than poor delusional Dan.

She loved someone who didn't love her in return.

"Right." She pulled away from him. "Does everyone know now?"

"Know what?"

"That we're not actually engaged."

"Say what?" Beau said from next to the front door where he stood. "You two are *not* engaged?"

"Well, if they didn't before, they will now." Colton gave Beau a tight smile. "Word will spread by morning."

"He was actually my bodyguard."

Why hold back now?

"Get out of here!" Beau said, holding the long-barreled rifle over his shoulder now. He almost resembled a young Paul Bunyan with his thick beard and big grin. "You two made it seem so real."

Colton scowled as if he was unhappy she had chosen this moment to tell everyone. But she assumed she'd be leaving here soon and better to leave without people blaming her for breaking off an engagement and leaving one more man of Stone Ridge heartbroken. As if.

"We should call your father now," Colton said, taking her hand. "Let's get back to the house and regroup."

Regroup. Figure out a plan of action and how to get her the hell out of Dodge with the least amount of damage to Colton's reputation as a liar.

They walked out together, passing Beau, who said he would remain to clean up and secure the scene. The Scene. The scene of her kidnapping. Her *kidnapping*! She felt Colton's strong hand on her lower back, guiding her to the group of men gathered outside. Surely, he could feel her spine shaking with the fear that only now seemed to grip her.

Levi, it turned out, had been deputized last month when they'd arrested an out of towner for driving drunk. He had handcuffs and the authority to haul somebody in. Dan would be carted to the jail in Kerrville after first being checked out for any injuries at the clinic in town run by Dr. Grant.

"I'm not pressing charges," Jennifer said.

"He kidnapped you," Colton said. "And this might not be entirely up to you."

"But he wasn't going to hurt me." It sounded crazy to her

own ears, but it was also the truth. "I'll…testify on his behalf if that's what it takes."

"He was going to hurt himself in front of you. You're telling me that wouldn't have changed who you are?" Colton took her by the shoulders. "If you don't press charges, he won't get the help he needs."

Maybe that was true. She'd have to look into it because she wasn't going to give up on Dan. She'd heard his cry for help. Hell, the entire town had heard him. He would get help now because even though she'd failed before, she couldn't give up. Not after hearing his story.

It was Joe's influence. Joe, who for a while, didn't look like he *could* or would change. But he had because she hadn't given up on her own brother. Maybe it wasn't her place, but someone had to believe in Dan. Either she'd find someone who would, or it would be left up to her.

"I'll think about it."

COLTON CONSIDERED SWINGING by the clinic with Jennifer to get her checked, but with Dan there he didn't want any more run-ins. And she claimed to be fine. Except "fine" was said in a tone of voice that probably meant "not really but I'd rather die than tell you more." She'd skinned her elbows while attempting to get away from Dan, but that appeared to be her only physical injury. Colton was at least glad to hear that she'd tried to get away.

Her hands were still shaking as he drove them back to the Grange and she clasped them together, holding them on her lap as if to disguise the movement. She wasn't fooling him. She was a wreck, and he didn't blame her.

Either way, she was ready to go back home to LA now that she was safe from Dan. She'd rushed to tell everyone the truth the second she could. It would all be in the open now and Colton didn't know what he'd say to Delores. She'd be heartbroken to get her ring back, hurt to see Jennifer leave Stone Ridge.

So would he, by the way.

More than anyone else. But he'd done what he set out to do. Keep her safe. If in the process he'd grown used to her always being home to greet him at the end of the day that was his own damn fault. No one told him to expect anything in return. He'd had a great two weeks, better than he could have imagined, and eased back into life on the ranch. The past few nights had been particularly amazing, life changing, and he'd miss her in bed most of all. He'd miss the way her body curled into his, the see-through T-shirt she kept wearing to bed, the smell of her hair. The way she'd moved over him, sure in her own body, shattering in pleasure and calling his name.

While he'd had a great deal of loss in his life, something told him this was the one he'd remember.

Inside the cabin, he called Horace Walker on the landline and explained everything.

"He's in custody."

"Thank you. Thank you. I don't know how I'll ever repay you for this favor."

If Colton didn't know any better, he'd say Horace sounded close to tears.

"You won't have to." He gave Jennifer the handset. "Want to talk to your father?"

"Sure," she said, taking the phone.

Colton busied himself in the kitchen to give her privacy, but he managed to hear every word.

"Yes. I'm okay, thanks to Colton. He saved my life." She paused. "Daddy, I know you love me but try to show me with more than your actions. Sometimes your children need the words, too. I know Joe did."

Another pause, and she kept going. "No, I'll make the reservations. Don't you worry. Sure, I'll be home soon. I'll call you with the information."

He would make a warm chocolate cake tonight. That would probably solve this ache in his chest. It worked for nightmares, why not for heartache? He rubbed at the spot and pulled out all the ingredients he would need.

Butter, milk, chocolate, sugar, flour, oil, eggs.

"Colton."

He glanced up to find Jennifer standing in the kitchen as if she'd been watching him.

"Yeah? What's up? What did your father say? How quickly are you headed out?"

She paused. "How fast do you want me out of here?"

He cracked an egg and cleared his throat. "Well, it would be nice if you could stick around and say goodbye to everyone. You have been here for a while, and I think they'll miss you."

"I would like that, too. But I didn't want to intervene with your plans."

"What plans? Riggs knows and he's not pissed. He'll get over it."

"Everyone will."

Except for him. Most definitely not him.

"Why don't you take a shower and get cleaned up? I'm making another cake. You finished the other one."

"Isn't that why you baked it?" This was said with an edge of annoyance he didn't miss.

He wasn't accusing her of eating too much. He'd had quite a bit himself. Jesus, he'd apparently completed his word count for the day with Dan and now he didn't know how to talk to people.

"Of course. Why else?"

"Never mind."

She stalked off, passing the kitchen table, and went to the spare bedroom where she was likely packing. Packing up her life here, getting ready to leave.

Damn it. What was he going to do now? Carry her to his bed and show her how he loved her? How could she not know he loved her, with everything he'd done? It hadn't been out of obligation. He'd told her he was crazy about her. He'd fallen for her the moment he'd first seen her in that smoky restaurant looking lost but trying so hard to be brave.

And every day since the she'd settled into his heart, digging a trench inside. He was never going to be the same without her. She had to *know* this and was choosing to ignore it. If she wanted to go, there wasn't anything he could do to stop her.

An hour later the cake was ready, he was a lot calmer and clear-headed, but Jennifer still hadn't come out of the room. Still wasn't talking to him. Heading down the short hallway, he passed by the table and recoiled to see *it* sitting there all alone.

The ring.

She'd taken it off, which quite frankly was a statement in and of itself. It wasn't a ring he'd picked out, or one she'd wanted. He hadn't even slipped it on her finger. But it was a slap in the face to see Delores's family ring, practically an heirloom, discarded this way. An heirloom that meant so much to her and that she wanted *Jennifer* to have. And Jennifer had left it there like it didn't mean a blasted thing to her. Well, he could take insults and rejection, but he wouldn't accept them when directed at Delores. The woman was practically a saint.

He found Jennifer sitting on the bed, staring out the window. As he'd suspected, her suitcase was open, but everything seemed to be in disarray. Her chucks were on the floor, jeans and shirts scattered over the bed.

"What's this?" He held the ring between his thumb and forefinger, knowing of course, exactly what it was.

She turned and gave him a long look. "Delores's ring."

"Why did you just leave it on the table?"

"Isn't that what you wanted?"

"Did I say I wanted it back?"

She stood, straightening, and crossing her arms. "That is *exactly* what you said when you gave it to me. You said Delores would want it back."

Damn it, that was *true.*

"But that was then. Things are different now."

She blinked. "They are?"

She honestly didn't seem to have any idea.

"Well, yeah."

"Then why don't you tell me how they're different. Because it seems like you can't *wait* to get rid of me."

"What in the hell gave you that idea? The minute I asked you to stay and say goodbye to everyone before you go? If I had ever for one second wanted you out of here, you'd *be* out."

"No, I wouldn't. You can't do that because of my father. He's your mentor and you owe him a lot. Now, he owes you big time. I'd take advantage of that if I were you."

"Is that what you think? You think I'm the dutiful soldier not making waves with his superior?" He stepped closer to her, still holding the ring in his palm, so tightly he might draw blood.

"Well, aren't you?"

"*No.* I left the service and I have no obligations to anyone other than myself, my family, and the ranch."

"I *know.* But you were forced to fit me into your plans."

"Wrong again, I didn't *have* to do anything. I don't take orders anymore. From anyone. That part of my life is over. I was very close to telling your father no. That I just couldn't help this time around."

"And then he said 'please.' I was there and I remember. He never says please."

"That's not why I said yes."

"No? Why, then?"

"I had to say yes when you walked into the room. Because you…"

He didn't have words for more because the feelings were too big.

"I walked into the room, and…"

Right. He should probably complete that thought. It was like peeling back his skin, that's what this was like. Not that simple.

"Oh my God, how did I fall in love with a man who can't talk?"

Wait. What? She was in love with him?

"What did you say?"

"You heard me." She lowered her head and seemed to be fighting a smile.

"I think I did but you don't sound happy about it."

"That's because it's hard to feel the way I do about you and even think about leaving. I don't know what I'm supposed to do when I go back to LA. Because everything is different, and it will never be the same. Not without you. I'm going to miss your surly attitude and the way you think cooking is art. I'll miss watching you walk with Freya, not riding her because you think she's too old and you want her last days to be good ones. I'm going to miss the way you hang on to me every night like you're afraid I'm going to take off."

"Did it ever occur to you that's *exactly* what I'm afraid of?" Colton took another step toward her.

She lowered her gaze and shook her head. "You'll be fine without me."

"No, I won't be." He tugged her into his arms and pressed his forehead to hers. "Here's what happened. You walked into the room, and I fell in love. Just like that. And every single day I spent with you I fell more in love with you. Even when you annoyed the hell out of me, I loved you. That's what happened. I know it doesn't make any sense, but it's all I've got."

"That's everything." She smiled up at him. "All I need."

"Except for this." He pulled back to open his hand and show her the ring.

"But it's not that simple, is it? We lied to everyone. It wasn't real."

"Not the engagement, no, that wasn't real. But you can't deny this…" Threading her fingers through his own, he held up their entwined hands. "This is real."

"What do we do? How do we make this work?"

"We could go slow for a change."

"Hm. It's an idea."

"We covered a lot of territory in these two weeks. We met and within a few hours we took a road trip together, were engaged within twenty-four hours, survived Sean surprising us with his rifle, a highly publicized wedding, and an attempted kidnapping. Maybe we can slow down and chill for a while."

"Take some time, get to know each other?"

"Might be a good idea. No more faking a thing. What do you think?"

"I love you, Colton, and I'm in no hurry to go home. But how are we going to do this?"

"Would you marry me? For real this time? Whatever else happens, we can figure it out."

"I'll marry you whenever you want. Tonight, tomorrow, or next year."

"It can't be soon enough for me."

She held out her finger and he slipped on the ring. "Now it's real."

"You realize this is going to require a great deal of explanation. First, we lied about being engaged. Now, we are. Is anyone actually going to believe us?"

"I don't care if anyone else believes me, just so long as you do." He hauled her up into his arms, heading toward his bed across the hall.

"What about the cake? It smells *so* good."

"Tell me the truth. Do you love me because I'm such a great cook?"

"No, but it's a nice perk."

She laughed when he threw her on the bed and joined her, rolling her into his arms.

"If you're good, *really* good, we can have cake as a midnight snack."

EPILOGUE

ONE YEAR LATER

*I*n continuing with the brothers' tradition, Jennifer and Colton decided to get married at Trinity Church.

"Are you ready?" Joe ducked his head between the partitions of the door leading to the entrance to the chapel. "It's now or never."

"Now, please." She slipped her arm through her father's extended one.

"Let's do this," he said in his usual commander-style voice, his posture straight as an arrow.

It didn't bother her anymore.

The best thing about her ordeal, besides meeting the love of her life, was the way it had eventually brought both her father and brother together again. After hearing of the attempted kidnapping, they'd both scheduled flights to Texas, so they could see with their own eyes she was no worse for the dire situation.

She'd count those days as some of the best of her life, quietly watching Colton and Joe, their backs to her, boots on the rail of the fence as they spent hours talking about…

everything, she guessed. She didn't pry, though Colton would have told her if she'd asked. It was only fair that these two men who'd shared a war together would have a quiet understanding between them.

Hundreds of photos of her two favorite people in the world were taken in a matter of days. And they'd become good friends over the past year. Colton was actually the facilitator of a reconciliation between father and son. It could not have gone any better if she'd planned it. So much had happened in the past year, much of it unexpected.

The *Truth Salad* podcast never managed to regain the popularity it had once enjoyed. But she no longer viewed this as a loss. These days the podcast centered on wild horses, gourmet bison cooking, and a mix of special interests. She had acquired a few dedicated sponsors which were just enough to keep her going. This was just fine for Jennifer, who enjoyed her anonymity. Listeners understood the show was now recorded "somewhere in Hill Country" and all other information was, as both her father, brother and Colton liked to say, "above their pay grade" and "on a need to know basis."

Oh, and Dan. Apparently, he had an older sister in Boston who'd had no idea her brother was suffering. When she finally heard, she and her family were there for Dan, who had agreed to a plea deal. It involved a year's house arrest, ankle monitoring, and *plenty* of therapy. He'd also offered to speak to others on the dangers of obsessive love.

Wisely, he hadn't contacted Jennifer to be on her podcast. She wished him well, always had, but the boundaries were in solid place and would remain. Forgiveness didn't mean forgetting.

The wedding march played and the doors to the chapel swung open. There was her devastatingly handsome soldier cowboy, waiting for her at the altar, smiling the grin that made her heart go as floppy as a fish caught in a net. He'd caught her alright, even if he liked to joke that he didn't deserve her. She was too young, too pretty, too perfect for a cowboy like him.

He was all kinds of wrong. *He* was the perfect one.

They reached the altar and her father handed Jennifer over to the man he'd always considered a second son. He'd now officially be part of the family and to say her father was thrilled would be an understatement. Jennifer joked that her father had old-school arranged her marriage. Not really, but there was a little bit of truth to that. If not for him, she might have never met Colton. And if not for Dan…well, best not go there.

Even through some of the ugliest times in life, a ray of beauty could be found, though one might have to look closely.

Oh, and the dress! Once she'd explained to Aunt Betty the whole flower versus stem thing, it seemed a light bulb went off. She did her thing, shopped till she dropped, and found a sleek dress that made Jennifer's body look like a svelte stem. Her head was the petal. Jennifer could live with that. It wasn't that she didn't like feeling beautiful. But she preferred feeling strong.

At the altar, she handed Eve the bouquet of spring flowers and took Colton's hand. Turning briefly, she took a good look at the packed house. Joe and her father in the front pew. There was Delores, beaming, so happy her heirloom would always be a part of the family she adored. Riggs and Winona were here, him having finally accepted an LA transplant as a sister-in-law. Sean and Bonnie, of course, Eve (who had become a close friend) and Jackson, Beau, and Lenny.

So many good folks who'd become like a second family. She adored them all, but none more than the cowboy next to her.

"Ready?" he said with a wink.

"Oh, yes."

She was ready for this moment, this man, and this kind of love.

And ready for a lifetime with her soldier cowboy.

ABOUT THE AUTHOR

Heatherly Bell is the bestselling author of fifty-six published titles under two different pen names. She lives for coffee, craves cupcakes, and occasionally wears real pants.

She lives in Northern California with her family and loves to hear from readers.

You may reach her at
heatherly@heatherlybell.com